THE SEARCHERS

THE SEARCHERS

NAOMI GLADISH SMITH

SWEDENBORG FOUNDATION PRESS

West Chester, Pennsylvania

This is a work of fiction. Names, characters, places, and incidents either are the product of the author's imagination or are used fictitiously, and any resemblance to actual persons, living or dead, business establishments, events, or locales is entirely coincidental.

Library of Congress Cataloging-in-Publication Data
Smith, Naomi Gladish.
The searchers / Naomi Gladish Smith.
p. cm.
ISBN 978-0-87785-334-3 (alk. paper)
1. Future life—Fiction.   2. Hell—Fiction.   3. Heaven—
Fiction.   I. Title.
PS3619.M5923S43 2011
813'.6—dc22
2010035645

Edited by Morgan Beard
Designed and typeset by Kachergis Book Design

Printed in the United States of America

For more information, contact:

Swedenborg Foundation
320 N. Church Street
West Chester, PA 19380

www.swedenborg.com

For the third generation:
May you enjoy the story and take from it
what you will.

CAST OF CHARACTERS

DAN
A desperate, not-quite-twenty young man

KATE
Dan's aunt. A professor on earth, now Kate is a student
in a world she never thought much about, let alone
believed in

FRANK
An ex-cop from Chicago who has been with Kate since
his arrival

BIRGIT
Loves her roses and gardening; shies from everything
and everyone else

PEGEEN
A young radical who may or may not be what she seems

GREGORY AND HANNAH
Husband and wife; one an administrator and the other
a teacher at the Academy; angels

JANET
Newly arrived and certain she knows more about the
afterlife than everyone at the Academy but the teachers

PERCY
A man whose past mistakes have not buried his hope
for the future

ZAROTH
A person who is very different things
to different people

THE SEARCHERS

PRELUDE

The slouching figure in the leather jacket, more boy than man, slipped the tiny revolver into his jacket pocket as he let himself into the street. He pulled his torn jacket closed, hunching against a swirling wind that pelted hard pebbles of icy snow against his exposed face.

There had to be another way out.

But there wasn't.

Dan had been over and over it from every direction like a rat running an impenetrable maze. There was no way out but this. It hadn't been his fault. But they didn't care about that. All they cared about was that one of their own had bought it because Dan had chickened out. Hell, who knew? He hadn't taken the job all that seriously—not until he saw the cop car. Willie had warned Dan that if he talked, no matter how much information he ended up giving the law, he was going to jail. Willie told him it was for certain. And Willie had smiled when he'd told him Tiny's friends in there were waiting for him. Dan's hand tightened on the small lump in his pocket.

At least Mom and Phil needn't know anything about it; maybe they'd never know. If he did this right away.

Dan's face was numb by the time he turned into the U-shaped courtyard of a dingy brick apartment building and trudged to the nearest door. His shoe slipped on a patch of ice beneath the snow on the unshoveled steps. As he grabbed at the railing to catch himself, the rough, ice-covered metal sliced into his palm.

He swore and righted himself, sucking at the torn skin. The freezing cold would stop the bleeding out here. And he wasn't going to worry about a couple drops of blood inside.

The littered room into which Dan let himself was cold and smelled of dirty clothes and the garbage he'd forgotten to take out. He picked up an empty pizza carton from the floor and stuffed it into an overflowing wastebasket, started to flick a sweatshirt from the sagging couch, and then let it drop back. He sat down heavily. Why clean up? A little trash was the least of what whoever had to clean the place would face.

He dug the tiny pistol from the leather jacket and held it in the palm of his damaged hand. It wasn't more than four inches from the black plastic inset handle to the nickel-plated barrel. He sat long moments staring at it. The guy said it would work as well as anything bigger. He carefully eased an inch of finger into the nickel trigger guard. Though his hand was slender, his finger barely fit between the guard and the half-moon of the gold-colored trigger. Dan considered the little gun a moment more, then pushed aside the little flame of fear that caught at his chest, took a deep breath, and closed his eyes. Quickly, before he could change his mind, Dan raised the gun to his head—and flexed his finger against the trigger.

I

Kate tapped her pencil on the desk. She looked out at the figure bending to pluck a weed from beneath a sprawling rose bush. It would be nice to have some of Birgit's fragrant yellow roses here in her room. Kate put down the pencil and turned back to the blue computer screen. *Get to work and finish the assignment—then think about roses.*

But before she could return to the paragraph on which she was working the blue screen disappeared, replaced by a woodland scene. Kate blinked. She'd been at the Academy—how long had it been now? "Time" lost its meaning here. It had been long enough to know the ropes, but she hadn't gotten used to some of the things that happened. Like having her computer screen change into a kind of television.

She peered intently at the scene. Three people were bending over a fourth figure lying on sunlit grass. Something in their solicitous posture reminded Kate of Birgit tending her roses. Kate leaned toward the screen. She couldn't hear the shining figures speak, only a musical murmur. Kate felt a prickling at the back of her neck. She knew the three must be angels. Celestials? She'd never seen Celestials, though she knew they must have been with her before she'd awakened in this transitional world.

The young man on the ground straightened a leg and sighed, stretched an arm in the air, and then tucked it beneath his chin again. The angel nearest the sleeping boy's head smiled at the gesture and reached out to gently roll something that looked like gauze from the young man's eyes. The dark-lashed lids opened lazily; the boy looked about, his eyes serene, unfocused. The three moved away, their shimmering forms becoming indistinct. One of them, a woman, stepped back, and for a moment Kate could see her clearly. The woman leaned to stroke the boy's cheek, then returned to her companions. The boy smiled at the feathery touch and turned on his side, his eyes already closed again.

Kate wasn't surprised to find herself transported to the smooth lawn beside the sleeping figure. She knelt, not knowing what was expected of her but willing to do whatever might be required. The thought of the assignment on her computer checked her only a moment. Hannah wouldn't mind if she didn't complete it.

Her breath caught, and any concern about her assignment vanished. This wasn't just any arrival. It was Ann's son, Dan. A twist of pain lodged in Kate's chest. How her sister-in-law must be grieving.

The boy's eyes opened and his glance drifted to Kate but swept past her. He frowned; the peaceful expression faded from his thin face. "Where am I? What happened?"

Kate sat back on her heels. Surely this wasn't right. She knew from her classes that when the Celestials left an arrival, the peace and joy they brought with them faded somewhat, but surely that wonderful state shouldn't be replaced by this bleak despair.

The boy held his hands before him, his shoulders slumped. He looked at his fingers and groaned. "I can't believe I'm still alive. I can't believe I fouled up this too."

Kate touched his shoulder. "Dan. I'm here. You're all right."

He raised his head and looked straight into her eyes without a glimmer of recognition. "What went wrong?" he muttered. He felt the pocket of his chinos and pulled out what looked like a toy pistol. "I swear I pulled the trigger." He pulled out the tiny magazine and examined it. "The guy said that close up this would work as well as any regular-sized one."

"Oh, Dan," Kate breathed, shock making the words almost inaudible.

His eyes cut to hers, then closed again, dismissing her as he lay back and drifted into sleep.

Kate looked about her. What should she do? Where was someone to help? And at the thought, she saw a woman approaching them.

"Hannah," she said thankfully, "what should I do?"

Kate's instructor looked at Dan, her eyes tender. She said nothing, but when she turned to Kate she spread out her hands in a gesture that plainly said, "This is your job. Stay with him." Kate bit her lip and nodded. Hannah smiled, her form already fading as she began to turn away.

Okay, evidently she was supposed to take care of this herself. Kate placed a hand on the boy's shoulder and shook it gently. "Dan, wake up."

He roused reluctantly and shrugged off her hand. "Who are you?"

"Don't worry about that," she said. "Everything's going to be all right. Believe me."

"Everything's going to be all right? That's the most asinine statement I've heard yet." He shook himself awake and frowned at her. "Hey, do I know you? You used to sit next to me in high school, right? History?"

Kate's mouth opened, but no words emerged. Her mouth snapped shut; when she spoke, asperity cooled her voice. "It's been a long time since I've sat next to anyone in a high school class, Daniel. Matter of fact, I was standing in front of college classes before you were born."

"Hey, you can't be old enough . . ." Dan's eyes grew round.

He looked at her closely. "Aunt Kate?" he whispered. "You sound like her, but you look so, so young." Panic stiffened his face. "You're dead. You died in Europe on that trip with Uncle Howard last year."

Kate stood up and brushed her slacks. "I don't know why you're supposed to find out like this, but yes, from your perspective, you could say I've passed on. And now, my dear, so have you."

"This is heaven?" the boy said, his eyes wide.

"No, but it's a place where you can be prepared for heaven, if that's what you want." Kate paused. "Why did you do it, Dan?" she said. "What possibly could have been so bad that you felt you had to do this terrible thing?"

Fear warred with wonder as he looked at the pistol still in his hand and then at her. "Did I, did I really do it?" he asked. He placed the pistol on the grass beside him. "I didn't think I'd wake up. And even if it turned out I was wrong about that, I sure didn't think I'd wake up feeling like this."

"Feeling like what?" Kate said quietly.

"Like crap," he said. "Just like I felt before." A puzzled look crossed his face. "Except at first. At first it was great. Can't remember ever feeling so—" the boy hesitated, groping for words. "—so safe and, and happy."

"You are safe and you will be happy," Kate said, hoping it was true.

"I'm so tired," he mumbled, rubbing his face. "It's hard to think."

They both saw the cottage beneath the oaks at the edge of the clearing at the same time. Had it been there moments before?

"Come on," Kate held out a hand. "I've a hunch I know where you can find a bed."

He got up, ignoring her hand, and followed Kate to the little cottage. A fire crackled in the fireplace of a single bright, whitewashed room. The coverlet of a bed beneath the window that looked out on the meadow was neatly drawn back to show crisp, white sheets.

Dan headed for the bed like a lemming for the sea. He paused only to kick off his sneakers before flopping down and pulling the bedclothes over his head. He gave a sigh that seemed to come from his toes.

Kate stared at the patch of dark hair that was the only thing visible above the coverlet except for a hand clasping the quilted cotton. The hand relaxed, loosening until the coverlet fell from his grasp. Poor, poor boy. What could have driven him to this? She hadn't seen her nephew often, but when she had, he'd always seemed a normal, if self-absorbed and over-indulged, teenager. But he wasn't a teenager; Dan had to be twenty. A spike of anger replaced Kate's compassion at the thought of her sister-in-law, and Kate had to fight the impulse to shake her nephew awake and ask him how he could do this to his mother.

"I don't think that would help matters very much." Hannah's light tone took the sting from her words. The woman moved from the doorway and entered the room. "Don't worry, he can't hear us. He's going to sleep for a while."

Kate's mouth curled in a wry grin. "Thanks for coming back. I certainly need some help with this. Since it seems obvious I'm hardly the kind of person Dan needs with him right now, can you tell me why I was chosen to be with him instead of someone like you?"

Hannah cocked her feathery blond head. "Actually, I haven't a clue. Of course, you are his aunt, and relatives are often among the first to greet newcomers. But you're something of a newcomer yourself and, well, a bit of a loner."

"I've been called worse."

For the first time Hannah looked flustered. "What I mean is, you're a very good student, Kate, but you haven't been with us long, you barely mingle with the other students, and really, my dear, you came here not knowing very much at all."

Not knowing much? Kate tried not to show either her amusement or the annoyance just beneath it. Had this lovely young woman the slightest idea whom she was talking to?

"Oh, I know you were a professor and had a Ph.D.," Hannah said.

"Two," Kate said shortly.

"And I'm sure you know a lot of things, but we're not talking about facts here, we're talking about knowing whether or not a thing is true."

Kate decided not to touch that one. Not right now. Like everyone here, she was a student. She could live with that. She knew she had a lot to learn about this new world, and about what she needed to know to graduate, to be ready to find her home.

Home. That's what they called heaven. Kate gave herself a mental shake and gestured toward the bed. "How can I help him?"

"Suicides are particularly difficult cases." If Hannah noticed Kate's flinch, she didn't comment on it. "Dan will be cared for while he's sleeping, but since you were brought to him on his first awakening, you're the one he'll need to see when he awakens again. Why don't you go back and work on your assignment? You'll be called when he needs you." She gave Kate a long look. "It won't be easy to work with him, but keep in mind that hard as it may be for you, it will be even more difficult for him."

"Any pointers you could give about how I should handle it?"

"Do you think I'm the one you should be asking?" A shade of impatience crossed Hannah's face at Kate's blank look. "Who would be able to help you far better than I can?" she asked, and then went on as though coaxing a backward child, "Come on, Kate, whom do we ask for help?"

"Oh, you mean God. Prayer." Kate flushed uncomfortably. "Well of course I do pray; at least I'm learning to," she said hastily. "And when I do I feel a lot more . . . content, connected. But as far as Daniel is concerned I was thinking of something more concrete, something I could . . ." She paused.

"Take to the bank?" Hannah said, smiling. "I'm glad you've found that you feel happier when you pray, but it's not just the talking to God that's important, it's the listening part."

Kate raised her eyebrows in an unspoken question.

"Are you listening to what the Lord tells you?"

"Can't say I've ever had a reply."

"Perhaps you're not paying attention." Then Hannah turned her head, caught by something Kate could not hear. "I'm needed in the gardens." Hannah half-turned, her form already beginning to fade. "Good luck, Kate. You can call me anytime you need help, but you might want to consider what I said about prayer—the listening part." And she was gone.

Pray? For Dan? For herself? Kate sighed. Maybe this would be easier in a church. And immediately Kate was in the center aisle of a church, looking at the front row, where a woman and a man were seated. Ann and Phil. Phil's head was bowed, but Kate's sister-in-law scowled at the pulpit, where a white-haired man raised a hand in a graceful gesture. Ann's lean, angular face tightened and her hands gripped each other, as though it was the only way she could keep them still. At first Kate couldn't hear what the man in the pulpit was saying, but then the rich, mellow tones became audible in mid-sentence. ". . . we can't know all the reasons this bright young man has been taken from us; we can only realize we must submit to what is God's will."

It isn't *God's will,* Kate thought, annoyed. But then her attention shifted to the stoic woman in the front pew. "He's all right now, Ann," Kate whispered. "He's here—with me."

Ann's scowl softened, and for a moment Kate thought her

sister-in-law had heard the words. Then she saw both Ann and Phil were looking at a man walking to the podium, supported by two canes.

Kate felt as though she'd stepped off a ten-story building. "Howard," she breathed. The name emerged as a moan.

The man had hooked his canes on the shelf beneath the podium and carefully positioned himself, clutching the sides of the podium with both hands. "The shock of losing someone suddenly is one of the most difficult things we encounter in life," he began. "We don't know why things like this happen. In Dan's case, we must remind ourselves that no one can understand what pressures another person has been facing, what drove Dan to the place where he thought there was no alternative to taking his life. But all that is immaterial now. We have gathered to remember the good times he gave us during his short life. We must trust Dan has found peace." Howard paused, his fingers on the podium showing white. "It's been more than a year since the death of my wife deprived me of the closest friend I've ever had," he said, his voice strained but controlled, "the companion and colleague with whom I spent the greater, the best part of my life."

A year, more than a year. There they were again, the words Dan had used. Here, where there was no time as people on earth knew it, they seemed strange, meaningless.

"Unlike the reverend, I don't claim to know what lies beyond this life," Howard was saying. "But there is something I'd like to share with you." He looked directly at Dan's parents. "Since my wife's death I've felt Kate with me. Often. And I've been astonished by the serenity I've felt at those times. So I'm beginning to wonder. I, I'm beginning to think there may be something to the idea of a world beyond this one." He glanced at the minister, but did not react to the thin-lipped smile of surprise—or was it consternation?—that flashed across the minister's face. Howard continued, "I simply decided to tell you this in the hope it may give you comfort." He grasped his canes and made his way back to the front row of seats.

Kate let out a slow breath. Only she knew what an effort it must have cost this reticent man to speak such private thoughts. In all the years they'd been together she'd never heard him speak about the possibility of a spiritual world, of life after death. Religion simply hadn't been a part of their shared conversation. Values, yes. Decency and compassion and commitment, yes. But neither she nor Howard had been raised in religious families, and though Kate had privately pondered the question of God, it wasn't a subject she'd shared with Howard.

But Howard had felt her presence. He had begun to wonder.

Kate felt tears well and then spill. She blinked, but the scene did not become clear, and she realized it wasn't her tears that blurred the picture before her. Instead of Howard and the church chancel there was only mist—and then a boy sleeping on a bed before her.

Kate brushed her cheeks with her fingers as she watched Dan's even, regular breathing. Yes, she should pray. But how? She'd been saying a lot of thank yous lately, but she just wasn't used to praying for something specific. Hadn't really gotten the hang of it yet. *What about those times she'd been in her office preparing to meet a troubled student?* She'd made a practice of gathering her thoughts, of trying to find the right words, advice that might help. Hadn't those quiet moments been a kind of prayer?

She bowed her head. *Help me say the right things to Dan. Help me to not mess up this kid any more than he's already managed to do.* Now what? Oh yes, Hannah had talked about listening. Kate bowed her head again, closed her eyes, and listened. But the only thing she heard was the sighing breath of the boy on the bed.

2

Frank Chambers pulled the door of his room closed, patted his pocket for a key, then let his hand fall. It was embarrassing that he still occasionally forgot there was no reason to lock doors at the Academy.

He shoved his hands in his pockets. Things were pleasant enough here. So why this urge to get away, just take off? It wasn't that the classes weren't interesting; one or two had hit at an uncomfortable gut level. But what use it was for a Chicago cop like him—an ex-cop—to delve into things he'd never given much thought to, like considering just what your idea of God was? And they wanted him to write about it, for Pete's sake. Who did they think he was, some kind of philosopher in training? Frank felt a twinge of guilt at the thought of the unfinished assignment on his computer. Kate had probably whipped it off without half trying.

Kate. He was going to have to stop thinking about Kate. Was the fact that she was unavailable part of the attraction? Frank flinched at the unwelcome thought. The fact was, she was attached to her Howard as firmly as a barnacle even though her husband wasn't here—yet.

There it was again, here, as opposed to . . . on earth. It still took some getting used to, especially in his present mood. *Let it go.* Right now he just wanted out of here.

Frank let himself into the garden, oblivious to its distilled summer beauty. He strode unseeing past the tall delphiniums that showed vibrant against the stone wall, past the stock and foxglove that waved over clusters of cosmos and daisies and snapdragon. Though dimly aware of the heavy fragrances wafting from Birgit's roses, Frank unlatched the garden gate without giving them a glance.

He frowned. The flagstone path beneath his feet led in a different direction than he remembered. And the plants were different. Cone-like seeds drooped from huge cycads growing in the sandy soil. The pointed leaves of great agaves threatened to pierce anyone who dared venture from the path, and beyond the agaves giant-leafed philodendra grew in wild profusion. Frank's pace quickened. As he passed through the desert garden to the area of massed philodendra, the earth beneath his feet became damp and spongy. A raised wooden walkway appeared, leading to a thicket of cypress trees. Frank gingerly crossed to the walkway and found himself immediately enclosed by a forest of tall, rangy trees hung with blooming bromeliads. The trees' foliage formed a canopy overhead that partially blocked the sunlight, though a few rays glinted on the thick-stalked anthurium that spiked the lush greenery. At the second turn Frank stopped short. There was nothing in the peaceful scene to cause disquiet, but twenty-nine years as a cop alerted him. If he were a betting man he'd give odds something was about to happen. Something he wouldn't like.

Without changing his position, Frank glanced left and then right as far as his peripheral vision would allow, and caught a whisper of movement. He rose on the balls of his feet and spun around—back on the force he'd surprised more than one perp by moving more quickly than they expected a big man to maneuver—but saw only a slowly bobbing leaf. Frank examined the still-quivering leaf. Could have been a small animal, maybe even a large insect. He waited, quietly watching the underbrush until his eyes grew accustomed to shades of green foliage and brown earth. Then he saw it, the outline of something beneath one of the huge leaves. It was large, had to be four, five feet long.

Frank consciously slowed his heavy breathing and took a cautious step forward. The thing moved. Frank stopped, his eyes darting about the forest floor, looking for a dead branch, a rock, anything he could use if he needed it. Nothing. The lizard-like creature's head lifted, and its beady eyes held Frank's for a long moment. Its teeth-lined jaws opened. It hissed, then flicked its tail and slithered away. Frank let out a slow breath. *Whoa.* What was this? What was an animal like this doing around the gardens?

Hold on. They'd been told at the Academy that the things you see in this world correspond to something you or someone whom you were with loved or wished for. So did this mean he, Frank Chambers, wanted something that looked like that slithering thing? Frank thought of the teeth that looked as though they could take off a finger or a toe as easily as slicing though butter. Not a chance. Yeah, he knew he still had a lot of baggage, but surely there wasn't anything in him bad enough to call up the creature he'd glimpsed beneath the plant. Was someone else around? Frank stood still, watching, listening.

He slapped his neck. *Mosquitoes!* Another first. And it had grown darker since he'd entered the forest. Frank's eyes narrowed. Maybe he wasn't the sharpest knife in the kitchen, but he knew enough to realize he should get out of this place. His pace brisk, Frank headed back the way he'd come. After a few yards he stopped. The walkway seemed less well cared for, the boards splintered, creepers curling their tendrils in tangles at his feet. Frank peered ahead and saw only a continuous vista of waist-high plants, scrawny trees, and hanging bromeliads. This couldn't be the way back.

Frank ran, his breath soon coming in short gasps. He hadn't been this out of condition since the days of chemo sessions and cancer. The thought of those chemo sessions startled him—it was a time he could scarcely remember. No, face it, he wasn't breathing this way because he was out of condition, it was because he was scared. *God help me.* And at that instant a shaft of light appeared to his right. Frank's head snapped toward it and he saw sunlight streaming on a portion of walkway that branched off at a right angle from the main path.

"Need help, Frank?"

Though he could not have named the man walking toward him, Frank recognized one of the senior staff at the Academy. Not one of the regular teachers, an administrator who sometimes came to assemblies. Like everyone connected with the Academy, despite his youthful appearance, the guy gave an impression of maturity.

Sunlight seemed to move with the man as he walked. When he approached, it enveloped Frank as well. "I'm Gregory," the man said, holding out his hand.

"Right. I remember." Frank squinted in the bright light, glad of its warmth. "Yeah, I guess I just might need some help," he said, shaking the outstretched hand. He hoped Gregory hadn't seen his momentary panic. "For a moment there I thought I wasn't going to find my way out of this place."

"If you really didn't want to be here, you could have found your way out," Gregory said, his tone nonjudgmental but brooking no dispute.

Frank felt his jaw tighten at this, but he said evenly, "That was one nasty-looking reptile back there. I know things don't happen here without a reason, so I'm guessing I saw it because there's something I should know and you're here to tell me about it."

Gregory smiled. "Not me, friend. Not my job." He was politely silent, waiting for Frank to say more. When Frank did not speak, Gregory merely smiled again, put a hand on Frank's shoulder, and gestured to the branching wooden walkway behind him. "Keep on going this way, take the second turn to the right, and you'll reach the grounds behind the Academy buildings."

"Thanks," Frank said. But he didn't move. "Why do I have the feeling I've missed something here? That there's some connection I should be making?"

Gregory looked at him intently. "If, as you say, you have missed something, you're going to have to find out about it for yourself." Frank could have sworn a twinkle came into the man's eyes. "After all, that's what you're here for, isn't it?"

"Right," Frank said. He hoped his tone did not betray the annoyance that mixed with his very real gratitude. Sure he was glad Gregory had turned up, but it was embarrassing. If only the guy didn't look so damned young! It was like having a rookie cop tell him how he should be conducting a case. No, not tell him—worse than that—silently stand there and wait for Frank to get with the program and figure it out for himself.

"Thanks for the directions," he said. "Glad you happened along."

"No trouble." Gregory stood aside to let Frank pass. The light in the grove increased, but the brightness that had accompanied Gregory vanished with him.

Frank's step quickened. So the rescue mission had been accomplished; there was no longer need for Gregory's presence. And it had been a rescue mission. A sobering thought. Evidently things had gotten dicey enough for help to be sent. Of course he was grateful, but the whole thing was disturbing. Had his little walk through the woods occurred because there was something he should be thinking about? Apparently. But for the life of him, Frank couldn't figure out what it was.

Birgit's trowel jabbed the rich loam. She dug into the moist black earth with a quick, competent motion and tossed a clod of dirt onto a growing pile beside her. A tremor shot up the corded muscles of her arm as the trowel caught a large root, the tool's sharp metal point spearing the fibrous tuber. Birgit clamped her lips shut on a guttural cry before it emerged. How could the root be here when the bush itself was gone without a trace? She squatted in a catcher's crouch and warily surveyed all that remained of her best plant.

Her dark eyes flicked to the bushes on either side of the hole she'd dug. She saw leaves speckled with black spot, and buds that only this morning had reached slender, dew-glistened heads toward the sun now drooped like cheap hot-house flowers left outside in freezing temperatures. Had this happened because she wouldn't speak, because she wouldn't go to their classes and listen to them talk about God? The teachers always talked about praying to their God. Why should she pray? What had God ever done for her?

Birgit carefully placed the trowel on the black earth and looked at her dirt-stained hands, flexing the short, stubby fingers. There was strength in them, strength that endured. She had learned to endure. Ever since the dark time when she'd been taken, when she'd met the terrible weariness of each new day, when forcing herself to go on though every movement seemed an intolerable effort, ever since then, she'd promised herself she would bear what she must. And she had. Things were different here, it was true. Plenty of food to eat, a room of her own, a garden where she could work for as long as she liked.

Birgit's shoulders slumped. What use was it being able to work in the garden when this happened? What use were the mornings of weeding and watering and digging the rich soil if her loveliest rose vanished, if she had to sit and watch the remaining ones wither and fade?

Birgit reached out and touched a curled, dark-red petal with a gentle finger. Her breath caught. Had she imagined it or had she seen it shrink at her touch? No, it must have been the breeze. To have her roses shrink from her would be more than she could stand. Did the plants here shy from you the way people did? No, the people here didn't shy from her; no one looked at her with that hint of disgust she was used to seeing in people's eyes. The only trouble with the people here was they wouldn't leave her alone. If only they would leave her alone. Her roses were all she needed. But now something bad was happening to her roses. What could she do?

Maybe she *should* pray, like they were always trying to get her to do. Birgit stared up at the bright bowl of blue sky. "Please help them," she whispered, "please make them well."

She started, her attention caught by a movement she sensed rather than saw, and looked down to see a baby rabbit crouched in the rich loam beside the hole. A mere handful of fur, it surveyed Birgit, its tiny nose quivering. Birgit reached out a tentative finger. The rabbit crept closer, sniffing at her earth-stained hand. Birgit felt the whisper of a touch as its whiskers feathered her forefinger. She held her breath as the tiny creature finished its inspection of her fingers and then moved off in a series of baby hops across the emerald grass that edged the garden.

A faintly spicy scent borne on a slight breeze reached Birgit. She looked down and saw a rose bush where a moment before there had been only a baby rabbit and a hole in the earth. The bush was small; its blossom did not even reach the knee of her dirt-encrusted pants, but the creamy, peach-colored rose that glowed in the middle of a cluster of shiny, dark-green leaves was one of the loveliest Birgit had ever seen. Two buds of a darker peach peeked from behind the opened rose. Birgit rocked back on her heels, putting a hand beneath the plant's leaves. Yes, the little bush's stem was planted firmly in the hole she'd dug, earth mounded about the sturdy stalk. Birgit brushed her cheek with the back of her wrist, unconscious of the streak of dirt left on her broad, flat face. She inspected the bushes on either side of the new arrival. There were still black spots on the leaves, but there seemed fewer than before and the buds no longer drooped forlornly. Birgit wiped her nose on her shirttail. She knew she should at least think a thank you for this answer to her plea, but she couldn't bring herself to do more than let a flicker of gratitude flash through her mind. It was enough for now that disaster had been averted; she'd say a proper thank you if the roses continued to recover.

Birgit sat on the damp earth to inspect the new rose, admiring each glorious petal that glowed peach with a soft cream at its center. It wasn't until she leaned over, careful not to touch the blossom, and breathed in the peach rose's sweet-spicy fragrance that Birgit allowed herself to acknowledge more than that first tiny shaft of gratitude.

She carefully clasped her hands, copying what she'd seen her teachers do as accurately as she could. "Thank you," she whispered. But she peeked at her new rose before, reassured, she got to her feet.

Dan's eyes opened slowly, then snapped wide as he became instantly alert. He remembered this cottage, remembered heading for this bed, aware of little but his desperate need for sleep. There had been someone with him. Who? Aunt Kate. Aunt Kate was dead.

So was he.

He didn't feel dead. Dan sat up, tossed aside the quilted coverlet, and got out of bed. Yeah, he was still wearing the same torn jeans. The full-length mirror on the closet door showed the same face he'd seen in the cracked bathroom mirror yesterday.

So there wasn't just nothingness afterward. Aunt Kate said this wasn't heaven; she'd made it sound like it was some sort of way station before you went there. But if there was a heaven, did it mean there was a hell too? Dan saw the image in the mirror flinch.

He frowned at the bulge that showed in his jeans pocket and slipped his hand in, his fingers closing on metal. An involuntary shudder shook him as he pulled out the little gun. Hadn't he left this outside on the grass? He stared out the mullioned windows at the greensward where he had awakened. Holding the pistol gingerly, Dan crossed the room and placed it on the washstand beside the bed. He took the linen hand towel from the washstand's rod and carefully covered the snub-nosed gun.

He became aware that he was hungry at the same instant the entwined smells of coffee and bacon wafted to him. He turned to see a neatly laid table before the fireplace set with a plate of bacon, toast, and eggs. Dan took a strip of bacon from the plate and stuffed it in his mouth. Maple cured. He remained standing as he lifted the plate to his mouth and used a piece of buttered toast to shovel in one egg, then the other. Good. Better than good. He sat down and took a swallow from the mug. *Starbucks?* He drained the mug.

"More," he demanded. He waited a moment. "More?" he said again. He looked in the empty mug and frowned.

"You might try the pot."

Dan's head snapped up to see Kate in the doorway. "Oh, yeah," he said, lifting the carafe. "I was just testing."

"Right. It's fun seeing how things work around here."

"Food just appears whenever you want it?"

"At first it does," she said cautiously.

"But not always?"

"Not always."

Dan decided to let that pass. He poured the last of the coffee into his mug and went to the fireplace, where he made a show of inspecting the rough-hewn timber mantelpiece. "So what do we do now?"

"I'm not sure. I'm new at this." She studied him. "Want to talk about what happened?"

"You mean when I decided to kill myself?"

Kate waited.

"Do I have to?" he said at last.

"No. You don't have to do anything you don't want to."

"I can do anything I want? It may not be heaven, but it sure sounds like it to me."

When Kate did not comment, he turned to her. "I didn't know I'd wake up," he said, his voice cracking. "I thought I'd be asleep forever; I'd be out of it, away from, from everything."

"And here you are, drinking coffee and talking with your Aunt Kate."

"Yeah." Dan managed a grin but it faded. He stared at his sneakers. "Wish I'd known—about, about here."

"Would it have made any difference?"

He looked at her, his face twisted. "I don't know." He glanced about the room. "Listen, Aunt Kate," he said, his tone guarded, "does everybody come here? I mean, is everyone who, who—died—somewhere near here?"

"Everyone from earth comes here at first. But this is a big place—you might say it goes on forever." Kate allowed herself a twitch of a smile, then sobered. "We remain here, or in other places throughout this intermediate world, until we discover what kind of people we became while we lived on earth." She caught herself. "But you shouldn't be bothered by all this right now. It's not your concern. Getting to know the place is. Look, it's glorious outside; why don't we go for a walk? I want you to meet a friend of mine."

"What for?" Dan's eyes were wary.

"No agenda. Just someone I've gotten to know since I came here."

"Okay." Dan made no attempt to sound enthusiastic, but he followed her outside. Giving a last look around the little room, his glance rested for a moment on the lump beneath the linen towel on the washstand. "Will I be coming back?"

"I guess. If you want to. Why?"

"Oh, nothing," he said. "Let's go." He caught up to his aunt in two long-legged strides.

"Frank, I was hoping we'd meet. This is my nephew, Dan."

Frank Chambers took in the boy's lean, nervous face, his hunched shoulders, the haunted eyes peering at him from beneath dark, tousled hair. "You from Wisconsin like Kate?"

"Chicago."

"Now wait a minute," Kate frowned at her nephew, "don't you live in Philadelphia?"

"Mom and Phil do. I haven't lived there for more than a year. Moved to Chicago, actually just outside Chicago, a couple of months before you—" Dan paused and swallowed. "Before you and Uncle Howard went to Europe."

Frank quickly stepped into the small hush. "Good choice. Chicago's a great town."

"Frank was on the Chicago police force," Kate explained. "He's a detective."

Dan's sudden stillness was more noticeable than any movement would have been. He ventured a quick glance at Frank as he attempted a nonchalant inquiry. "You been here long?"

Frank regarded the young man, his gaze disconcertingly steady. "Kate and I arrived pretty much together. But as for how long ago, those words don't mean much here."

"I thought we'd take a tour of the campus and end up at the recreation center where I can introduce him to some of the other newcomers," Kate said easily. "Want to come with us, Frank?"

"I have to finish that assignment for tomorrow; why don't you go on ahead and maybe I'll mosey over later and see if you're still there." He paused. "And Kate, maybe we could talk—when you're free?"

She was alert. "Sure."

"Had an interesting walk off campus a while ago. Like to see what you think about it."

Kate nodded and began to walk away. She didn't notice that Frank reached out a hand to touch Dan's shoulder. "If you're going to carry heat, you'd best not wear jeans, friend," he said quietly. "You can see the outline way too easy."

Dan's hand went to his pocket, an abrupt, involuntary gesture. He looked sick.

"You coming, Dan?" Kate called back.

The look Dan gave the Chicago cop was half defiant, half pleading. "Sure, Aunt Kate," he said.

3

"How about we check out the rec center?" Kate said. "You've probably seen enough bricks and mortar. I'm sure you're ready to meet some of the people here."

If Dan didn't look particularly eager to have his aunt introduce him to anyone, Kate didn't notice. She was frowning at the building at the end of the long, winding, gravel pathway ahead of them. "Funny, that should be the recreation center, but it doesn't look like it—at least not the one I'm used to." Her eyes searched the groups standing about the quadrangle, the couples lounging on the lush green lawn that fronted the low stucco buildings. "And I don't see anyone I know. Everyone seems younger than the people in my classes. Not that anyone in my class looks old, at least not after a while." She glanced at her nephew, who was slumped against a nearby tree, hands in his jean pockets. "You could at least pretend to look interested, Dan," Kate said, her voice tart.

Dan pulled himself upright. "Sorry, guess I'm still tired. Maybe this Academy stuff is just for people like you. People who like school. I gotta tell you, college wasn't high on my agenda when I was uh, back there, and it hasn't moved up since I've come here."

"It's not a college; some of the people in our classes who seem to be having the easiest time haven't had much formal schooling at all." But Kate's voice softened as she regarded her nephew. "I shouldn't be pushing school at you, should I?

24

You've had a rough time of it lately. I guess it wouldn't be high on my agenda either."

Dan inspected the laughing groups lounging on the grass. The one nearest them consisted of three admirers clustered about a girl with tousled, curly, black hair. She wore a black vest over a tight, open-necked, sleeveless blouse and jeans.

"I don't know," he said with a grin. "That one might be on my agenda."

"It's not only ridiculous, it's unnatural," the girl was saying. "We're past the time of women allowing themselves to be constricted in the semifeudal contract people call marriage. The whole thing doesn't make sense. Social studies have shown that trying to restrict a man's sexual appetites to one person is a losing proposition, and if men can enjoy more than one meaningful relationship, why not women?"

"Good point," said the long-haired boy sprawled next to her. "Like I said to—"

She cut him off with an upraised hand and continued, "A woman is well able, both physically and psychologically, to accommodate many partners over a lifetime. Limiting herself to one is just something that's been foisted on her by generations of male-driven cultures."

"Not," Kate said firmly.

The woman looked up at Kate. "Who are you?" she demanded.

"I'm Kate. And that garbage you're spouting isn't social science, it's the sort of psychobabble I'm apt to hear from undergraduates trying to rationalize their behavior—and maybe some graduate students who haven't grown out of it."

"Well said."

The calm voice took them all by surprise. No one had noticed the arrival of the slight, official-looking man wearing a khaki uniform. The patch on his sleeve showed a jagged bolt of lightning across a blue cloud.

The younger woman's green eyes flashed as she turned her attention to the new arrival. "This is a private discussion, or at least I thought it was. Now it seems to have become a town meeting. Who the hell are you?"

The uniformed man seemed completely unfazed by her attack. "You've come back to the Academy recently, Pegeen," he said. "I just want to remind you that while you may choose to do and say what you wish when you're off campus, the views you've been expressing aren't welcome here." He turned to the long-haired acolyte who had so eagerly affirmed Pegeen's little lecture. "And you too are welcome to voice whatever views you wish, but when anyone attacks the idea of marriage, it brings a discordant sphere that affects us all here. We would, therefore, ask that if you wish to continue this discussion you to take it elsewhere," he politely gestured to the far gates, "where both you and we would be more comfortable."

"Oh for God's sake," the girl snorted, but she didn't meet the man's gaze. Instead, she drew a pack of cigarettes from a clutch purse, selected one, and lit it. "Look, I'm not talking about promiscuity," she said reasonably, "not that I have anything against it. But promiscuity doesn't foster meaningful sexual relationships, and meaningful relationships are what it's all about. Marriage, hooking up, call it what you want." She did look at him then, as she blew a waft of smoke at the leaves above her.

The man shook his head, but said only, "I simply remind you that there are limits beyond which you may not go if you choose to stay here." With that, he turned on his heel and was gone.

"How's that for academic freedom?" Pegeen held up her hands in mock dismay. "Looks like they have guards around here whose sole job seems to be snooping on intellectual conversations." Dismissing him, she ran a hand through her wiry black hair and turned to Kate. "So you teach? Me too. I've taught," she frowned, "—in more than one university, good ones, but teaching's not a part of my life at the moment." She stubbed her cigarette butt into the green grass. "Where do you teach? Some Midwestern college?"

Kate felt herself flush, but the younger woman didn't wait for Kate to answer, instead cocking her head at Dan. "And you are?"

"Dan," he mumbled.

"Want to join us?" Pegeen drew up her long legs to give him room to sit beside her on the grass.

"I don't think so," Kate said quickly. "He has things to do."

"Too bad," Pegeen shrugged a suntanned shoulder. "Maybe some other time?" Her cool green eyes lingered on his until he had to look away.

"I—well, sure," he stammered.

"Come on, Dan." Kate's tone was crisp.

He followed his aunt, but glanced over his shoulder at the little group. Some of the men who'd been listening to the beautiful Pegeen had slipped off, but others clustered about her.

"Don't even think about it," Kate said.

"You have to admit she gets your attention," he said. "Any chance I could get into a class with someone like her?"

"Dan!" Kate said. But she smiled. "I don't seem to be doing too well at getting you to meet people. To tell the truth, I'm not quite sure what it is I'm supposed to do with you." She checked the sun. "It's nearly time for vespers. I don't suppose you'd like to come with me? It's a lovely service, and you'll meet a lot of people afterward."

"I'm really not into that kind of stuff, Aunt Kate."

"Okay, I can understand that. Neither was I—at first," she said.

"The only place I really want to go is back to that cottage where they let me sleep." His hand brushed his jeans pocket and jerked away. "I can see all this stuff some other time, can't I?"

"Of course you can." Kate decided her nephew did look tired, very tired and very young. She resisted an absurd impulse to brush back the hair from his forehead. "Would it help if we just went somewhere and talked?" she said.

His eyes darkened. "About what?"

Perhaps she was supposed to help this man-child face up to things. "About what you were running away from," Kate said gently. "What was happening in your life when you . . ." she paused.

"Shot myself?" he finished for her.

"Yes." She looked at him, her eyes sober. "You must have been desperate."

"Ever been raped, Aunt Kate?"

Kate stopped walking. She stood absolutely still. "No," she said quietly.

"I would have been. They told me someone like me wouldn't stand a chance. They told me I would be—" the last word was strangled, unintelligible. Dan hung his head, his arms dangling at his side. Then, to Kate's amazement, he raised his head, and with mouth slack, eyelids at half-mast, sucked in a deep breath and gave a giant yawn.

"God, I'm tired." He yawned again, and this time as his breath exhaled, his legs buckled.

Kate lunged to catch him before he fell, but despite the astonishing lack of heft in Dan's slim body, she could barely keep hold of him long enough to ease him to the grass.

"You okay there?" The large brown man who rushed to help Kate to her feet turned and picked up the sleeping boy as effortlessly as if Dan were a marionette made of balsa wood. "Name's Percy," he nodded to Kate. "Like me to take your friend somewhere? Looks like the kid is out for the count."

Kate rubbed her knee where it had been caught between Dan's limp body and the ground. "If you wouldn't mind,

I guess maybe I should take him back to his cottage." She looked at Dan's lolling head. "Think he's all right?"

"Oh, sure," the big man said. "Sometimes it hits them like this. All they want to do is sleep. Don't worry, it's only temporary. You show me where to go and we'll get him back to bed."

Kate led the way and watched thankfully as Percy laid Dan on the bed and drew the white coverlet over his sleeping form. "I don't know how to thank you," she said, holding out a hand that disappeared in the big man's. "I haven't seen you around; are you at the Academy?"

"I'm with security," he said, smiling.

"No khaki uniform?"

"I'm, well, sort of an apprentice." The big man smiled again. "You need anything, any help with the boy, you just call, you hear? Ask for Percy."

Kate's reply was heartfelt. "Believe me, I surely will."

She saw him to the door and then came back to stand a long moment watching the sleeping boy, thinking of the savage scrap of information Dan had thrown her. Of course, he really hadn't disclosed much of anything except how terribly he feared going to jail. He hadn't begun to tell the whole story. Well, that could be left for another day. Right now, apparently, he needed sleep. No, it was more than that; he seemed to crave oblivion.

How could she help him? Introduce him to some of the younger arrivals, some students like those they'd seen on the campus green? She smiled wryly at the memory of the girl sitting on the grass, surrounded by her acolytes. *Someone other than that one.* There was one young woman who had things thoroughly ass backward. Was Pegeen really a sociologist? She seemed far too young to have taught in any university, let alone in several, as she claimed. Of course, Kate reminded herself, things were not always as they seemed here.

Kate lifted her head at the sound of bells. Vespers. Should she go or stay with the sleeping boy? Would she be alerted if Dan awoke? She opened the door and gazed at the sun's westering rays, which cast a golden glow on the tall trees, on the grass, and on the stone buildings in the distance. Hannah would be at vespers; Kate could ask her.

Kate frowned. She should be able to figure this out for herself. After all, for several decades she'd guided students, had held their hands not only through adolescent heartbreak, but cases that involved life-threatening despair. Surely she could handle this. But then Kate thought of the wisdom in Hannah's calm smile. *There's no shame in needing reinforcements.* Kate lifted the door latch, closed it carefully, and walked toward the gardens and the ringing carillon.

She'd ask Hannah.

Gregory spoke to the massed flowers at the back of the garden. "Come out, Birgit. I want to talk with you."

There was nothing for a long moment. Then the tall flowers quivered and Birgit's head, with its cap of short, straight, black hair, emerged from the blossoms. She moved through the flowers with slow, careful steps and came to stand before the tall man, her head bowed, shoulders hunched.

"Don't worry about your flowers," Gregory said. "You wouldn't have stepped on or harmed them, my dear. Not when you love them as you do." He sighed. "Since you refuse to come to my office, I've come to you." He waited a moment. "You don't have to speak, but you'll have to look at me, Birgit. I have to see your face."

Birgit did not raise her head. Her fingers nervously picked the fabric of her cotton shift.

"Birgitanittha."

At the command in the quiet voice, Birgit raised her head to expose dark, frightened eyes.

"You've been badly hurt," Gregory said gently, "and you don't want to be hurt any more. We understand that. You've developed some pretty effective strategies to protect yourself, strategies that were important for your survival. Fair enough. But they're getting in the way here." He paused to give her a chance to speak, and when she didn't, he continued, "I can understand why you've made suspicion and distrust so much a part of you, but if you're going to progress here you will have to learn to function without them. You won't be happy until you give them up, and you won't be able to give them up unless you let us help you. Unless you speak."

For an instant it seemed as though Birgit might say something. Then her head sank lower and she gave a minute shrug of her thick shoulders.

Gregory folded his hands before him. "All right. Until you let Hannah know you feel ready to attend classes, it would be best if you stayed away from your roses."

The anguished sound that emerged from Birgit was too guttural to be a cry. Her square hands clamped tight over her mouth.

"I didn't mean you can't come to the gardens," Gregory said quickly. "You can walk in them all you'd like. It's just that it might be better if you didn't work with your roses at the moment. They wouldn't prosper under your care right now. Don't you see, my child, the anger and distrust inside you are what make your roses wilt." He sounded almost as unhappy about it as she looked. "Will you consider it, Birgit? Will you come to the special class Hannah has arranged for you? Will you try to listen, to learn what you must know to be happy?"

Birgit remained silent. When finally she darted a glance at the tall man, a flash of rebellion lit her eyes before she lowered them.

He sighed, but smiled at her. "Please come see me any time

you wish, or go to Hannah, if you'd prefer." He paused to give the girl a chance to speak. She didn't. Gregory reached out and gave Birgit's shoulder a comforting pat and turned away, vanishing into the golden evening.

Birgit covered her face with her square hands, pressing them tight against her eyes so the tears wouldn't fall. She remained on the path until the sun gleamed low in the evening sky. Then she wiped her nose on her sleeve, slipped her hand in her pocket, and took a shuddering breath of thanks as her fingers met a bundle of soft fur.

At least she still had her rabbit. She hadn't given in. She felt a small puff of pride. And she wouldn't.

Kate sat at the end of one of the carved wood benches that formed a semicircle of seats. She should quiet her thoughts—pray for the troubled, sleeping boy, for herself—but she couldn't, not until the first notes issued from the choir of half a hundred as they began to sing. Kate felt the muscles in her neck relax, the clenched fists in her lap open. She couldn't quite make out the words, but the blended notes that filled the fragrant evening air seemed to sing of trust and love, of hope and safe harbor. She let the meltingly glorious music swirl about her, and when the call for silent prayer was announced, she was ready.

The shimmering vision came before Kate had a chance to frame a plea. She saw a man leaning heavily on two canes. The image sharpened. He was standing on a boardwalk looking out over a lake with white-capped waves. Wind tousled his thinning hair as he transferred the cane in his right hand to his left so that he could hold both canes in one hand and grasp the handrail of the boardwalk with the other.

Howard was at their summer home in Wisconsin. He was thinking of her.

Kate's whole being yearned for the damaged man before

her. She drew a quick breath as Howard looked up, his eyes slit against the wind.

"Will I see you again, Kate? Are you somewhere out there waiting for me?" Though the words were uttered softly into the rising wind, Kate heard them as clearly as if they had been whispered in her ear.

"Dearest," she said, her voice breaking on the word, "I'm not 'somewhere out there,' I'm here with you. And yes, my love, I'm waiting for you. We will be together."

Howard rubbed his acne-pitted face and the gray stubble on his chin. Howard, who shaved carefully every morning, hadn't shaved in several days. Kate longed to reach out and brush that bristly cheek, to scold his negligence. Instead she breathed a prayer that the words she'd just murmured to him would come to pass, that it was God's will they'd be together.

Howard stooped awkwardly and picked up a seagull feather from the boardwalk. He twirled it idly between his fingers, then let the wind take it, watching as the feather spiraled on currents that took it across the dune and over the trees. "Kate," he breathed. "If only I could come to you."

The feather floated toward her. Kate reached out to take it and touched—nothing. She became aware of the people beside her, those on the benches below, all heads bowed in silent prayer. She blinked away tears. "Thank you," she murmured. But her lips quivered, and she had to bite back a wail of despair. She took a deep breath and said again, "Thank you, Lord."

Did it count? Did a prayer of thanks count when you were furious that the gift, the precious glimpse, had been taken away as swiftly as it had been given? Kate caught herself and pressed her hands against her cheeks. She almost laughed aloud. Here she was, acting like a rebellious teenager who hadn't been allowed to go on a date! "Oh, I'm sorry," she whispered. "I'm truly grateful. I am. And I do thank you."

The short service was soon over; people strolled about the

grounds outside the chapel. Kate stood looking over the crowd until she spotted Hannah's feathery blond head. "Hannah," she called out, slipping through the chatting groups.

Hannah waited, smiling. "How's that young man doing?" she asked.

"I tried to show him around, but I'm afraid it wasn't a great success. He doesn't seem to want to do anything but sleep."

"That will pass. And yes," Hannah said, answering Kate's unasked question, "you'll know when he awakens. That is, if he wants to see you."

"What if he doesn't?"

"Ah, now that's a different thing. Usually arrivals are happy to see a family member, someone they know."

"But I didn't really know Dan. I've always had a pleasant relationship with Ann and Phil, but the family lives in Philadelphia and we mostly saw them at weddings and funerals. I didn't even know that Dan had moved away. He remembers me, I think with affection, but we have virtually nothing in common." Kate cocked a wry eyebrow. "So it wouldn't be surprising if I'm not at the top of his list of people he wants to see."

"But from what I intuited when I was with him, there is a person, or perhaps more than one, he doesn't want to see. Quite possibly you aren't giving enough weight to having the comfort of a familiar face around when you're frightened."

The vague annoyance Kate had been feeling melted. "You think? He didn't seem frightened, except when he talked about—" her voice trailed off.

"Yes." Hannah put a hand on Kate's arm. "Do as much for him as you can, and be available; that's all that is expected." And she turned to the elderly man, clearly a new arrival, who stood beside them, anxiously waiting to speak to her.

Kate saw Frank Chambers' head moving above the cluster chatting beneath one of the great maple trees just as he spotted her. She waved him over, surprised how pleased she was to see his large, sturdy form.

"How's the kid coming?" Frank said when he reached her.

"I'm not sure; he's sleeping—again. I was just talking to Hannah and she seems to think I can help with his adjustment."

"He's a lucky young man to have you to help him," Frank said shortly.

Kate looked at him, arrested. "You wanted to talk to me, didn't you?" she said.

Frank shrugged. "Oh, I was just in a funk. You have enough on your hands without having to listen to my bellyaching."

"If you need to talk, I'd be happy to listen." She gestured to the building opposite. "Why don't we go get a cup of coffee? My treat." She grinned.

"That's because we don't pay for things here?"

"You got it."

4

Kate poured a cup of coffee from the carafe on the sideboard and took it to a couch beneath tall, diamond-paned windows that looked out on the darkened lawn. Frank snapped open a soft-drink bottle and nodded at two men who sat in low-slung chairs in front of the fireplace as he crossed the room to take a seat in an overstuffed chair beside the couch.

"Thanks for coming, Kate. Not that there's anything you can do. Guess I just wanted to talk to someone I know, and well, we've been together since we came to this world." Frank took a long swallow and carefully positioned the bottle in the middle of a coaster on the low, glass-topped table that separated his chair from the couch. "I just realized you and I are the only ones left from our group of arrivals now that Maggie's transferred to her gymnastic school," he said.

"Maggie was the first person I thought of introducing to Dan when he came here. But of course she's gone, and considering his problems and her track record with men, I'm not altogether sorry it's not in the picture." Kate leaned forward. "Okay, what is it, Frank?"

"Don't let the perp change the subject. You'd make a good cop."

"Frank."

"Okay, I'm worried." He thumbed the top of the bottle. "I figured that if we made it this far we were on our way, y'know? To heaven. Sounds conceited, but I don't mean it that way.

I just figured I must not have fouled up my life completely, because they let us come here, didn't they?"

"The thought's crossed my mind too," Kate said. "I wouldn't worry, Frank. You're one of the nicest people I've met. One of the first things we learned here is that the good we do isn't really ours, it's in us because we've allowed God's good to flow into us, allowed ourselves to be a conduit for his love so that he can help others through us. Well, the good you do may not have your name on it, Frank, but from what I've seen you certainly have allowed God to work through you; matter of fact, you seem to make a habit of it." She smiled at him. "If you don't make it I don't see how any of us have a chance."

He brushed this aside. "There's a lot of stuff I've been thinking about lately, and 'nice' has nothing to do with it. Some of the stuff surprises me. Always thought I pretty much lived up to my code. Paid my debts—and I don't mean cash—expected other people to pay theirs."

"Your code. Sounds like something from the gunslinging Wild West."

Frank shifted in his chair. "Guess it's not far from it. I pretty much had to figure things out for myself. I've told you about being on my own ever since I was seventeen."

Kate nodded. "You did."

"Don't know if I told you about when I decided that at six one and weighing in at one eighty I was big enough to take on my dad."

"And were you?"

Frank's grin was wry. "He damned near killed me. You're not a cop for as long as my dad was without knowing how to handle a howling mad seventeen-year-old. Besides, I may have had a couple of inches on him, but he weighed over two hundred. He had the beginnings of a gut, but back then most of it was muscle.

"After I could make it down the stairs and out of the house I took off. Like I said, I've been making my own decisions ever since. Not too many of them were that bad. I think I've accepted responsibility when I made a mess of things, didn't break my arm patting myself on the back when things turned out okay. I know I'm mostly to blame that my marriage didn't work. But I figure Marge came out of it okay with that dentist of hers. Since I came here I've remembered a lot of things in my life, some good, some not." He fell silent for a moment, then said, "So that's why the thing I saw this afternoon scared the hell out of me."

"What thing?"

"It was outside the grounds, a swampy place I've never been before. This scaly alligator-type critter comes out of the underbrush." Frank stared at the bottle on the table. "I've been here long enough to know the things we see are a picture of what's—" he paused, "—of what's inside someone around us or what's inside us."

"And you think that thing personified something inside you?"

"I didn't see anyone else around I could sic it onto," Frank said with a short laugh. "And when I think back, I realize that before the thing hissed and showed a mouthful of teeth and slithered away, it had been staring at me like it wanted to crawl on my shoulder and make itself at home." He gave an involuntary shudder.

Kate couldn't help a shudder of her own. "But it did go away."

"Thank God. And it didn't follow me when I took off. Not that I knew where I was going; I was pretty lost when Gregory came on the scene."

"The one in administration, Hannah's husband?"

Frank nodded.

"Did you tell him about the thing you saw?"

"He already knew. When I asked him what it was all about he said I'd have to find out for myself." Frank took another swallow from the bottle. "Been thinking maybe I should take off for a while, leave all these fancy buildings and pretty gardens and keep going until I figure out whatever it is I need to know."

Kate reached out her hand to touch his. "If you feel that strongly about leaving, it may mean you should." She clasped her hands together. "I'll miss you, Frank. You're not the only one who likes having a friend around to talk to."

He looked at her sharply. "Here we are, me venting about myself without giving you a chance to open your mouth. You got trouble?" His expression became carefully neutral.

Kate sighed. "I know Howard and I both have things to do before we can be together. I think perhaps one of the reasons I arrived before Howard is that my leaving has made him consider a lot of things he wouldn't have thought much about otherwise. But he's so lonely! And I can't tell him we'll be together . . ." Kate bit her lip. "I know I should be more patient. I know I'm behaving like a spoiled child, but I don't want to wait. I want to be with Howard now." She grinned at Frank. "So sue me."

Frank, looking out the darkened windows, didn't see her smile. "I hope Howard knows how lucky he is, lonely or not," he said.

Kate sobered. "You know what terrifies me," she continued, her voice low. "Hannah says people who've worked on their marriages on earth are together in heaven, and while I truly think our marriage was the most important thing in both our lives, I wonder if we worked on it hard enough? Did I value it then as much as I do now? And what if—what if one of us didn't make enough of the right choices in other areas of our life, what if those choices lead one of us to . . ." Kate stopped.

Frank couldn't help the spark of pleasure he felt at the

idea of Howard limping his way to hell and leaving Kate to her own journey. He pushed it away. "Hey, giving that kind of thinking a lot of room sounds about as sensible as me encouraging the swamp thing to come hop on my shoulder."

"Should I pretend the possibility doesn't exist?"

"No, but I think you'd do better to spend your time learning what you need to know while you're waiting for Howard."

Kate raised an eyebrow. "Any suggestions as to what that might be?"

"I have enough to occupy me without giving anyone else suggestions," Frank said brusquely. He rose.

"Oh don't go, Frank."

"It's getting late." He stopped. Kate wasn't listening. Though she was gazing at the glass tabletop, her eyes were blank and unseeing. Frank saw her cock her head and realized he'd been wrong. Kate was listening—intently—though not to him. It was as if a mist had come between them. Her tall frame became indistinct; her beige slacks and the bright aquamarine of her silk blouse faded in the haze.

She was with Howard, of course. She was with the cripple who had absorbed her energy throughout their marriage. Had it been Howard's flawed condition that held her in the unequal partnership? Was it his illness that enabled him to continue to claim Kate's devotion? Frank felt a prickle at the back of his neck. Was that a leathery snout poking from beneath the curtain that encased the tall window frame? Could it be a smaller version of the reptilian creature from the swamp?

"No!" Frank breathed. "No!" Fragments of thought swirled about him. *Not a picture of what I want. I don't want to harm Howard, or harm Kate's relationship with him. I don't want these thoughts.*

"Frank, what's the matter?" Kate's voice roused him.

He wiped the sweat from his face. "Nothing. I was just waiting for you to, to come back."

"You knew I was away?"

He nodded. "Did you know that when you're with Howard you become fainter, less distinct?"

"Really?" Kate said, diverted. "You mean you can't see me when this happens?"

"I can see you, but it's like there's some sort of plastic sheet between us." Frank made an attempt to sound offhand. "You and Howard talk about anything special?"

"We don't talk. At least, I hear him sometimes, but I don't think he can hear me. Maybe I only think I hear him because I know so clearly what he's thinking. Just now he learned his Milan piece is being reprinted in a book of literary essays. He's so happy. And he felt my presence. I'm sure he knew his thoughts had called me to him and that I was happy too." Kate's face lit at the remembrance. Then she gave an embarrassed little laugh. "Here I am, going on about us. What were you saying?"

"I was telling you I had to get back. Look, don't worry if I'm not around for a while, Kate. I think you may be right about paying attention to my gut instincts." Frank took his empty bottle from the glass table.

"You don't have to clear that," Kate reminded him. "Around here they whip things away as soon as anyone leaves."

"I clean up my own mess."

She looked at him and nodded. "I know." She stood up as he turned to leave. "Take care, Frank."

Dan stretched. Should he wake up? Maybe not. His eyes still closed to the soft sunlight that washed his face, Dan snuggled deeper into the down comforter.

His eyes snapped open as a flash of memory seared his consciousness. He kicked aside the comforter and sat up, his bare feet finding the floor as his gaze sought the bedside table. He stared, riveted by the bump beneath the white towel. It was still there.

"Oh God." Dan held his head in his hands. How did he get back here? Had Aunt Kate hauled him back and put him to bed like a baby? He had to get out of here. Go somewhere, anywhere. *Not to Aunt Kate.* She was old, no matter how young she looked. He needed to be around someone his own age. Someone fun. Dan loped to the little bathroom sink and splashed water on his face.

That was it, he'd see if he could find his way to that quad lawn, the one with the guys and the good-looking babe, what was her name? Pegeen.

Dan took his time finding the way through the gardens to the quad near the recreation hall where he and Kate had seen the girl and her entourage. He wasn't in any hurry, content instead to enjoy the grounds with their incredible vistas. *Must have an army of workers to maintain them.* Dan stopped short, his sneakers scudding on the pebbled path.

He stared at the clump of spiked, red flowers at the back of the garden. They waved slightly, as though brushed by a breeze. But there was no breeze. The feathery plumes of the tall grasses next to the spiked delphinium stood motionless. Someone was in the garden, hiding between the tall flowers and the stone wall behind them. Intrigued, Dan stepped into the garden. Nudging aside the broad leaves of a low-lying white flower cluster, he picked his way through a series of waist-high asters that ranged from the lightest pink to vermillion. A muted scuffling caused a spike of delphinium further back to sway violently.

For a moment Dan was uneasy, but then he saw a glimpse of black hair and realized there was someone, a rather small someone, crouched behind the sturdy stalks. "Hey there," Dan called out softly. "Don't be scared. I won't come any closer."

The flowers' motion stilled.

"My name's Dan. Come on out and tell me yours."

There was only silence.

Dan reached out and carefully pulled aside a handful of thick stalks. A girl cowered in the dirt. She was quite still, head turned away, her face hidden by a silken, blunt-cut layer of black hair.

"I said I wouldn't come closer, and I won't—if you're still scared," Dan said. "But you're not, are you? You're not afraid of me."

The girl's head turned a fraction and she shot a quick glance at Dan through her mass of hair. She gave a minute shrug of her shoulders.

"Okay, then come out of the garden before you mash the flowers."

She raised her chin at that, a belligerent flash in her dark eyes. She was more woman than girl, Dan thought, maybe mid-twenties, Asian, small, solidly built. She cautiously rose from her knees and, after a moment's indecision, followed Dan as he made his way through the asters to the pathway.

"I never hurt flowers," she said, her voice rusty. She stood before him, arms crossed, hands tucked into her armpits.

"Of course you don't." Dan took a step back to observe her. "I've told you my name, but you still haven't told me yours," he said, smiling.

For a moment it seemed she wouldn't answer, but then she ducked her head. "Birgit," she mumbled.

"Birgit. Nice name. So what were you doing hiding in the flower beds?"

Her head lowered. "They don't want me to be with my flowers. I must stay out here on the path like everyone else. So when I want to get near them, I hide."

"Hey, your secret's safe with me. You want to check on your flowers, you go ahead. I won't tell."

"They will know," she said glumly. She turned abruptly. "I go now."

"See you around?" Dan said easily.

She looked back at that, startled. Then Birgit's dark head nodded up and down and she padded toward the far gate.

Dan turned his attention to a pathway leading in the opposite direction. The quad must be over this way. What were his chances of finding the girl he'd seen yesterday? Was it yesterday? Not that he particularly wanted to join her circle of devotees, but unless he was mistaken, there had been a message in her green eyes, a message directed at him alone. Seemed a shame not to check it out.

Kate gathered her papers and prepared to leave the classroom. There had been no call from Dan this morning, telepathic or by phone. She'd better get over to his cottage and see whether the kid was still sleeping or had decided to go off on his own. And if he had gone off, how was she supposed to find him? Added to that, when and if she found him, how could she help him? Was there any way she could help Ann? Kate sighed and devoutly hoped some guidance would be forthcoming. Even a little would be nice.

Then there was Frank. Kate's stomach clenched at the thought of the hurt in Frank's eyes when he'd talked to her last evening. She'd miss the ex-cop, but she'd felt vaguely relieved when he hadn't shown up in class this morning. It meant he'd gone off to face his demons, and though his story about the scaly monster had been unsettling, it was good he'd decided to take charge. Taking charge was something she'd always been good at. Or at least she had been once upon a time.

She stepped into the hallway, only to halt at the murmur of voices. Though the door to Hannah's office across the hall was closed, Kate could hear every syllable as clearly as though she was in same room. Hannah was speaking with someone who, from the sound of it, was a new arrival. Kate quickened her stride, but the whining words followed her.

"I taught for twenty years in our church schools, and I

went to church schools myself from kindergarten on through college," the newcomer was saying. "I don't need to take classes, at the least ones you have here. I can see why you have them; the people I've met around here don't seem to know much about the spiritual world. As a matter of fact, they seem to be finding out about it as they go along."

"You have a point," said Hannah mildly. "They do have a lot to learn."

"Exactly," the newcomer said. "And I'm happy they are being given the chance to do it, but why should I take classes with them? Judging by the one I just attended I'd say they're pretty basic."

Kate felt a flicker of annoyance. So that's who the newcomer was. The woman who had come to class and sat through it, visibly bored, but taking any opportunity to add her thoughts to Hannah's explanations. *What was her name? Oh yes, Janet.*

"Perhaps you can share with them what you learned while on earth?" Hannah was saying.

"I wouldn't mind that," Janet said, sounding mollified. "As I mentioned, I taught for years. But it may be a challenge considering the lack of a firm religious foundation in most of these people, let alone the ones who seem, well, rather limited, intellectually. As I was walking over for class I tried to engage a young woman in the garden in polite conversation and she looked at me as though I was speaking a foreign language." Janet's tone was aggrieved.

"Ah, yes. Birgit doesn't talk to strangers. As a matter of fact, she rarely talks to anyone. Janet, there's someone I'd like to introduce to you, someone who can act as your guide. I think you'll enjoy getting to know her." Hannah's quiet voice rose slightly. "Kate, would you come join us?"

Kate had been edging toward the building's exit. Now she stood still.

"Kate?" Hannah's gentle call came again. "I know you're

intending to go to your nephew's cottage, but at the moment he's content to explore the grounds by himself. I thought perhaps you'd show Janet around the campus while you're checking on his whereabouts."

Hannah couldn't foist this new arrival on her. Surely Hannah couldn't expect her to help this ill-tempered, self-important woman when she already had Dan on her plate? Kate knew she was scowling. She tried to smile, but her face felt encased in cement. *Oh please, Dan's enough.*

By the time she walked into Hannah's office Kate found she could smile. Just.

5

What was it about Janet that she found so annoying? Kate eyed the petulant woman on the stone bench next to her. Had she had been given charge of this woman precisely because she annoyed her? A fleeting thought, but it returned with the persistence of a mosquito.

"So Hannah says you were a teacher, too. Where did you teach?" Janet said as she stretched her short legs in front of her.

"Madison. University of Wisconsin."

"Good university." Janet managed to make it sound patronizing. She looked out over the soft blue hills in the distance. "Nothing like watching young minds develop. Of course we teachers learned a lot ourselves—and in this world we'll keep on learning. For instance, do you see those trees?" She pointed to the valley beyond the gardens where palms and laurel trees were planted in spirals that formed an intricate helix. "I'll bet you didn't know there's a spiritual significance to that."

"No I didn't," Kate said, interested. "What does it mean?"

For a moment Janet looked uncomfortable. "Actually, I forget. But it's something heavenly. I know that palms and laurels correspond to good things."

"I've noticed the view of the valley changes. It's never exactly like the day before and sometimes there are different varieties of trees."

Janet's confidence returned. "That's because the view reflects the state of whoever is looking at it. Look! What did I tell you?

The trees are in a sort of a grid pattern now. Neat, isn't it?"

Kate preferred the helix configuration but did not say so. "For someone who has just arrived you seem to know a lot about this world," she said. "It's pretty impressive."

Janet shrugged, clearly pleased. "I do know quite a bit." She paused, frowning. "But that doesn't seem to be getting through to the people here at the Academy. I can't understand why I was put in the Rookie Religion course."

"Is that what it's called?" Kate asked.

Janet looked flustered. "Well, no. Actually Rookie Religion is what we called a basic course those kids had to take who hadn't been exposed to much religion before they came to our high school."

"You taught at a parochial high school?"

Janet flushed. "I taught in the elementary school. Fourth grade," she said shortly. "And yes, it was a school of our religion." She tweaked a twig from the arbor above them. "My father and grandfather were ministers of a church that teaches a lot about the spiritual world; my grandfather was a bishop, actually. I grew up hearing what heaven and hell were like."

"Lucky you," Kate murmured.

Janet looked around. "Turns out it's pretty much the way they said it would be. As soon as I saw Hannah and Gregory I knew everything I'd heard about angel couples, about marriage being central to heavenly happiness, was right on target."

"I've got to say it came as a surprise to me." Then Kate thought of her undiminished love for Howard. "Or maybe not." She took a breath. "So what does this church of yours say about a person who takes his own life?"

"Suicide?" Janet's eyes widened in astonishment. "You?"

"No. I just wondered about it."

Janet pursed her lips. "Well, unless they're mentally ill and not responsible for their actions, they'll find themselves in a whole lot of trouble. I'm not sure whether they'll end up in hell, but I do know suicide's a heck of a bad move."

"In what kind of trouble will they find themselves?"

Janet eased to a more comfortable position on the stone bench. "Well, say a person gets into a funk and slits her wrists. She'd probably wake up here and find she couldn't get rid of the knife she used." She didn't hear Kate's quick intake of breath. "I always imagined it would be sort of like it was stuck to her hand with sticky glue."

"But that's so cruel."

Janet considered. "Maybe the person has to come to terms with what she did? One thing I know for sure is that the Lord is loving, not cruel. And no matter what we come up against, he's always with us—even though at times it's hard to accept . . ." She stopped.

Kate did not particularly want to hear about whatever hard times Janet had experienced. "You know, I'd better get going. Would you like to come with me while I scout the campus to see whether I can find where my nephew has gotten to? He's a new arrival like yourself." She did not add that her nephew was one of those whose fate Janet had pictured so vividly.

Janet's response was unequivocal. "If you don't mind I'll check out the campus some other time. Actually I'd rather sit here for a while."

"Of course. Another time." Kate rose from the bench. A disinterested observer might have wondered at the haste with which Kate bolted down the path.

Janet's fingers curved around the smooth stone edge. Yes, there had been a time when she'd felt angry. More than that, she'd been totally devastated at the turn her life had taken. And who wouldn't? To be left a widow at twenty-six. But after the first days she'd borne it courageously. It had to count for something, the fact that she'd gone on with her life, taught fourth-graders year after year, gone to church Sunday after Sunday, sat through innumerable doctrinal classes, not to mention helping cook the dinners before the classes, all the while remaining faithful to the memory of, of . . . Janet bit her lip. What was his name? He was tall. When he held her, the top of her head just reached the sharp knob of his Adam's apple. Tall and skinny, and at twenty-nine his reddish hair had already begun to thin.

For a whole two weeks after the accident Janet sat on that uncomfortable beige plastic chair beside his hospital bed, ignoring the murmuring of the TV on the wall, watching the wisps of pale red hair that peeked from beneath his massive bandages, wondering how long it would take the hair to grow back on the shaven parts. It hadn't. He died before it was more than stubble. *What was his name?*

Shouldn't she have met him by now? When you came here you met the person you'd been married to, if that person arrived before you did. Actually, she hadn't thought all that much about it, about being his partner in this world. A small shiver crept up the back of Janet's neck. She wasn't sure she wanted to be anyone's wife, especially someone whose name she couldn't remember. But still, he must be around—somewhere.

"Hello, Janet."

Janet stared at the man standing before her. He was a redhead, but the color was a vibrant auburn rather than the washed-out shade she remembered. "You're—?"

"Richard," he supplied. "At least that's how you knew me."

Richard. Of course. She stared. He wore chinos and a golf shirt and he wasn't skinny. Not by any means. Richard was, well, Richard was a hunk.

He held out a hand, enclosing hers in a brief, friendly greeting. "Shall we go for a walk? I'd like to see the Academy gardens again." He held open the wrought-iron gate.

Richard had been an enthusiastic gardener, Janet remembered. How annoyed she'd been at his insistence on immediately changing into old clothes as soon as he got home from work so he could putter in his garden. More enthusiastic than knowledgeable, her skinny young husband had watered the little garden so assiduously the flowers developed rot.

"I don't water nearly as much these days," he said with a grin.

Janet flushed. She'd forgotten her thoughts would be apparent to an angel. *Richard—an angel?*

The man beside her stopped to admire a patch of daisies artlessly set in the middle of a curving bed of ivy. "Nice combination, isn't it?"

"Look, Richard, we should talk," Janet said abruptly. "I've just arrived and I'm not up to speed on everything here, but I, I think we should get some things straight."

"Right." He smiled at her. "I always admired your take-charge, can-do attitude. What do you want to talk about?"

Janet looked at him, nonplussed. "Well, you and me. We were just kids when we were together. I mean, we're totally different people than we were then, at least I am." His smile broadened at that and Janet had the sudden, uncomfortable feeling she had little idea just how great that difference was. "Of course you've had all this time to learn everything," she said.

"True." He waited for her to continue.

Janet ran her fingers through her short hair. "Well, what I want to know is, are we expected to, will we be together?" When he hesitated, Janet's face showed both her uncertainty and her exasperation. "You've been waiting for me, right?"

"No," he said gently. Seeing her wide-eyed shock, he continued, "You don't really want to be with me, do you, Janet? My endless pottering and puttering wasn't the only thing that annoyed you. We never fought, but we never really shared much, either. After the first shock of my leaving you rather enjoyed living your life as you liked."

She looked away. "I don't know what you're talking about." If only he weren't so darned good-looking. Janet imagined being held in those arms against that muscular chest, imagined lifting her lips to his. A noise that was no more than a soft sigh caused Janet to look up. Richard had turned away, his form so indistinct it was almost invisible.

"Richard!" she said, her voice sharp.

His figure became more defined, but when he spoke it was as though from a distance. "I'm sorry, Janet, but I have to leave." At Janet's sudden movement he turned back. "I am truly sorry," he said, his face registering both her pain and his regret at having caused it. "Is there anything you want to ask me?"

To her surprise Janet found she couldn't think of a thing to say. Why was she suddenly shy and tongue-tied? "I, well, I thought we would, we could—" Janet looked into Richard's thoughtful blue eyes and felt as though she was drowning. "Why didn't you wait for me?" she demanded.

"I live in a community that's very different from one in which you would feel comfortable," he said gently. "My wife and I—"

"Your wife!"

He looked at her steadily. "Come now, Janet. You haven't given me a moment's thought in years. The only reason I came to mind now was because talking to Kate reminded you of your days as a courageous young widow."

"I was terribly unhappy. I did grieve."

"Of course you did. But mostly it was for the loss of a certain comfort zone that being married gave you. Your unhappiness didn't last long, did it?" he said gently.

"That's unkind!" Janet's eyes narrowed. "I didn't know angels could be unkind."

For a moment he merely looked at her. "I'm not handling this well, am I? Look, you'll enjoy it here, Janet. I came to the

Academy too; it's a great place to make friends and meet people interested in the same things you are."

Janet felt like a wayward child given a consolation prize. "I don't know why you think I'll find friends," she snapped. "From what I've seen the students here have to start with basics; not many of them knew or cared much about anything spiritual while they were on earth."

"Give it a chance, Janet. You'll find that once they're here they learn fast." He smiled at her. "And maybe you'll meet someone whose name you'll remember."

"I did remember—after a while." She thought an interminable moment; then her face cleared. "Your name is Richard!"

"Actually, it isn't."

"What do you mean?" Janet said, her voice sharp.

Though still smiling, the man before her was beginning to look the slightest bit harassed. "It's a conceptual thing. Our names signify who we are, or the particular use we perform. That's probably one reason you had such difficulty recalling what I was called on earth." He lifted a hand in farewell. "Now I really must leave."

"Don't go!" She reached out to grasp his sleeve.

He waited until she released him, then placed his hand on her shoulder. "Dear Janet, I wish you well in your new life." There was tender but firm finality in the words. He gave her shoulder another comforting pat and was gone.

Janet looked down at the daisies and ivy. So he hadn't waited for her. That rankled. Despite the fact that what he'd said was true. In the past years she hadn't thought much about him, not as a person. When he'd come to mind it was as an adjunct to her widowhood, the name she'd mentioned when explaining her marital status. With a brave lift of her chin. Janet flinched at that last fleeting thought. Had she played it for plaudits? She pushed the unwelcome fancy from her. She wished he hadn't known how attracted to him she'd been just now. Because he must have known. And here he was, married and living in some heavenly society. Janet felt tears well. She let them spill down her cheeks as she crossed her arms tight about her chest. It wasn't fair. Here she was, struggling to fit in and there he was, all settled and happy in his new life. It just wasn't fair. She frowned and bit her lip as she tried to recall . . . *What was his name?*

Dan surveyed the quadrangle from beneath the big oak. He inspected the groups of young men and women in deep discussion sitting on the broad steps of the stone building, the laughing couples and the wandering paths that curved across the clipped green grass. She wasn't here.

Why had he thought she would be? The invitation in those green eyes, that's why. Wouldn't a smart babe like her realize he'd get away as soon as he could, that he'd come back the first chance he had? Dan moved further into the shade of the great tree. Probably best she wasn't here. Maybe it hadn't been such a good idea to come. What could he possibly have to say to someone as beautiful and vibrant as Pegeen?

"Well, if it isn't Dan the man."

Dan whirled about, catching his foot on an exposed root and saved himself from tumbling to the ground only by grabbing a handful of rough bark. Dan brushed his smarting hands on his jeans, blushing furiously.

"I'd love to have you at my feet, but I wouldn't want you to hurt yourself, lover."

"Pegeen?" Dan stared at the woman's thick blond hair. "You, you look different."

Pegeen touched the blond mane that fell to her shoulders in smooth waves. "A woman can change her hair color, can't she?"

Dan swallowed. "Sure, but it's so—different. It was shorter, wasn't it? And real curly?" What was he doing, talking about hair? Maybe it was a wig. Who cared? How was it he had no problem chatting with a frightened girl hiding in a garden and putting her at ease, and yet here he was, standing tongue-tied and stupid. How long before this fascinating woman laughed at his blundering attempts at conversation and walked away?

But she didn't laugh or walk away. "See that red Beemer parked on the side street over there?" She pointed to a fire-engine-red convertible. "It's mine."

"You're kidding."

"Like to go for a ride?"

They were beside the shiny red convertible before Dan had a chance to think. "Wow, an M6! Aren't they over a hundred thou?"

"Want to drive? Be my guest." Pegeen tossed him a set of keys as she opened the passenger door and slid into the leather seat.

"You're kidding," Dan breathed. Damn! How could he have said that again? She'd think he was a total idiot.

"Come on, let's blow this place and get beyond these ivy walls."

"Think we should? I mean, aren't there rules about leaving the campus?" Dan had a mental picture of an annoyed-looking Aunt Kate coming across the campus looking for him accompanied by that khaki-clad policeman. "I just got here and I don't know about stuff like that."

She batted her long-lashed green eyes at him. "Didn't you hear that campus cop? He practically ordered me off campus, so we're just following his suggestion. Come on, lover; if there are any rules about exploring outside this place, as the old saying goes, they're made to be broken."

Dan hesitated only a moment. "You know the way out?" he said, pulling the little car away from the curb.

"Just drive up to that big gate over there and see if it opens."

It did.

Dan couldn't see that much difference between the scenery outside the gates and the campus inside. There were fewer flowers and trees and no manicured lawns. The winding road led through towering hedgerows until the landscape leveled out and they found themselves traveling next to dusty fields that stretched out to rolling hills in the distance. It might not be anything special, but it seemed nice enough. Dan took one hand from the wheel and rested it on the door. "So, you've been here a while. You like it?"

"Let's say it has—possibilities. I've let them know back there," she nodded toward the disappearing towers of the Academy, "that I'd be available to teach a course or two, but so far it seems they're not that interested."

"You're a teacher?" Dan didn't sound particularly pleased. "I mean, you look too, too—"

"Young?" Pegeen gave a throaty laugh. "Don't give it another thought, lover. Let's just say I'm as young—or old—as you'd like me to be." Pegeen stroked his knee, squeezing it gently.

Dan flushed. "Uh, is there any place in particular you want to go?"

"There is a person I want to check out in these parts, someone I've heard about who might be useful for my future plans, but I don't have to see him today. We don't have to do anything right now but have some fun."

"Hey, it's getting late," Dan said in surprise. Strange, he hadn't noticed the sun was low in the afternoon sky.

"So what? You afraid there's a curfew?" Pegeen looked at him from beneath her curling lashes. "We're both adults, aren't we? We go where we want and stay where we want."

"Sure." Dan cleared his throat. "Absolutely."

6

Frank emerged from the tree line, panting as he stopped to catch his breath. He looked back at the ribbon of road he'd just traveled, at the undulating expanse of maple and oak and beech trees, the dots of grazing sheep on meadows that fronted the distant walls of the Academy campus.

Then he turned and clambered the rest of the way to the top of the dune. The far side sloped less steeply and led to a gentle series of smaller, grassy dunes with sparse trees—*cottonwood*, he thought—and in the distance was a sandy beach and a body of water that stretched as far as Frank could see. The scene was completely unlike the landscape he'd left. He might be in a different country. Had he been led here? Was he being told he should go off to explore another part of this new world? But he'd been there, done that; he'd joined a group of wanderers to explore this new world when he'd first arrived. The little group had found several fascinating communities, some delightful, some definitely not, but in the end only he and Kate—and, for a short time, the gymnast Maggie—had come to the Academy. Being accepted at the Academy had been a big deal. Had he blown it? Would he be welcome if he went back?

Was it wise to even consider going back? For a second there when he was talking with Kate, Frank hadn't been able to catch his breath. He could have sworn his heart stopped. It didn't take a genius to analyze his response to her presence, and it was obvious his attempts to sublimate his feelings, to dismiss them and get on with his life, weren't working. Matter of fact, they had failed abysmally. So what should he do? He didn't need to meet more scaly, alligator-like creatures to know he was treading on dangerous ground. He needed advice, but who could he talk to? Gregory had seemed friendly enough, but Frank cringed at the thought of exposing himself to someone who seemed so, so damned perfect.

Frank set off, slipping and sliding down the large dune in great running steps, then slogging up the smaller ones. When he came at last to the beach, he dropped onto the warm sand and sat, legs outstretched, arms propped behind him. He lifted his face to the slightly fish-tinged breeze. This place reminded him of—where? The back of Frank's neck prickled. Sure. This was a lot like the place he and Kate and the rest of the group had stopped and met Maggie's grandmother.

Where Frank had met Ben.

He'd met his son, the child who had died as an autistic four-year-old when he ran out into oncoming traffic. Now a handsome, articulate young man, Ben had appeared to Frank on a beach much like this. Was Ben somewhere nearby? Though Frank had often thought of his son since that afternoon, he had never called him. Somehow he'd felt diffident, unwilling to summon Ben from the busy, productive life his son described that day on the beach.

"I'm never too busy to come and talk. Glad you wanted me."

Frank looked over at the smiling young man with curly, black hair squatting on the sand beside him and felt only mild surprise.

"You've been accepted at the Academy. Congratulations."

"Thanks." Frank paused. "I think."

"What's up?"

"I didn't exactly know it was you I wanted to talk to, but I guess I do. Look, before we get into it, I want to ask you something about the Academy. I haven't had the balls to ask anyone there, but does getting into the Academy mean you're going to get into . . . I mean, is the next step . . ."

"Heaven?" Ben finished for him. "Most of the students 'graduate,' as they call it, but not all. Some need more instruction and are sent to another school, and there are some," his blue eyes clouded, "who are able to be at the Academy only because they've insisted on it."

"They can do that?" Frank said, diverted.

"It's much the way those who insist that they be able to enter heaven are able to. But of course they find they don't want to stay." Ben's clear eyes looked at Frank in puzzlement. "Y'know I've never been able to understand why anyone would want to chose evil. Of course I realize that's because I came here as a child; I never had the chance to rationally choose for myself between good and evil while I was on earth, but still . . ."

"I heard about that in class." Frank studied his son. "I didn't ask Hannah at the time, but I wondered. It wasn't possible for someone in your situation, but most kids, even young ones, can chose between right and wrong."

"Sure. But not rationally. That's the key word. You gotta be an adult for that." Ben lay back on his side and, digging his elbow into the sand, rested his head on his hand. "You didn't ask me here to discuss the Academy. What's the matter?"

Frank found it difficult to answer. How could he tell this wise yet naïve young man about Kate? About having thoughts that caused reptiles to appear? "Nothing that important. Mostly I just wanted to see you."

Ben's eyes were kind. "The creature you saw is a manifestation of the thoughts that have been enticing you. You didn't want them around you and you've been fighting against them. That's good."

Frank felt himself color. *Damn.* Of course Ben could see his thoughts. Frank picked up a handful of sand and let the grains trickle from his fist. He stared at the tiny pyramid they formed. "So do you know about it—the thoughts I've been having about Kate?"

Ben looked at Frank intently and then looked away, distressed. "Yeah," he said.

"Sorry," Frank said softly.

"Kate is married. She's another man's wife."

Frank's jaw tightened. "A man who is living out his life on earth. Who knows, maybe he's with someone else by now."

Ben's level gaze was compassionate. He said nothing.

Frank looked out over the sparkling water. He dug his hand into the sand, clutching the hot grains as though he could squeeze the scattering particles into a ball. Frank's hand was big, but the one Ben placed over it was bigger.

"You're trying. You're paying attention," Ben said quietly. "That's important."

Frank reached in his back pocket, took out a handkerchief and blew his nose. "Who's the parent around here and who's the kid?" he said, his voice ragged.

"From where I sit, I don't see either parent or child," Ben said easily. "Anything else you want to ask me?"

Frank looked away. "What should I do? Leave? Go off on my own? Or go back and fight it?"

"I'm not the one you should be asking, Frank."

Frank scuffed the sand with his heel. "If you're saying I should pray, I've done that. A lot."

"But have you listened? First you ask, then you listen. That's how prayer works."

"Don't suppose it's some voice coming from the sky," Frank said grimly.

Ben grinned. "Not that simple. But you might hear a voice in your head. Pay attention if you do."

"How do I know it isn't me telling myself what I want to hear?"

"You'll know." Ben stood up and reached down to put

a hand on Frank's shoulder. "Try it. It'll be okay. You'll see." And, giving Frank a dazzling smile, he vanished.

Frank rose slowly from the sand and took a few steps toward the water. *Lord, tell me what to do. Please.* He seemed to be speaking to lapping wavelets that endangered his shoes. *Should I leave the Academy, or would that be just running away? Should I go back, or is that inviting trouble?* He waited, but heard only the soft susurration of the water, the twitter of barn swallows darting to their holes in the high dunes behind him. Frank stood looking at the thin line of the horizon. What did he expect? An airplane to appear and skywrite his answer across the blue expanse?

With a weary shake of his head, Frank plodded back the way he'd come, navigating the small dunes, then up the great sloping one at the rear. It was as he slip-slid down its steep incline to a stand of fir trees at the bottom that a thought darted through Frank's mind like a shaft of light. His feelings for Kate were not only wrong; they were dangerous, dangerous for him and possibly for Kate. Did he want to take the chance of hurting Kate? Another thought followed quickly. Going back to the Academy might give him a chance to make things right.

Where had that come from? Was this the "answer" Ben told him to listen for? Frank looked through the branches of the fir trees to the cloudless blue sky. He hadn't actually heard anything. And he hadn't the slightest idea what he could do that would "make things right." *What gives? There has to be more.*

Frank waited, concentrating. He couldn't do this by himself—surely he would be given some inspiration about how he should go about it, some comforting hint of what to do. But no spark of enlightenment came.

Right. Frank gave a wry smile, but he straightened his shoulders and briskly continued his trek through the trees to the road that led back to the Academy.

THE SEARCHERS 61

It was velvet black night when Dan woke up, a flickering pain behind his eyes. Where was he? Oh yes, they'd been at this country inn—how long? Two days? Three? The days ran into each other—and the nights. Dan wrinkled his nose as a foul odor wafted from the open window. *Fertilizer? Who would be out fertilizing at night?*

A heavy snore shook the bed. Dan willed himself to lie still. Didn't want to wake her. But what a woman! She was incredible. What stamina, what imagination! And gorgeous, too. However she'd done it, she really was a blond. As he was now in a position to know, that blond hair was definitely not a wig.

Why did he feel so uneasy about being with her? He liked it here in this untraveled wilderness, and it wasn't as though he'd signed a contract to stay at that school or whatever it was. As for the past few days, they were adults, weren't they?

Have to do something about this headache. Dan reached out to flick on the lamp on the bedside table, then quickly snapped it off again. Even the soft, shaded bedside light pierced his eyes and zoomed around inside his head like a bouncing laser. In the brief instant the lamp had illuminated the room it had showed Pegeen lying ramrod straight, her head thrown back, mouth slightly open.

No, don't wake her. She was great, but man, she was insatiable. Dan eased the pillow into a tight wad and pressed it against his aching head. What was with this headache? Bad booze? Maybe the uppers Pegeen had persuaded him to take? Shouldn't have done the uppers. That was the sort of thing that had gotten him into trouble before. A wave of panic swept him as he remembered the horror of that time.

He'd started the whole thing as sort of an exploration into an exciting world, something he had intended to sample and walk away from. But it had become a nightmare, one that had taken over his existence, a spiraling descent that seemed to happen overnight. The kid he'd been a few short months before he'd arrived in Chicago could never have imagined the things he would do to get what he needed.

Thank God Mom hadn't known what had happened in the year after he'd moved to Chicago. It had been a relief when the guy at the store had given him the pistol. And he'd been right. In the end it had done the job as well as anything bigger.

Dan cautiously inched to the side of the bed, eased off the sheet, and swung his legs to the floor, clenching his teeth at the jagged slash of pain that seared through his head. For a long moment he sat in the darkness, his hands clutching the side of the mattress. He leaned forward and felt for the jeans he had flung onto the chair beside the bed. Yeah, there it was, the small, solid lump in the pocket. He could take it and throw it out the window, but what was the use? He'd find it in the jeans pocket when he dressed in the morning.

He shouldn't have let Aunt Kate see the fear that had driven him to use the pistol. What he'd said had been God's truth, but he shouldn't have blurted it out like that. Men kept those things to themselves.

"Hey, lover babe?" The sleepy voice came from the darkness.

"Yeah?" Dan answered softly.

"Anything wrong?"

Dan hesitated. "Headache," he said.

"Poor baby. Come here and let Mama make it all better." The lazy words were a command as much as an invitation.

"Geez Pegeen, we just, I mean you can't mean—"

"Oh, but I do, lover, I do."

Despite the pounding in his head Dan began to slide under the sheet obediently, but halfway into the bed, he paused. "I really gotta get something for this headache, babe. Let it have a chance to work and I'll be back."

"Pooper," Pegeen said, yawning. "Well, wake me up. Promise?"

"Sure." Without putting on the light, Dan grabbed his jeans from the chair and, arms outstretched in the dark, sidled to the foot of the bed and made his way to the bathroom. He clicked on the bathroom light only long enough to open the medicine cabinet and take out the aspirin bottle and swallow two pills. He dressed hurriedly, then stood with his ear to the door and waited until he was certain the snores had resumed in the next room. He quietly opened the door, holding his shoes against his chest, and tiptoed across the bedroom to let himself into the hallway.

No one saw Dan creep down the uncarpeted stairs of the inn. No one saw him cross the empty lobby, ease open the front door, and disappear into the night.

"Actually, I suppose Kate's nice enough, but she's so, I don't know, so professorial. I don't feel comfortable with her, and anyway, the one time we talked it didn't seem like she enjoyed being with me all that much, either."

Hannah suppressed a sigh. "You certainly don't have to have Kate or anyone else show you around, Janet, I simply thought she'd be a good person to introduce you the rest of your classmates. Are you sure you don't want to make an effort to get along?"

"Oh, I suppose I'll try. But I still don't see why I've been put with people who know so little." Janet brushed her fingers through her short hair. "Aren't we supposed to be placed with others like us? People of the same religion, the same culture?"

"Not necessarily," said Hannah, her voice mild. "We don't always know why certain people are sent to us rather than elsewhere, but we can be sure each person who comes here has special needs that are best met at this particular Academy. Our job is to do our best to meet those needs as they are presented to us." She looked at Janet thoughtfully. "It's not only the teaching staff who can meet the needs of the students, you know. Have you considered that there may be someone here who needs something that you're uniquely able to give?"

Janet brightened. "You're right, I did answer some of Kate's questions," she said. Her shoulders slumped. "But I'm not sure about everything I told her. I mean, some things are different here than what I expected, different from what I was taught."

Hannah pushed away from her desk and leaned back in her leather swivel chair. "Perhaps what you were taught was true, but your understanding of these things might not always have been correct—or perhaps I should say not complete." As she examined Janet's face, her gaze sharpened. "But something else is bothering you, Janet, not just your classmates' lack of knowledge about the spiritual world."

"It's not fair." Janet picked up a damask pillow and cradled it against her stomach. "I thought when I got here I wouldn't be alone any more!" An ending hiccup became a wail.

Hannah's look was gentle. "You expected to be with Richard, didn't you?"

How did Hannah know his name when she couldn't remember it? "I don't want to talk about it."

"Nor shall you—not until you want to." Hannah got up and came around her desk. "My advice is to look around," she said briskly. "Be alert for the chance to be of use to someone. It will make you feel much better."

"Thanks," said Janet, sounding anything but grateful. She tossed aside the pillow and got up. "I'll do that little thing."

Hannah grinned. "And Kate thinks you have no sense of humor."

Janet halted, outraged. "She said that? And how would she know anyway? She didn't make much of an effort to show me anything. Like I said, she hasn't been around since we were in the garden."

"She's been extremely concerned about her nephew, another new arrival. It seems he has chosen to leave us for a time." A frown creased Hannah's forehead, but she returned to the business at hand. "I'm sure Kate didn't mean to be unkind or inattentive, Janet."

Janet didn't look mollified. She gave an abrupt little nod to Hannah and left the office. She clomped down the hall to the gardens outside and headed for the arbor. She needed to think, and the place that immediately came to mind was the stone bench in the little arbor that looked out over the hills. But before she reached the garden gate, she heard something, a keening sound that seemed to come from the spikes of purple-blue delphiniums by the garden wall. It came again.

Janet hesitated, than came back. "Who's there?" she called out.

A choking sob came from the delphiniums. Janet stepped into the garden and immediately a small, dark-skinned young woman darted from behind the delphiniums, waving her away with frantic hands. "No! You hurt the flowers! Everyone who come here step on flowers!"

Janet took an awkward step back onto the path. Of all the nerve, when she'd only been trying to help.

As the woman picked her way to the path, Janet saw that it was the silent girl she'd tried to talk to earlier, and that her round young face was blotched and swollen.

Janet's annoyance disappeared. "What's the matter?" she said gently.

The young woman shook her head dumbly.

Janet tried a different tack. "My name's Janet."

The woman ducked her head, then darted a distrustful glance at Janet and said softly, "I am called Birgit."

"Well, Birgit, if I'm going to be able to help you, you'll have to tell me what's wrong."

Great tears rolled down Birgit's broad cheeks. "She's gone! Someone has taken her."

"Who?"

"My rabbit." Birgit glared at Janet. "I think they take her to try to make me talk."

"I doubt it," said Janet. "The people here wouldn't do anything like that. But talking does make things easier, doesn't it? Now about this rabbit of yours, when did you last see it?"

"Her," Birgit corrected Janet.

"Her," Janet agreed.

"I came back to my rooms from taking a walk and before I get my rabbit I go to the kitchen to get the food that is left for me when I am hungry. I bring my dinner to the table, but when I go to get my rabbit so she can eat too, she is not in her basket. She is gone! I look everywhere. I come out here to look in the garden, but she is not here. She is not anywhere." Birgit's dark eyes sought Janet's. "Do you think she run away?"

"I haven't the foggiest. But I shouldn't think you have to worry," Janet said comfortingly. "If you truly need to have this rabbit of yours—does she have a name?"

"Shoma." Birgit barely breathed the two syllables.

"If you truly need to be with Shoma, you'll find her—or she'll find you."

Birgit's lower lip quivered. "Did she, did she go because of me?"

Janet considered the possibility. "Probably," she said, but compassion took any sting from the word. "Look, Birgit, if you've done something you ought not to have done, or not done something you should have, and if you're sorry and try to do better, I'm positive Shoma will come back."

Birgit was silent, resting her chin on her chest. She knew what she'd done. But it wasn't anything so bad. She'd been curious, just wanted to know where the boy who'd said his name was Dan was going. He had been so nice to her, had made her laugh—well, not out loud, but he'd made her smile. So she'd followed him when he left the garden. She had watched from the trees at the edge of the quadrangle as he talked to the beautiful blond-haired girl. It was then that the darkness had filled Birgit's head, a darkness that rose like bile as she saw the blond girl's gracefulness, the easy way she and Dan stood as they spoke to each other.

A dull anger gnawed at her stomach even now, as she stood here with this sharp-voiced woman. *It's not fair!* Why must she always be on the outside, why must she stand watching a world where she could never belong? When Dan and the girl got in the little red car and drove off, a pain pierced Birgit— so sharp she had to clutch her chest. And in that moment Birgit had wanted the silly blond girl to know what it was like to hurt, the way Birgit knew. She wanted the girl to know how it felt to lay curled in a tight ball of pain, moaning her despair to the dark.

Shoma had gone because of the envy and hate Birgit had felt at that moment; Birgit knew it as surely as if she'd heard the verdict spoken. That hatred had caused the other thing she hadn't said anything about to Janet. When she'd picked up her plate to take it to the kitchen, in place of a succulent salad there had been a slimy tangle of seaweed. Birgit bowed her head, her hands in tight fists at her sides.

"Birgit!" Janet's voice brought Birgit back to the garden path. "Don't just stand there quivering. I told you Shoma will come back to you if you're truly sorry for whatever it is you've done. Goodness, it can't be that awful."

"I thought bad things," Birgit said, her words expressing a world of repentance. "And I am sorry, I am so sorry."

It wasn't the young woman's obvious grief and regret that caused a catch at Janet's throat. It was the realization that Birgit's transgression had been merely a thought. The girl hadn't actually done anything wrong! How many times had Janet allowed herself the luxury of thoughts she knew were wrong? *Wrong?* Some had been downright wicked.

"Well now," Janet said hurriedly, "let's see what we can do. Have you spoken to Hannah about this?"

"Oh no. She, she would make me go to class!"

"Is that the worst that can happen? You sit with a bunch of people and listen to them talk for a few hours each day. Come on, I'll go with you; let's see what Hannah has to say."

And so Janet found herself in Hannah's office again, a reluctant Birgit in tow. "You see, Birgit's really sorry for whatever it is she thought," Janet said, finishing her tale. "So don't you think she should get her rabbit back?"

Hannah had listened to Janet's explanation of Shoma's disappearance in silence. Her eyes were filled with compassion as they rested on Birgit's tear-stained face. "What do you think, dear?" she asked the thickset girl. "Were those thoughts something you want to be a part of you?"

Birgit bowed her head. "I do not want the girl hurt," she said softly. "I do not want anyone to be hurt like me."

"Of course not."

Janet looked from one to the other, mystified. Neither Birgit nor Hannah seemed to be aware of her presence.

"Interesting that those thoughts only came when you were near those particular people," Hannah murmured thoughtfully. She drummed her fingers on her desk. "Janet's quite right. I think you may find your rabbit in her basket when you return to your rooms."

Birgit looked up, her eyes bright. "Shoma has come back?" She cast a longing look at the door, but made no move toward it.

"I think so. But Birgit, will you try coming to class tomorrow?" Hannah coaxed.

"If she comes with me," she said, motioning to Janet.

"All right. I was going to have one of our assistants tutor you, but it might be good for you come to the classes and participate as much or as little as you like."

"And can I bring Shoma?"

A small smile tugged at the corners of Hannah's mouth. "Absolutely. Now off with you." Hannah watched Birgit scuttle from the office. "Well done, Janet," she said. "Thank you."

"Hey, buddy, wait up!"

The jeep came to a halt on the dirt road fifty feet ahead of the hitchhiker. The large man rested his hand on the wheel.

"You know me?" Dan said. And then he caught sight of the woman beside the dark-skinned man. "Aunt Kate! What are you doing here?"

She was out of the jeep and striding toward him. "It's more like, what are you doing here in the Trackless Parts?" she said, her tone tart. But she gave him a short, hard hug. "I've been worried sick about you, Daniel."

"They call it the Trackless Parts?" Dan asked, diverted. He looked about. "Doesn't look trackless to me."

"What does it look like to you?" the man at the wheel asked.

"This is Percy, Dan," Kate explained. "He hauled you back to the cottage when you were in your sleeping phase and keeled over on me."

"Hey man, thanks," Dan said. "The, ah, the friend I was with thought it looked like Georgia. Personally, I think this part is sort of like the New Jersey Pine Barrens."

"This is all fascinating," said Kate, "but why don't you get in the jeep and we'll head back to the campus. It's getting near sunset."

"So what's so special about sunset?" Dan showed no immediate inclination to join his aunt, who had climbed in the front of the jeep beside the big man. "I'm not sure if I want to go back; matter of fact, I'm not sure exactly where I want to go."

"Get in," Kate pointed to the back seat. "We'll discuss your travel plans later."

"What happens at sunset?" Dan persisted as he climbed in.

"Never stayed to find out," Percy said noncommittally. "You been out here a few days; what happened to you?"

Dan shifted his position. "Oh me and this friend have been driving around checking the place out. But we always seem to land at an inn by late afternoon, and I can tell you the inns around here have all been pretty comfortable."

"This friend of yours is a woman?" Kate looked back at him. "Is this Pegeen we're talking about?"

Dan gave an acquiescent shrug, but refused to return her steady gaze.

"Where is she?" Kate demanded.

"I left her at an inn a few miles back," Dan mumbled. "I know it's sort of a lousy thing to do, but things were getting a little too serious. I mean, the situation was getting kind of weird."

"Weird? I'll give you weird; it goes by the name of Pegeen." Kate snorted. "Listen Daniel, we're going to have to talk, and I don't mean just about young women who spout stupid ideas about sex."

They were still on the dirt road, but the scenery had changed. Palms towered above thick palmetto bushes. A fresh, salty breeze swept around the jeep, and a moment later a glimpse of blue-green water and a beach appeared beyond the palmettos.

Percy pulled over and stopped in the shade of a giant banyan tree. "Your aunt's right, my friend. Did you know she's been looking for you the past three days, even shanghaied me to take her outside the Academy grounds for the past two?"

Kate twisted around to face Dan again. "We've found you and that's all that matters right now. But Dan, do you know where you've been? We call where we are now 'the world of spirits,' a place between heaven and hell, but I can tell you this sector of the Trackless Parts is a lot nearer hell than heaven.

You worry me when you say you felt pretty comfortable at the inns here. Dan, believe me, you don't want to feel comfortable in the Trackless Parts."

For the first time, Dan seemed disturbed. "Are you saying that the, the bad guys who arrive might be here instead of up there where you guys are?" He looked around. "They might be right around here?"

"Probably not." Kate sighed and pushed a stray lock of hair from her forehead. "It's not as simple as bad guys go here, good guys go there. Everyone awakens in this world feeling pretty much the same as he did before. It's only after he or she is here for a while that what's inside begins to surface. That's when a person discovers what he loves more than anything else, and it's that love that pulls a person toward heaven or hell."

"What he loves? Like what, for instance?" Dan said, a frown furrowing his forehead.

"Like, does he have any interest in or empathy for anyone but himself?"

For a moment Dan was silent. "Sure. Sure I do," he said, looking relieved as he remembered the shy girl in the garden. *What was her name?*

If Kate was surprised, she concealed it. "Well, that's fine then," she said. "I just wanted you to realize that it would be better if you stayed on campus, at least until you know how things work around here." She turned to Percy. "Think we should get back?"

Percy nodded and gunned the motor, sending the jeep scudding up the sandy dirt road, and in what seemed an incredibly short time, they were driving through the great iron gates of the Academy. They pulled into the parking lot beside what looked like equipment sheds and Kate got out. She looked questioningly at her nephew. "Coming?"

Before he could reply, Percy put a big hand on Dan's shoulder. "Why don't you leave him with me, Kate? I think it wouldn't hurt if we had a little talk of our own."

He and Kate exchanged glances. "Right," she said. "Please keep in mind that I'm here for you if you need me, Dan. Make that *when* you need me." She gave them both a brief smile and left.

Dan sat silent for a long moment, rubbing his hands together and examining his nails as though searching for hidden dirt. "What?" he said finally.

"Suppose you climb up here to the front and we start with that 'weird' woman you were with. Kate said her name was Pegeen?"

Dan clambered into the seat beside Percy. "She, it, wasn't weird at first," he said. "I gotta say she was everything I ever dreamed of in a woman—and then some. But boy, has she got some ideas. Like she thinks we're still on earth, at least some of the time she does." Dan looked away. "And sometimes it's like she's in a frickin' classroom. She lectures me about how women have been subjugated by men since forever and how it has to stop. She says she's going to show the world the way things should be handled. Like how her and me are going to have a relationship that'll show the way it should be between a man and a woman when they're both 'centered in reality.'" He brushed his hand over his eyes. "Sure. And she's telling me this right after she's wrung my sorry ass for the fourth time and still won't let me be. Man, it's like she's doing some kind of research and I'm her laboratory specimen."

"Do tell?" The deep rumble of Percy's voice sounded suspiciously like laughter.

The glance Dan flicked him was sullen. "Let's see how you'd perform if you had someone giving you sociology lessons every time you turn around."

"Still got that little pistol with you?"

Dan's expression was answer enough.

"I saw it in your jeans when I carried you back to the cottage. You might give some thought about how to get rid of it, you know."

"You've got to be kidding!" It exploded from Dan. "I haven't been thinking of anything else." He caught Percy's sideways look. "Well, the past few days it's sorta been on the back burner," he admitted.

"Here, let's take a look at it." Percy held out his hand, and after a moment's indecision Dan handed it to him.

The big man examined it, the black handle and nickel-plated barrel almost disappearing in his large hand. "Nice little piece," he said. "Haven't seen an FN Baby Browning since, well, let's say in a long time." He detached the magazine, inspected the bullets and reloaded the tiny pistol. "Semiautomatic, made in the fifties, I'd guess. In Belgium."

"You want it? You can have it."

Percy handed it back. "It's not yours to give away. At least not yet."

A noise escaped Dan. "What do I have to do?"

"First off, you stop chasing tail. Second, you start attending classes. Haven't thought of number three yet, but I will."

"What makes you an expert?"

Percy crossed his big arms over the steering wheel. "Your Aunt Kate told me about why you used that Baby Browning. Told me how you figured using it was better than what might happen to you in prison."

"She told you? Damn."

"She's worried about you. That's why I was out there with her." Percy met Dan's eyes, his own somber. "Kid, I know about prison. That's where I—transitioned."

"Where you died," Dan said bluntly.

"Where I got a shiv in the back during a fight."

"You were a guard?"

Percy shook his head.

"You were a prisoner?"

Percy gave the briefest of affirmative nods.

Dan took a moment to digest this. "So when you woke up here, you weren't in prison?" he said tentatively.

"I was in the prison infirmary, at least that's what I thought. Then when I was fully awake, they told me I was free to do what I wanted."

Dan stiffened. "They let people who've been in prison be with everyone else here?"

"All I know is what happened to me. I was told I could go anywhere I wanted."

Dan drew a quick breath, about to ask a question, but just as quickly changed his mind. Instead he rubbed his finger along the dusty dashboard, then looked up and said, as though a thought had just occurred to him, "What were you in for?"

"Maybe someday, I'll share that with you, bro. Right now I'd just as soon not get into it." Percy took the keys from the ignition and put them in his pocket. "You must be hungry. You get a move on and you'll find they lay out some pretty good food here." He gave an amiable nod and sauntered off toward the sheds.

7

The creature waited in the brush not far from the bottom of the hill. From where it crouched it could just see the spires of the Academy towers. From time to time it absently reached down to scratch the sandy ground, but mostly it remained quietly attentive, eyes searching the road that led from the desert region below. It liked this moment in the day, when dusk gave promise of the night ahead. The creature tilted its head and sniffed the breeze. It stretched its long neck to peek above the twigs and branches and was rewarded by the sight of a woman striding up the road, clenched fists swinging at her side. The creature waited until she was just past its clump of brush to step into the road.

"May I ask where you're headed?" it asked.

The woman whirled about, fists raised, her combative stance belied by the fright in her eyes. She swallowed and thrust out her chin. "What the hell do you mean, jumping out of the bushes like that?"

The creature raised a placating appendage. "I didn't mean to frighten you; I'm a traveler like yourself. I simply waited until you were near enough so I could see who you were before announcing myself. Can't be too careful around here, I've found."

She relaxed slightly and lifted an eyebrow. "So who did you decide I was?"

"A very beautiful young lady," it said promptly. "Not only a beautiful young lady, but one obviously more than willing to take on anyone who might try to do her mischief."

"You got that right, friend. But I have to tell you that if we're going to have any kind of conversation you're going to have to cut out the sexist remarks."

"I beg your pardon?"

"That 'beautiful young lady' crap."

"Sorry." The creature hung its head. "We don't meet too many, ah, women like you in these parts. Gorgeous, assertive, and brainy into the bargain."

"And how would you know I'm brainy?" the woman asked. She put a hand on her outthrust hip and cocked her head.

"It's obvious," he purred. "I'm Zaroth, by the way. At your service."

"Pegeen," she said. "At least that's the name I'm using at the moment."

"Any name you choose is quite all right with me." Zaroth's voice deepened. "I see you're headed for the hallowed halls of learning." He gave a disdainful flip of his appendage toward the Academy. "But perhaps I should be more circumspect. You're enrolled up there?"

"Not really," Pegeen said with an angry shrug. "It's ridiculous that they would even consider asking me to attend classes, especially when I'd offered to teach a session on my specialty. After all, I've been a full professor for the past twen—" she stopped. "For quite a while."

"I like your spirit." Zaroth dusted off a large rock at the side of the road with a sweep of his furled appendage and gestured to Pegeen to take a seat. When she did, he perched beside her. "So you're just visiting these parts?"

"I decided to check out the area with a friend. I'd heard it had possibilities." Pegeen's face darkened. "At least I thought he was a friend until he ran away like a scared rabbit."

Zaroth looked appropriately shocked. "He ran away? Is

that why you're reduced to walking along this dusty road? He left you without transportation?"

"No, he isn't that much of a bastard," Pegeen said. "Anyway, by now he knows I'd have his head if he made off with my car. No, the damned thing wouldn't start. Won't even turn over. And no one at the inn seems to give a damn. So here I am hoofing it."

"Ah. May I venture to say I can't be sorry you were put to such trouble, since it meant you happened by my, ah, resting place." He sidled closer. "If I may be so bold, my dear, I hope you won't find it sexist, if I also say I find you very, very attractive? Quite a tempting morsel, in fact."

Pegeen looked at him, puzzled. "Why do you talk like a character out of a Victorian novel, and a bad one at that?"

Zaroth put the palm of his clawed appendage to his forehead and closed his eyes. "How clumsy of me. You see, due to my calling I'm used to speaking in what may seem to be a rather pedantic style. Quite right that you call me on it. I should have said, let's see, that you're the type I really dig, the kind of chick I'd like to move and groove with." At the look on Pegeen's face, he stopped. "I still didn't get it right, did I?"

"Better stick with the Victorian rhetoric. At least it has a certain charm." But she smiled at him. "Look, it's getting dark, and I ought to be thinking about heading back the school. I haven't been able to locate the person I came to see and I don't fancy staying out here at night. At least they have good beds and decent food. You going there too?"

"I think not."

"Oh?" There was a tinge of disappointment in her voice.

"Frankly, my dear, the people up there are prejudiced. They can't bear to have anyone around who is a little different. If you look a bit different, if you espouse dissimilar ideas, you're not welcome."

"Isn't that the truth? The powers that be wouldn't recognize a new concept if it smacked them in the face." Pegeen frowned and leaned back so she could look into Zaroth's eyes. "What's this about your looking different? I hope you're not being coy, because I'm not into coy. To state the obvious, and I have a hunch you're very aware of the fact, there aren't many men around here as good-looking as you, Zaroth." She tilted her head and gave him a small smile.

"How nice of you to say so." Zaroth tucked Pegeen's hand beneath his appendage. "Let me walk with you a short way. I have a feeling we're very—shall I say, simpatico—and there are certain things I'd like to talk to you about."

Pegeen let him help her to her feet, but when she looked up at Zaroth her eyes were shrewdly appraising. "You were expecting me, weren't you?"

"What acuity! You have a mind like a steel trap, m'dear! Yes, I was expecting you. You see, when I heard you were asking about the university here, I must admit my curiosity was piqued."

"Yeah, nobody would tell me where it was or anything about it, except that there were important people in charge. They wouldn't even tell me who they were." Pegeen's eyes narrowed. "Hey! You're one of them, aren't you?"

"One of what, my dear?"

"One of the movers and shakers at the university down there. I've heard you people are on the cutting edge of new thought."

Zaroth bowed his head modestly. "We try to be. Look," he said, "you tell me what you've heard and I'll tell you about us from my perspective, and we'll make our way up to this institution where you've made your home—your temporary home, I trust."

Pegeen felt a slight shiver as Zaroth led her up the road.

She told herself it wasn't exactly fright she felt, but it wasn't exactly excitement, either. It was, she decided, a delicious combination of the two.

⁓

"He was waiting when I got here," Kate said, surveying the large black, brown, and white dog beside her on Dan's doorstep. "What kind do you think he is? He's not quite big enough for a St. Bernard." She patted his shaggy head.

Dan eyed the dog without interest. "Looks like a Bernese Mountain Dog," he said. "You're here because . . . ?"

"I thought you might want company for dinner."

"Not really." Dan flushed at Kate's level glance. "Sorry, but I've had a lousy day; I was looking forward to just coming back here and crashing."

Kate's lips thinned.

"But since you're here, come on in," Dan said hastily. He fumbled open the door. "Really, I mean it."

Kate hesitated, then followed him inside. The dog lumbered after them as though invited. "What do we do with the pooch? Since he was on your doorstep, I'll bet he's meant for you."

"I have more than I can handle without taking care of a dog," Dan said. "You found him; maybe he's yours."

"Mine? I wouldn't know what to do with him. Howard and I never considered having a dog; couldn't with our schedules." But it was Kate who took a bowl from the kitchen cupboard, filled it with water, and placed it on the scrubbed wooden floor beside the sink. The big dog lapped the water gratefully and Kate knelt beside him, sinking her fingers into his shaggy ruff. "What's your name, fella?"

Dan, collapsed on the couch beside the fireplace, raised his head to look at the dog. "Percy?"

At Kate's questioning glance, he said, "You gotta admit, they're both plenty big, and I wouldn't mind having either one of them between me and anyone I met in a dark alley."

He thought a moment. "But maybe the real Percy wouldn't appreciate it."

"How did it go with Percy?" Kate said quietly. "He is a good guy to have around, you know."

Does she know that Percy was a con? Dan thought briefly of telling his aunt and seeing her eyes widen in surprise. *No. She's right. Percy's a good guy. Whatever he did.* "Yeah, I know," he said to Kate. "How about Buster?"

Kate took the change of subject without comment. She considered the big dog. "He does look like a Buster."

Dan snapped his fingers. "Here, Buster. Come."

The big dog sat.

"Hey Buster, move your butt over here."

Buster's tail thumped the floor, but he did not move.

"Buster, you've been summoned," Kate told him sternly. "Get going."

Buster rose, ambled across the room to the couch, and put his head on Dan's knee. Dan jerked away from the drooling dewlaps. "Damn," he said. He sat up and surveyed the wet spot on his jeans. "They have gardens without weeds and roses without thorns here. Can't they do dogs that don't slobber?"

"You'd think so." Kate handed Dan a paper towel. "Look, Daniel, I can understand if you want some time alone, but will you promise me you'll call me tomorrow? I won't bug you about going to classes, though I think you might like them. There are things you need to learn and the classes are a good way to find out about them."

"Can't I stay here even if I don't go to classes?" Dan looked about the cozy room.

"I'll have to check on that. If you decide you'd rather not go, maybe we can figure out something else."

Dan adjusted the pillow beneath his head. "What's so special about the classes anyway?"

The question caught Kate off-guard. After all her time at the Academy it should be simple to answer him, but she found she hadn't the slightest idea how to tell this edgy, apprehensive nephew of hers what these wonderful classes were like.

"What makes them special? Well, to start with, they're unlike any others I've experienced, and I've experienced more than most. They are interactive: a question is posed, and the class usually divides into groups that consider it and come up with their best answer. The teacher lets each group give their take on the subject and then when we've finished, we're given the real answer. The truth."

"From the teacher?"

"Sometimes. Not always. Sometimes another angel appears, one from a different heaven, that is, and," she gestured helplessly, "he or she tells it like it is."

"So, like, tell me a 'truth.'" He put an arm beneath his head and looked at her with earnest eyes.

"Don't try to con a teacher, Daniel. Do you think I haven't had students ask me the same kind of question with the same kind of phony, 'tell me more' look in their adorable eyes when they want to avoid classwork?

"But if you really want to know—we learn how God's love is the basis of both the natural and spiritual worlds, that it is God's love that enables us to think and breathe and live every moment of every day. We learn how he is with every one of us every moment, whether we are in heaven, or hell, or on one of the myriad earths in his universe. We learn the truth that, paradoxically, though all life is from God, each person is given the gift of freedom and rationality so that he or she can choose, and can act as if he lives from himself alone, can feel that the life within her is her own." Kate stopped and grinned. "You know, your eyes are glazed."

Dan gave a sheepish blink. "No, no, it's interesting."

"Buster was more interested than you, and that's just

because he thinks there's a chance I might feed him. Look, I ought to get back to my rooms. Don't let my little lecture scare you off. Five will get you ten if you decide to go to a class you'll discover it's fun. Don't look like that—I mean it. Meanwhile, what do we do with Buster?" She eyed the big dog who sat looking at her hopefully. "I can't take him back to the dorm."

"Why not? He likes you."

Buster looked from Kate to Dan and thumped his tail on the floor.

"Don't be ridiculous. I can't." Kate's voice was wistful. "I do wish you could come with me, Buster," she addressed the dog. "I've always wanted a dog, though I hadn't imagined one quite as sizeable as you."

Buster's tail did double time.

"Oh come on, take him, Aunt Kate. You know you want to."

Kate smiled. "You want me to be a rebel too, right? Let the folks around here know you aren't the only troublemaker in the family?" She snapped her fingers at Buster. "Okay fella, since you seem to have decided to stick around, you may as well come along. Let's see what happens when a large dog decides to take up residence in one of the dormitories."

Buster gave a cheerful woof and ambled past her toward the door, plumed tail high.

8

Frank wiped the remnants of dew from the bench and closed his laptop, placing it beside him. That was enough for today's assignment. He stretched, folded his arms across his chest and leaned back, closing his eyes. The morning sun filtered through the clustered leaves of the grape arbor that arched over him, the rays warming his upturned face. Only an occasional twitch of clenched jaw muscles betrayed the fact that Frank was not the picture of relaxation he seemed.

Would it work? Would sheer resolve and dogged concentration take his mind off Kate? He had never worked at anything this hard. Since he'd made his way back to the Academy, he'd worked on it. And prayed. Hadn't prayed as much or this earnestly since the time after the accident when he'd sat beside Ben's hospital crib. Kate, bless her, seemed oblivious of the fact that he'd been avoiding her. Probably too worried about that nephew of hers. Of course, the kid's act was all bravado. The way he still constantly fingered his jeans pocket, checking and rechecking, made it obvious he was scared out of his mind. The next time Frank was with Kate, should he offer to talk to the kid?

Frank felt a visceral pain stab at his gut. There wouldn't be a next time. He'd made a pact with himself. No getting into situations that would invite scaly creatures to come around.

A slight noise from the other sheltered trellis on the far side of the outlook jolted Frank from his thoughts. He craned to see through the grape vines, but could distinguish nothing but dappled sunshine on the thick tangle of leaves. There it was again. A muffled sob. *Oh great, a crying woman.* Frank rose and took a cautious step away from the bench, then another. A couple more and he'd be able to get away undetected.

A twig snapped beneath his foot. Frank froze. What the hell was a twig doing on these pristine pathways?

"Who's there?" The choked words came from the other side of the trellis.

Frank suppressed a sigh and walked back. He'd never been much good with crying women, though he'd had to deal with plenty of them. "Anything I can do?" he said, thrusting his hands into his pants pockets.

The woman wiped the heels of her hands across her cheeks and gave a brisk shake of her head. "No, no. It's just a cold coming on," she said. "I thought getting some fresh air might help."

Yeah. And colds leave tear stains on your shirt. He knew the woman. Janet. The one who always had her hand raised to answer any and all questions. "You're in my nine o'clock class."

"And you're a friend of Kate's. You're the Chicago policeman," Janet said as she brushed a stray leaf from her crisply ironed slacks.

Frank's eyelid twitched. "It's been quite a while since I've been on active duty. Look, you sure you're all right?"

"Of course." The tone was defiant, but Janet's mouth quivered. She turned suddenly, but not before Frank saw her eyes fill with tears.

This time Frank could not suppress a sigh. But he went to the bench and sat down. "Want to talk about it?"

"Why would I want to talk to someone I don't even know?"

"Sometimes it's easier that way," Frank said mildly.

Janet looked out over the hillside to where gardens stretched into the distance. "He didn't wait for me." The words came tumbling out. "I waited for him, but he didn't wait for me."

"Husband? Boyfriend?"

"Husband."

"He's here at the Academy?"

"No," she said. "He came here long ago, when we were both young. I waited through all the years until I was old, and here he is still young."

Frank considered telling Janet that she looked pretty much twenty-something to him, but decided this might not be the time for compliments. "You've met him?"

"He came a while ago when I thought of him and," a hiccup interrupted her quavering sentence, "and we talked. Then this morning I thought of him again and he came again, but he made it clear it was just to visit. He as much as told me I had to live my own life and find my own way. And then he left. And even though I've just been with him I can't remember his name!" It was a wail.

"Richard," said Frank.

"How did you do that?" Janet shot him an infuriated look.

Frank shrugged. "I guess it must be there in your mind somewhere."

The news didn't seem to make Janet any happier. "Anyway, he said it wasn't his name anymore. He told me, I, I wouldn't feel comfortable in his community, that we're completely different," she stopped.

Frank felt his gut twist; he knew how that went. "You loved him a lot," he said, his voice gentle.

"Well of course I did. Do." But for the first time she seemed uncertain.

Frank waited.

"I mean I liked being married; it wasn't like he said, that I didn't even think of him much after a while." She sniffled. "Well, maybe I did enjoy being on my own, making the decisions, doing what I wanted to do." She gave Frank a lopsided smile. "Do I sound like a horrible, self-absorbed person?"

"Not at all. You had to live your own life." Personally, Frank thought Richard was probably well out of it. The woman was, in fact, a pain. Frank made a move to rise. But she was so unhappy. He leaned back on the hard stone bench. Try another subject, anything to take her mind off her long-ago spouse. "You seem to know a lot more than the rest of the class about the stuff we're learning," he said.

She brightened. "I should think I would. After all, I've known all my life most of the things you're just beginning to learn about."

"'Zat so? You're saying the rest of the world's religions are wide of the mark? Back on earth there's one that has a lock on all we've been learning here?"

"No, no," Janet made a little fluttering motion of denial. "I didn't mean that. All religions contain great, basic truths, the ones a person needs to live a life that will lead them to heaven. But you could definitely say the religion I'm talking about has more clear, more detailed truths about how to live that life." She paused. "But I'm finding our understanding of those truths is limited and our interpretation of them can be flawed—or I guess I should say, *my* understanding and *my* interpretation," she finished with what seemed to Frank like uncharacteristic humility.

"Suppose you tell me about it," Frank said, grasping at the subject. At least she'd stopped crying. For now.

Janet raised an eyebrow. "In twenty-five words or less?"

At her supercilious tone Frank rose from the bench. "Or maybe not," he said, his voice cool.

"No, wait, I didn't mean to be rude." Janet gave him a rueful smile and then disarmed him completely with, "It just seems to come naturally with me." She gestured to the bench beside her. "If you like, I'll try, but, well, it's such an enormous subject."

He sat down again. "Use words of one syllable. Draw pictures."

Janet laughed aloud. "Now who's being rude?"

Frank joined her laughter. "You got me. Look, since you seem to already know a lot about this place, maybe you could fill me in on a couple of things."

"Shoot."

"I've wondered about the people who work here at the Academy. Are they all angels like Gregory and Hannah?"

"A lot of them are, but I think some are what they call 'good spirits'—people who aren't angels yet, but will be."

Frank mulled this over. "One time Gregory talked about going home with Hannah. Where's 'home'?"

Janet gave him an indulgent smile that made Frank want to reconsider his decision to help this annoying woman. But she saw his reaction and said quickly, "I assume they live in a heavenly community nearby—one of the natural heavens. Of course I'm speaking figuratively. Near and far haven't any relevance in this world. When they're needed here, they're here, sort of like being paged without a beeper. When they want to be 'home,' they're home." Janet cocked her head. "Anything else?"

"What about that light that shines around them when they're together? I've noticed it gets brighter when they look at each other."

"The Lord, God if you will, is the light of this world, of all worlds, and that light, filled with his love, is what makes all life, both spiritual and natural, possible. The light you saw around Gregory and Hannah is a reflection of their love, the special love married couples have from the Lord."

Frank nodded slowly, then looked at her. "You knew all this before you came here?"

Janet pulled a leaf from the vine above her and twisted it. "To tell the truth, I didn't really pay as much attention to it as I should have. Look, I don't know why I'm the one explaining this stuff to you. Oh sure, I know the basic spiel about good and truth, that good—doing it—is what makes truth living, that love is what activates and energizes truth, but I realize now that a lot of the time I was sitting in church I was just taking up space. I didn't always keep my mind on what was being said." She gave a short laugh. "If you want the unvarnished truth, more often than not I was thinking about classes I had to prepare or committee meetings that had to be scheduled."

Janet got up and paced the flagstone arbor. "I know I should have done more studying, more applying to my life what I knew to be true. Being in the classes here has made me realize how much most people would give to have had the chance to learn the things I grew up hearing." She paused and looked at him angrily. "Not that it was a picnic for me, you know, having such definite guidelines—knowing the choices you made were ones that affected your life to eternity. I mean, the choices I made . . . that affected my life." Her lips trembled.

At the memory of some of those choices, Frank guessed. "Maybe I've had my quota of religious tutoring for now," he said. He knew his voice sounded falsely hearty, but he continued, "You know about me; I was a Chicago cop. Tell me about yourself. What did you do?"

Janet wiped her eyes and lifted her chin. "I was a teacher. Elementary school, not college like your friend Kate. And I don't know if we can stay away from the subject of religion. All my adult life I lived in a small, suburban community where most of the people belonged to the church I was telling you about. My father was a minister, my grandfather too." Her voice gained confidence. "Grandfather was a well-known theologian, a bishop, in fact. And not just in theological circles; he was regarded as a scholar in the academic world. Everyone thought my father was headed in the same direction, but he died when I was twelve and he was only forty-three."

"You've seen him since you've been here?"

Janet darted him a quick glance. "No. I've been wondering about that. Haven't seen Grandfather either. I thought your relatives were the first ones you saw when you awakened." She picked at a fingernail.

"Have you thought about them? Wanted to see them? That's the way it seems to work here."

Janet brightened. "That's it! I've been so busy there hasn't been time to—" She stopped herself. "Who am I kidding? It isn't that I haven't wanted to see them, it's that I've been scared."

"Why?" Frank said, interested.

"To tell you the truth, I'd just as soon wait. I never really knew Daddy except as someone who was busy and shouldn't be disturbed. Or else he was away on trips. And Grandfather always seemed so, so righteous. I never felt I could live up to the example either one of them set." She gave him a half-grin. "Maybe I'll wait until Mother comes and paves the way. She's ninety-seven, so she should be along soon." She studied Frank and asked, her voice hesitant, "Have you seen your family?"

"Dad. Though I'd just as soon not have had the pleasure." Then Frank's eyes softened and the chill in his voice disappeared. "And I've seen my son, Ben."

"He's an angel?"

"He is that." And much to his surprise, Frank found himself telling this odd woman about the damaged little boy he had loved so much, the son who had come to this world and grown to be a wise adult, one who loved his work of helping the lost souls he was sent to comfort.

Neither Frank nor Janet heard the chimes that signaled the beginning of morning classes. Or perhaps, because of a slight shift in the freshening breeze, the sound of the chimes did not reach the shaded benches that overlooked the far valley.

Dan wiped the sweat from his forehead and leaned forward to grasp the handles of the loaded wheelbarrow. A couple more trips and he'd have every one of these damned bricks ready to be settled into the sand of the new pathway. Thanks to Percy's intervention, he hadn't been given more than a blunt warning about straying into the Trackless Parts, and the assignment of spending a good part of each day working on the paths being built to edge the new garden. Didn't seem fair that Pegeen had gotten off without having to do much of anything. At least he hadn't seen her around hauling bricks.

Dan steered the wheelbarrow across a wooden ramp and onto a grassy knoll. It had been a kick in the gut when he'd entered the school office and seen, not only Percy standing by the window, but Pegeen lounging in one of the two chairs across from Gregory's desk. The look that flashed across Pegeen's face made him hesitate before taking the empty seat, but it was gone so quickly Dan wondered if he'd imagined it.

"Look who turned up!" she'd said with a lazy smile. "Had a long walk home, lover? Take a seat and rest that good-looking body."

An involuntary shudder had swept his tense shoulders at the thought of the stifling room at the wayside inn, its sweat-soaked sheets, and the whisper of foul odors that crept in from the barely opened window.

Dan shuddered now, despite the hot sun on his sweaty T-shirt.

Luckily, Pegeen had turned her attention to the man behind the desk. "Why have I been called in here like some recalcitrant student? Who made you judge and jury anyway?" By the time she'd got this far, her voice had risen. Now it trembled with anger. "Who gave you the right to question me about concepts I've spent a lifetime studying, things I know a hell of a lot more about than the lot of you, if you really want to know."

Gregory cut her short. "I acknowledge that you're sincere

in your beliefs, Pegeen. That's the only reason you've been allowed to return to the Academy," he said. "Despite the fact that those beliefs are dead wrong, I know you really think they'll lead to happiness." He sighed and shook his head as though to clear it. "You have the chance to learn otherwise while you're here. All you have to do is pay attention." He adjusted the pile of papers in front of him. "And now I want both of you to sit there and listen while I tell you a few things."

To Dan's surprise, Pegeen had shut up. And she'd listened, though obviously resentful, to Gregory's stern lecture about what kind of behavior would and would not be allowed on campus. His reprimand finished, he'd given Dan the assignment of building new paths. Then he'd nodded to Percy, indicating that Dan's part in the interview was over, and Dan had followed the big man out of the office, leaving Pegeen with Gregory. Percy hadn't said much before he'd left Dan at the equipment sheds, but despite the fact that Percy made no attempt to hide his disapproval of Dan's behavior, Dan was glad the big man had been given charge of him rather than the flinty-faced, khaki-clad security guard.

Dan pulled up his T-shirt and used it to wipe the sweat from his forehead. Hauling bricks to the east campus garden might be backbreaking work, but the upside was that it had kept him out of Pegeen's way so far. Added to that, he was in better condition than he'd been since high-school football. Dan grunted, upended the wheelbarrow, and let the bricks slide onto the growing pile.

"Be careful! You will hurt the flowers!"

Dan spun about, his glower relaxing into a smile at the sight of the short, thickset girl heading toward him. "Hey Birgit, what's up? There aren't any flowers around—not yet."

"Oh yes." She pointed to a clump of daisies half-hidden beside the pile of bricks.

"They're just weeds," Dan protested.

"Oh no." Birgit shifted her backpack to a more comfortable position and knelt to examine the white flowers nestled in the grass. "They are beautiful. You would have crushed them if I hadn't called out."

"Then it's lucky Birgit, protector of all growing things, yelled at me."

Shy humor glinted in Birgit's dark eyes. "You are being funny."

"You ought to see me talking to the TV during Monday night football games. I knock 'em dead."

Birgit wasn't exactly sure what he meant, but she knew there was no harm in this young man's teasing. "You are nice," she said. "Before—when I would not talk—you helped make it easy for me to speak. Now I go to class and it is not bad like I thought. No one laughs at me."

"You let me know if they do, kid." Dan gestured to her backpack. "You're done with class?"

She nodded. "I only go in the mornings. In the afternoon I can work in the gardens and tend my roses and take walks to see new gardens like this." Birgit considered him. "I like to talk with you. I like the way you say things that make me laugh, but I wonder why you look so sad sometimes—the times when you think no one sees you."

Dan scooped up a brick near the daisies and tossed it onto the pile. "You're too damn observant, Birgit."

"Are you afraid because of the thing?"

"What thing?" Dan said, his voice sharp. His hand twitched, but made no move to his jeans pocket.

"The thing that follows you."

Dan's eyes narrowed. "What the hell are you talking about?"

"The black and gray thing, the one that sometimes goes behind you."

Dan's head snapped as he whipped about to look behind him. "Where?"

"It isn't here," she said.

"Hey, you had me going there." Dan attempted a chuckle. "You're kidding, right? There's no black and gray thing following me."

"Not now," Birgit agreed gravely.

"Not ever." He rasped it, demanding her agreement.

Birgit shook her head. "It has been near you. Sometimes."

Dan's face flushed, his muscles tightened. He took a breath and forced his clenched fists to loosen. "What did this, this thing look like?"

"Like a skinny wolf, but it stands upright. Its front legs reach out like arms and it has paws like hands with black, curved nails."

The color that had flooded Dan's face left it. He swallowed. "How can you stand there calmly and talk about something like that? Doesn't it scare you?"

"No. I do not fear it."

"Why not?"

Birgit thought for a moment. "Because I am safe here. Because it is not concerned with me." Then she added, almost as an afterthought, "And because there were many bad things where I was before—so many that seeing a strange creature does not make me fear."

For the first time Dan seemed distracted from his own disquiet. "Was it that bad? When you were on earth?"

"Yes." A shadow darkened Birgit's face and she turned away. Then she turned back and smiled at him. "I do not wish to remember the dark time. I do not have to. I am protected here. We all are."

"Except for me, apparently." At her look of incomprehension, he said, "If you're right about that thing following me."

"Oh, that. I don't think it can do any harm—it is always a

distance behind you. The Academy, the buildings and grounds, are protected. It will not come near you, I think, unless you want it to."

"I don't."

"Then you should not worry," the dark eyed girl said simply.

"Right. Don't worry." Dan touched his back pocket. Then he reached for the handles of the empty wheelbarrow. "Guess I'd better get back to my job before Percy pops up and reminds me. See you around?"

Birgit nodded. "Okay," she said as though trying out the word. "Okay. I see you around."

She watched Dan trudge along the unfinished path toward the utility buildings. She stood beside the pile of bricks until he disappeared from view. Then she slid the backpack from her shoulders and coaxed a rather large rabbit from its depths and held it in her arms. "Was I right to say he should not be afraid?" she asked the rabbit. She looked up at the high, scudding clouds in the bright blue sky. *Please protect him from what he fears. Please, help him.*

9

Kate kicked off her shoes, put her feet up on the upholstered couch, and adjusted her body to its comfortable curves. She picked up a book from the pile on the table beside her and opened it, but when Buster raised his head from the braided rug and rested his jaw on the edge of the couch, she let the book slip to her lap and stroked his silky pelt. At the invitation Buster rose, hind end wagging with delight, and put his paw up.

"No, Buster." She nudged him away with a foot. "Much as I appreciate the fact that you don't slobber on me, at least not so far, there isn't room on the couch for both of us. Besides, I'm reading." Buster reluctantly subsided to the rug, but Kate did not pick up her book. She sat watching the gently crackling flames that licked the logs in the fireplace, her face thoughtful. Dan may have been given to her charge, but she hadn't had much effect on her recalcitrant nephew, at least not that she was aware of. *What possessed him to take off with Pegeen?* Kate grimaced. *On second thought, it didn't take a rocket scientist to figure that out.* But now he was back and, after his meeting with Gregory, had apparently accepted the Academy policies—and the consequences of his little adventure.

Had her warnings about the Trackless Parts sunk in at all, or did he consider her attempts to help an unwelcome intrusion? Maybe Dan needed to hear these things from men like Percy and Gregory rather than his aunt. Still, she'd been entrusted with helping him, and if she could do anything to steer him away from what lay at the far edge of the Trackless Parts, she would. She'd always prided herself on her ability to take charge of the situation, to analyze a student's need, formulate a plan, and take action. Surely she could come up with something that would answer in Dan's situation.

You're not in charge here. Matter of fact, you weren't in charge during your life on earth.

The thought came with astonishing swiftness and clarity. Kate's lips curved in a rueful smile. How presumptuous of her to suppose she was. And how Howard would have chuckled. Howard, who had been known to claim that being married to Kate was like living with an academic version of General Patton. Howard would have looked at her over his glasses and—

Kate caught her breath. There he was. Howard, sitting at his desk in their combined study, the desk lamp illuminating his fine, graying hair against the background of that dreadful striped, floral wallpaper they'd always been too busy to have redone. She saw a spiral of smoke curl from the overflowing ash tray that perched precariously on a pile of papers.

"Howard! You're not smoking again!" Kate regretted the scolding words as soon as she spoke them, but of course Howard hadn't heard.

He flicked his cigarette toward the ashtray, and when the hot ash landed on the paper instead, he brushed the ash onto the carpet and stepped on it. He examined the scorched brown hole in the top piece of paper, shrugged, and stubbed out the smoking butt. Reaching into his shirt pocket for the cigarette packet there, he stopped. "How you'd hate my taking it up again, Katie," he said aloud. He grinned and replaced the pack in his pocket, then pushed away the two canes that rested against his desk and leaned over to rummage in the bottom drawer. He withdrew a wrapped hard candy, wincing as he straightened. "A smoke does help the pain though."

Kate's heart contracted. Howard never spoke of his pain. Not even to her. She'd always been able to guess when it was bad, but she never mentioned it either. It was a tacit pact they'd had. Then she realized that Howard had not spoken this last statement. She'd heard his thoughts.

"Oh, darling," she whispered. "If you're in pain, my love, please, please take your medicine. I know you're not as alert as you'd like when you take it, but what's a little less mental acuity if you can get rid of the pain?"

Howard adjusted his position and eased against the chair's cushion. "Not too bad," he said, considering. "Not bad enough to start taking pills, anyway." He gazed at the faded, ugly wallpaper. "Never did get around to getting rid of this damn wallpaper, did we, Katie?" He took off his glasses and rubbed his eyes. "Oh, how I miss you, Kate. Oh God, how I miss you."

Kate blinked tears from her eyes. "I'm here. I'm with you, right here, right now. And one day we'll be able to be together. Know that this is true, Howard. One day you will be here with me and your pain will be gone." She stopped, the impact of her words hitting her like a fist to the gut. She leaned forward. "Oh Howard—feel my joy at the thought of you without pain. Feel my joy when I think of us together again."

Her husband gazed into the distance, his face intent. "Is it possible? Is it really possible I'll see you again?" Kate heard the words as clearly as if Howard had spoken, and she heard the grumbling thought that came immediately afterward—*Just wishful thinking. Probably. But—maybe not. Maybe not.* As the man and desk and study began to fade, Kate saw a look of hope wash Howard's face, a look that for a moment erased the lines pain had etched on it. And with that flicker of hope she saw a fleeting reflection of her own joy.

Kate stared at the braided rug. Though she couldn't recall moving from the couch, she was on her knees. She absently brushed aside Buster's inquiring nose. Howard had heard her, though he hadn't realized it. More than that, he'd taken a step beyond wondering to tentative belief. Even though his stubbornly scientific mind urged him to dispute it, he had accepted the possibility of a life to come, of a world in which he would be with her.

"Help him," she prayed fiercely. "Please Lord, help my beloved scholar open his mind—and his heart."

She began to clamber from her knees but found her eyes level with Buster's and sucked in a sharp breath. She remained kneeling transfixed by the simple, all-encompassing love she saw in the Buster's big brown eyes and felt her own fill with surprised tears.

"What's this all about?" Kate whispered. She sat down on the rug. "Lord," she murmured, her gaze fixed on the big dog, "give me a clue."

Buster lowered his head to his paws with a sigh. Kate stayed where she was. *Okay, let's think this out.* Why had she seen that flash of pure, unconditional love? Was it a promise that the love she and Howard had was one that transcended time and space, a promise that her loneliness would end? And it was more than missing Howard, she admitted. There was something lacking in herself. She could accept with astonished wonder the things she was learning about God and his creation, revel at what she was beginning to comprehend of this spiritual world, but though awed by it all and excited by her daily-expanding knowledge, the love that created the natural and spiritual worlds was something she acknowledged rather than felt.

Was it sacrilegious to think that what she'd just seen in the eyes of a shaggy dog had been a reflection of that love? To imagine God would use Buster to illustrate his love for one religiously underdeveloped academician?

Kate squeezed her eyes shut.

Please Lord, help me to learn how to know you and do your will. Let me absorb the wonderful ideas I'm learning. Teach me to love you.

Something Hannah had told them came to Kate like an answer to this thought. "The person who repents his faults (*no, "his evils," Hannah had said*), and keeps God's commandments loves the Lord."

I do know something about love. You taught me about it when you gave me Howard, when you gave us the half a lifetime we shared. That was your gift, wasn't it? The excitement of those first months when we came to know each other, the wonder of all those years together—they came from you.

The smile that had begun to relax Kate's tense face faded as other, unwelcome thoughts crowded in. There had been bad times. The day before their fifth anniversary. She'd found the note stuffed underneath a heap of Howard's socks and had carelessly tossed it on top of his dresser. If the paper hadn't fallen open to expose a scrawled endearment followed by the signature of one of Kate's best friends, Kate wouldn't have read it. And afterward she wished she hadn't. The next months had been agony—for her, for Howard, and, she supposed, for the writer of the note as well. But she and Howard had survived and so had their marriage. Later Kate wondered whether Howard had intended her to find the note, whether this had been his way of having the boil lanced and the poison allowed to drain away.

There had been other dark times. The months after the diagnosis of Howard's illness. Its steady, inexorable progression in the years following. Yet Howard's courage and stoic acceptance had deepened their love and ultimately strengthened their marriage.

Kate opened her eyes and brushed her cheeks with a shaky hand. "You were there with us throughout our marriage, weren't you?" she whispered aloud. "The times we worked on it and those when we weren't paying much attention. I'm paying attention now."

And as she struggled to her feet, another thing Hannah had said came to her. "*The Lord works indirectly, through people who allow him into their lives, who allow themselves to be a conduit for him to help others.*"

This wasn't just all about her and Howard; it was about the opportunity to help Dan to find out what he needed to know about himself. And Janet. Kate stifled a slight flicker of exasperation. *And Janet*, she told herself firmly.

She got to her feet. "I'll try," Kate said. "I'll surely try." Fire crackled in the quiet living room. Buster sighed and put his head on his paws again.

Hannah raised her head from the pillow and propped her chin on her hand. A melody drifted through the open windows with the sun's early morning rays. Both music and light were faint at first, then, as the soaring sound of women's voices grew louder, the light that filled the room brightened to a diamond brilliance. The song's strains melded, rising and swooping, circling round to the opening theme and back again, ending in a final refrain of melodious humming. After a moment's silence the music began again, men's voices now, deep and rich, then another song with men and women joined in a joyous paean of praise. When this last song ended Hannah sank back on her pillow and looked at the tall figure of her husband leaning against the open window.

"Is it me or was morningsong especially lovely today?"

Gregory turned and smiled the smile that never failed to make Hannah's insides turn somersaults. "I was just thinking the same thing." He studied her and a tiny crease appeared on his forehead. "Something's bothering you." Then he gave a brief nod. "Ah, our problem students."

"Got it in one," Hannah said. She rose and went to the

archway and pulled aside a gossamer curtain to show an alcove. A small, marble bathing pool sat in its sunlit center.

Gregory followed and leaned against the archway, arms folded. "Who?"

"Take your pick. Who do you want first? Janet, who spent her time on earth doing committee busywork and telling everyone around her what they should do and what was best for them? With the result that not many people cared to be with her for any appreciable time—and she never figured out why, poor woman. I put her with Kate, but so far that's not working too well, mainly because Janet's jealous of Kate, but partly because Kate doesn't have much patience with people who aren't in what she considers to be her league. It's something she has to work on," she smiled, "which is precisely why I put her with Janet." Hannah smoothed an arm with a fragrant soap, and added, "I hope Kate will come to see that Janet doesn't have a bad heart and that she always did her duty as she saw it." Her smile turned wry. "It's just unfortunate that she spent so much of her time doing that duty she never had more than the odd moment for introspection. And this when she was in a place where she heard truths on a daily basis that would have made her life so much more meaningful, not to mention so much easier, if she'd put them into practice."

Gregory nodded. "She certainly could have used all the time she spent polishing the image of herself as a virtuous, grieving widow to better purpose, especially when for forty years she seldom gave a thought to the young husband who came here before her."

Compassion flitted across Hannah's lovely face. "And she can't even remember what he was called when he was with her."

"She'll find her way," her husband said. "If the Lord doesn't use us or Kate, there will be someone else to guide her. So who beside Janet?"

"Well, there's our suicide. While I grieve for the situation Dan has placed himself in, so far he's not acknowledging any real responsibility for his predicament. I hope you've put a stop to his roaming the Trackless Parts—to say nothing of what he was doing there. We can't countenance behavior like that." Hannah's voice sharpened. "Which brings us to the mad woman who's playing with his head."

"Pegeen." Gregory's mouth twitched. "Not the most receptive person."

"I can't believe that woman. You'd think she would pick on someone her own age; Dan's practically a teenager." Hannah stepped out of the pool and wrapped herself in the thick, white towel Gregory handed her. "She all but abducted him—not that he put up much of a struggle. And the ideas she spouts about marriage make me weep." She went back into the bedroom where she slipped on a lemon-yellow shift. "Tell me she doesn't really believe those ridiculous things."

"Oh, but she does. That's one reason she's still with us," said Gregory. "The trouble is, she can't resist trying to convert people to her point of view whatever their beliefs might be. Apparently during her life on earth, one of her favorite pastimes was stirring things up, and it looks as though she's still at it. We're going to have to watch that woman, especially around the younger students." He cocked an eyebrow at his wife. "I don't know much about these things, but I saw a picture of her in one of her articles and she didn't seem to me like the sort of person who would be so much into this constant hair-color changing."

Hannah smiled at him. "Yes, she certainly is getting a charge out of being blond, brunette, or whatever she decides to be at the moment. Just a phase, I should think. But what about Zaroth? Did you see that he accompanied her back here? Apparently he came as far as the gates."

Gregory's eyes shadowed. "That individual was one of my unhappier experiences in this job. I was certain he had such potential when he was here with us."

Hannah touched his arm. "None of us realized it at first. Zaroth had become so adept at deception during his time on earth that it took us a while to realize he wasn't to be trusted. A Celestial would have known it at once." She looked thoughtful. "If you'd like, I'll talk to Pegeen. But of course it's up to her whether or not she'll listen."

They were downstairs now, at the end of a comfortably sized dining room whose French doors opened to a patio and multihued gardens. A light, fragrant breeze ruffled the white linen tablecloth on a round breakfast table in front of the open doors. A steaming pot of coffee and a little bouquet of violets and lilies of the valley sat on the table where two places were set with bowls of fresh fruit. They took their seats and held hands across the table.

"We thank you, Lord, for all you have given us this day and for all you give us each day," Gregory said. "Guide us to know how we may perform our chosen use and help those given to our care."

Hannah kissed her husband and poured a cup of coffee. "Speaking of whom, what about dear Frank? Has he come to you for help?"

"'Fraid not. He's avoided me like the plague since that incident in the cypress forest. I thought he might open up to you."

She shook her head. "He comes to class, asks good questions and occasionally joins the discussion, but if anything gets too personal, he's out of there—mentally, if not physically."

"I wouldn't worry too much. He's a good man. From what

I've seen, despite the fact that he's going through a lot of stuff himself, he's someone the others here feel comfortable talking to. I have a hunch he might be able to help them; and y'know, in doing so there's a good chance he will find his way too."

"Of course." She flushed. "Oh dear, I should be ashamed of myself, getting into a swivet about our charges."

Gregory's hand covered hers. "No shame there; it's your job to be concerned. Listen m'love, you need a break. How about after classes are over for the day we catch the new play that just opened?"

Hannah brightened. "Three Times Seven? I've heard it's really good. We can see if Stephanos and Petra would like to join us."

"No question about that, even if they've already seen it." He grinned and answered her puzzled look. "Petra's brother is in the cast."

Hannah laughed. "Now I know it will be good." She took a last bite of muffin and reached for the satchel at her feet. "I'll be in the garden when you're ready."

Pegeen peered around the great holly bush. Stupid to leave the gates open and not have a guard on duty. She darted to the pillars beside the tall gates and, assuring herself that the guard house was indeed unmanned, slipped out to the grassy hillside. Yes, this was the road she'd taken when she had returned to the Academy. Somewhere over there in the distance was the city where the oddly exciting Zaroth lived. Somewhere past the hills and over the plains was that deceptively old-fashioned creature she'd promised to help. Pegeen shivered. Those wondrous, liquid eyes held more than a hint of danger, but it was delicious danger. She'd never felt such a powerful attraction for anyone as she had for Zaroth. Had there been a threat in his silky voice when she'd hesitated to agree to get him the information he wanted? She hadn't been afraid. Not really. She knew how to take care of herself. But she hadn't refused. Though Zaroth had been vague, it was apparent he was high in the administration of the university down there, and she was more than a little interested in seeing what they might have to offer. Still, she found herself wondering whether she should have let herself be talked into something she wasn't entirely certain she understood. Why would he want to entice anyone there? Pegeen kicked a pebble out of the way. Why should she care?

Her thoughts shifted to the lecture in Gregory's office. It had gone on interminably and been excruciatingly boring, but his reprimand was quite plain. She was on probation. Her conversations with the young students had to stop. Then there was the way Gregory had looked at her. Despite his calm demeanor, there was something in his eyes that made her squirm, a veiled strength she feared might be more dangerous than Zaroth's.

Maybe she should rethink this call. But then she imagined Zaroth waiting for her, his delightfully odd yellow eyes anxiously alight. The least she could do was check in with him. She opened the small red pouch slung over her shoulder, took out a cell phone and flicked it open. "Zaroth?" she said, "No, this isn't 'your Pegeen.' I'm not anyone's Pegeen. Look, they let me back in, but it wasn't easy and there are a lot of restrictions. This may take a while. Anyway, are you ready? Here's your first report from 'that place on the hill,' as you call it."

10

Frank had almost reached the end of the path when he saw the young man hunched over a wheelbarrow. Dan. There was a desolation in the droop of the kid's shoulders that caught at Frank's gut. Frank slowed his step reluctantly. He'd already missed yesterday's morning classes thanks to his session with Janet, though he had to admit it felt good to have helped the annoying woman through her misery. And he had been able to help. Frank eyed the gate that led to the campus grounds. He especially wanted to go to this morning's first class, because they were going to continue discussing the inner meaning of the Book of Isaiah. What had seemed like gibberish to Frank the few times he'd heard Isaiah read from the pulpit had now begun to make complete sense. He might not take part in the discussions, but that didn't mean he wanted to miss the class just because of Kate's exasperating nephew. He looked at Dan's bowed head and swore silently.

"Whatcha doin'?" He knew his falsely hearty tone must have annoyed the boy, but it was the best he could do at the moment.

Dan looked up. "Workin' out. What does it look like?"

Frank approached across the close-cropped grass. "No, really—how's it going?"

Dan let the wheelbarrow down with a thud. "You tell me." He wiped his forehead with the bottom of his T-shirt. He gestured to two neatly stacked piles of bricks beside the sand-filled pathway. "See those?" he said.

"Yeah."

"I've been working for days, ever since Gregory hauled my ass over the coals for ditching this place and going to the Trackless Parts and, and those piles don't stay the way I put 'em; some don't stay at all." He gave an angry grimace and wiped his nose with the back of his hand. "First off, when I just dumped the bricks any old how and they started disappearing, I thought somebody must be trying to jerk my chain, but when I complained, the guys at the brick shop said nobody takes stuff around here, said maybe the piles were gone because I wasn't paying attention." Dan's voice changed to an outraged whine. "Pay attention to *what*? Anyway, I tried. Started stacking them real careful like you see here, and they did stay—at first. But once I get more than two piles, the third one disappears by the time I come back, plus the pile I'm taking them from at the shop doesn't seem to be getting much smaller. And the guys say I have to haul every last one of 'em here before I can quit." He glared at Frank. "How the hell am I supposed to do that?"

"Looks like you've got a problem." Frank tried to look sober. He squatted on his heels beside the nearest pile and inspected it. "Seems like ordinary brick." He hoisted one, tossed it in the air and caught it. "You doing this as some kind of punishment?"

Dan's glower deepened, but he mumbled, "They said if I wanted to stay here I had to do this. Assholes."

"Do you? Want to stay?"

Dan considered. "For now I'd just as soon be here, but I dunno, I don't like being told where I can and can't go. Who knows? I might want to check out some of the places in the Trackless Parts."

Frank suppressed a sigh, but let this pass. "Ever think you're supposed to spend your time on the job thinking about what got you this duty in the first place?"

"I'm not stupid. I have thought, at least some, but I can't

go around doing it all day. People are supposed to help you in this place, for Pete's sake, but no one around here cares, not really. Except maybe Aunt Kate, and I know she's brainy, but she doesn't know anything about real life. Everybody around here talks a big line, but nobody really gives a damn."

"Really?"

"Well, I guess Birgit does. She's cool. She cares—but even with her it's mostly about her flowers."

"Birgit? The girl who has begun to talk?"

Dan's face lost some of its discontent. "I did that. Got her to talk. First time I met her she wouldn't say a word, just backed away and stood there in the middle of her roses. Me, I'm a guy who likes to talk, so I joked with her, tried to get her to speak. And she did. Does." Dan smiled at Frank. "She's even going to classes now. Guess she's had a lot of stuff in her life she doesn't want to go into, but she's an okay kid."

"Good her, and good for you," said Frank. "But, about this other business . . ."

"The bricks?"

"I was thinking about the gun."

The blood left the younger man's face; he stared at Frank, his eyes wide.

"Yeah, the one that's still in your back pocket."

Dan's hands twitched. He did not reach behind him, though it obviously took an effort not to. "Yeah, the guy that brought me back from the Trackless Parts talked to me about it, said I could get rid of the damned thing if I wanted to, but that's a crock. I've wanted to ever since I got here."

"Seems to me it's all of a piece. You don't want to think about why they've got you doing this yard work, so you don't, not really. You don't want to think about the fact that you took your life, so you don't." Frank gave him a level look. "But sooner or later you're going to have to, you know, and that's what might make that little piece disappear."

"I don't see why I have to have it on me." Dan's voice rose. "It's not like I'm going to use it or anything."

"Ever had a gun before?"

"Before?"

"Before you used this one to kill yourself."

Dan flinched. "I wasn't into things like guns."

"So what were you into? Drugs?" Frank waited, and then added, "I'm not going to arrest you or haul you off somewhere. The only reason I'm asking, aside from habit I guess, is that I know enough about how things work here to know you and I didn't meet by accident this morning. So how about we talk. It was drugs, right? Started running with the bad guys and couldn't keep up?"

"Sort of," Dan mumbled. "I kicked the habit though. I'd been clean two months when—" he looked at Frank and finished, his eyes defiant, "when I offed myself."

"Why did you do it?"

"Aunt Kate asked me the same thing; so did the guy who came with her." Dan inspected his fingernails. "I was about to be arrested and doing time was gonna be pretty much of a sure thing. You're a cop; you know about prison. I wasn't about to let myself in for that, okay?"

"You're right, it can be tough in prison. Matter of fact, it can be hell. But lots of people face it, cops included." Frank's face was grim. "Had a friend once—a beat cop like myself who made a mistake. He paid for it with a broken marriage and five years behind bars, until, well, until something happened. He didn't whine, didn't ask for anything from anyone. Spent his time doing a lot of stuff he'd never thought of doing before—reading, thinking, and finally, from what I hear, praying." Frank looked into space.

"You telling me I should have done like this friend of yours? Go to jail, repent, live happily ever after?"

"He didn't live happily ever after. Nobody promises that, at least not for life on earth," Frank said quietly. He toed the pile of bricks, pushing one back into alignment, and then looked up at Dan. "You don't have any ideas about why that pistol is still with you?"

Dan turned away, muttering under his breath.

"Say what?"

"I get the idea. I told you I'm not stupid," Dan snarled at him. "You're not supposed to kill yourself. I wasn't supposed to kill myself. Guess it's some kind of rule. But how was I supposed to know it was so bad?" His eyes filled with tears. "I know what it must have done to my mom. I'd moved to Chicago the year before and she didn't have any idea I was into drugs—or that I'd gotten myself straight. I don't even know if she knows now. Or what happened before I did it."

"Just what did happen?"

"I don't want to talk about it."

"Maybe that's part of your problem, friend. I'm a pretty good listener. Why not try me?"

After several moments of silence, moments in which Frank stood waiting patiently, Dan swallowed. "I was doing drugs and a few times I carried a couple of packets for some guys." He took a few steps down the sandy path of newly laid bricks and turned back to face the older man. "Once, and I swear it was just once, I took one of the packages, cut it, and sold it and pocketed the extra money. I was sure no one knew. But they found out. Said I had to make up what I owed, do stuff for them. It wasn't anything much, except this one time when they had me be the lookout on a job. I, I was so scared when I saw the cop car coming, I ran. Stuff happened. One of the guys got it. Not long after, this social worker I'd gotten to know got me into a rehab program. Didn't think it would work, but it did." Dan's inhale was shaky. "But a couple of days after I got out of rehab some guys came around to see me. Said the guy I sold the stuff to back when I cut the package was undercover, said I was going to have to take the rap for that and for the lookout job." He smiled bitterly. "I confess and do my time and they might let me live."

Frank nodded. "I don't suppose it crossed your mind that the chance your friends could make all this stuff stick was just about nonexistent?"

"They put incriminating evidence in my room and alerted the cops. They said the cops had an all-points out on me."

"I bet they did." Frank put a hand on the younger man's shoulder. "Well now, it wasn't all that difficult to tell your story, was it? What do you think now?"

"I wish I hadn't let Sammy talk me into using the damn thing. I—I'd do anything to have a chance to go back, to do things over, maybe find another way."

"You don't have that chance, buddy," Frank said. "None of us do."

"And now I'm stuck with this thing forever?" Dan's hand crept to his rear pocket. He froze.

"What?"

"It's gone!"

Frank's gaze sharpened. "Interesting."

"Is it gone for good?"

"I wouldn't know, but my guess is that now you've faced up to the whole story, you don't need it as a reminder."

"Just telling you made it go away?"

"It'd be nice if that's all there was to it, but no, I have a suspicion you're going to have to do some thinking about how you got to the place where you figured you were the one who got to decide when your life on earth should end. If you need to have the gun come back, it will."

Dan nodded, but he didn't look persuaded. He felt his empty jeans pocket again and let out a little sigh. "Right now the only thing that matters is it's gone." He brightened. "You suppose this means I can stop doing this stupid job?"

"If I were you I'd finish it up. See if those bricks stay where they're supposed to. Anyway, what are you in such a hurry to do?"

Dan shrugged. "Nothin'. But hauling bricks isn't high on my list of favorite things." He began unloading bricks from the wheelbarrow. "Okay, I guess I'll see if I can finish this," he looked at Frank, "and then maybe I'll do some of that heavy-duty thinking you were talking about."

"Sounds like a plan." Frank flicked a finger to his head in a salute. He walked back to the gate and let himself out of the gardens. He hadn't commented on Dan's mention of traveling in the Trackless Parts, but it occurred to him that he'd been outside the Academy grounds himself several times with no remonstrations or consequences. *Interesting.* Frank quickened his steps. If he hurried he shouldn't be all that late for class. He ducked beneath a broad leaf that hung over the dirt path. Frank halted abruptly. The path. Why was it dirt instead of one of the fine-pebbled pathways that led through the campus? Frank looked about him. *Hooboy.* No buildings in sight, no manicured lawns, no students hurrying to class.

He was in the Trackless Parts.

"Kate, d'you have a minute?" Janet balanced a pile of books against her hip and waved to Kate, who was already halfway down the stone steps. Kate paused to let the other woman catch up. *Remember to listen. See if there's a way you can help.*

"Everyone around here is so busy they don't seem to have time to talk to anyone but their buddies," Janet observed as they walked across the green lawn.

"Really?" Kate felt mildly pleased with herself, not only for resisting the impulse to correct Janet's grammar, but for pushing aside the thought that there were good reasons Janet's classmates did not seek her out.

Kate shortened her steps to match Janet's. The least she

could do was offer to be this woman's friend—she obviously needed one. The thought of friends brought Frank to mind. A crease furrowed Kate's forehead. She hadn't seen Frank lately and she missed him. Missed their talks, missed his large, comforting presence. Something, she wasn't quite certain what it was, had kept her from actively seeking him out. Whenever she considered it, she felt a slight warning tug. It might be her imagination, but Kate couldn't rid herself of the feeling that it might be better if she left him to reappear of his own accord.

"I wanted to talk to you," Janet was saying. "That is, if you're not busy."

"I was about to go to my rooms to get Buster and take him for a walk," said Kate. "Why don't you come with us?"

"And Buster is—?"

"My dog." A grin lit Kate's face. "I never thought I'd say that; never had a dog before. You can't imagine what a comfort it is to go back to my rooms and find him waiting for me. When I sit reading with Buster curled at my feet he seems to help me concentrate, and y'know, all I have to do when I feel worried is look at him and I know everything's going to be all right."

Janet's eyes widened. "You mean you're afraid things aren't going to be 'all right'?"

"Sometimes," Kate said simply.

Janet gave her companion a questioning glance, but, when Kate offered no explanation, did not ask more.

Buster greeted Kate with joyful woofs, tail wagging, hindquarters wiggling with barely suppressed exuberance. His attention shifted to Kate's guest and Kate grabbed his collar. "Don't even think about jumping on her," she admonished him. Buster gave her an injured look and sat.

"Oh, he's beautiful," Janet said, patting Buster's big, flat head.

"You might want to be careful; he's been known to slobber." Kate took a bright red leash from one of the bookcase shelves and snapped it on Buster's collar.

"What a lot of books! Where they here when you came?"

"A few. The rest appear from time to time." Kate pulled a small, leather-bound volume from the shelf. A look of pure pleasure swept her face as Kate traced the gold-tooled title. "This was here when I woke up this morning."

At Janet's inquiring look, Kate showed it to her. "They're poems from my husband."

"Your husband's a poet?"

Kate chuckled. "No way, no how. Howard's strictly a left-brain intellectual." Her face grew pensive. "But he knows how much I love poetry, and he's been reading it. He copied these into one of his notebooks; they're love poems, things he couldn't put into words himself." She snapped the little volume shut and returned it to the shelf. "Guess we'd better get going."

"Look, I all but invited myself," Janet said. "You're sure it's all right? Maybe you'd rather be alone."

"Of course not. Buster and I enjoy company," Kate said quickly. "Where would you like to walk?"

"How about in the orchard? Not many people go there, so we won't be interrupted."

The orchard was planted in spirals of apple and peach, cherry and pear, the trees all in different stages of bloom and fruiting, the mingled scents enveloping Kate and Janet in a heady yet delicate mix of aromas. "I can't imagine why I've never been down here before," Kate said, breathing deep. "This is gorgeous." She unsnapped Buster's leash and let him gambol, sniffing first one tree and then the next.

"I often come here," said Janet. "It's a nice place to think." She sank to the grass.

Kate sat down beside her. "So what did you want to talk about?" she prodded gently.

Janet picked up a fallen blossom and poked it behind her ear. "It's nothing important, really. I just wanted to ask you about—your friend."

Kate looked at her, perplexed. "My friend?"

"Your policeman friend. You came here together and you seem to have known him for a long time. I, I thought you might be able to tell me about him."

Kate's glance darted to the woman beside her. "Frank? I didn't know you even knew each other."

"Oh yes. The other day we talked for ages, we talked so long we missed class." Janet removed the blossom she'd stuck in her hair and twiddled it between her fingers. "There I was sitting in the arbor bawling like an idiot, feeling absolutely horrible, and Frank came by. He was so nice, so understanding. He just listened, and I talked—and talked." She flushed and tossed the bruised blossom onto the grass. "Afterward I realized it had been mostly about me." She bit her lip. "I tend to do that. Talk too much about myself."

Kate didn't hear this last, hesitant confession. Since Janet had begun the tale of her encounter with Frank, Kate had been aware of an uncomfortable pressure in her chest. *Janet and Frank? No!* Frank was simply too good for her. Could they really have spent hours together? He'd probably found himself trapped with a weeping woman and felt he had to stay to offer whatever help he could. *Of course. That's just what Frank would do.* And who knew better than she what a comfort Frank's calm, supportive presence could be? Kate drew a breath, feeling slightly better.

But the tightness in her chest returned as another thought flashed across Kate's mind like an unwelcome meteor. Why did she care so much? *Because Frank's a friend and I'm concerned about him,* she answered the meteor. *Or is it,* niggled the flash of light, *because since before you even came to the Academy you've been aware of Frank's feelings for you?*

I've never encouraged it, Kate protested. *Never.*

But you've enjoyed the fact that you are special in his eyes, that he thinks other women don't measure up to you.

Kate hung her head. The flashing thought wasn't something she wanted to acknowledge. But there it was. And admitting it hit Kate like a body blow.

"So do you know if he was married when he came here?"

It was a moment before Janet's careful question penetrated Kate's consciousness. She roused herself. "Divorced."

Janet was silent for a moment. "I just wondered. I know he was married once because he told me about his little boy—the one who died. I didn't want to ask about his status now, in case . . ." she paused.

"In case what?" Kate asked, a hint of asperity in her voice. "Look Janet, don't you think you should be asking him this kind of thing?"

"Well of course, but I'd hate to blunder into something sensitive," Janet said. She peered around the clearing as though suddenly interested in their surroundings. "Hey, where's Buster? He seems to have taken off."

Kate looked about, startled. "Buster!" she called. "Come boy, here!"

"Does he often run off?" Janet peered down the winding spiral of trees.

"No," Kate said, her voice sharp. "Never."

"Look, why don't you take the upper part of the orchard and I'll search the lower," Janet offered as she rose to her feet.

Kate got up heavily. "I don't think that's going to help," she said. "I have a feeling he'll come back to my apartment by himself." *Or not,* she added to herself.

"If you say so." Janet padded along beside Kate as the women headed for the path that led from the orchard. "I really appreciate your talking with me," she continued brightly. "I feel so much better having your input about this."

"My pleasure," Kate said, unable to keep a certain dryness from her voice. She'd come here with Janet intending to be the conduit of God's love to help the woman in any way she could. *Hah!* It hadn't taken more than a mention of Janet's interest in Frank to squelch that. She didn't want to think about the other reason she was hurrying back to her rooms. She was pretty sure she knew what Buster's sudden disappearance meant, and she was hoping, quite desperately, that when she got back she would find a small leather book still on her bookshelf.

11

Janet watched Kate sprint up the stairs of her dormitory building and swing open the plate-glass door, clutching the bright red leash to her chest. Funny that she didn't want to go looking for the dog. Why was Kate so sure Buster would come back on his own? Although from the way Kate had rushed back to her rooms it looked as though she wasn't all that certain. And even before their race back to the campus Kate had tensed up and gone all quiet and preoccupied—she must really love that dog.

Janet rounded the curved path and was headed toward the arbor up on the hill when it struck her that there might be more to Buster's disappearance than met the eye. Was it something like the temporary disappearance of Birgit's rabbit? *If so, that's Kate's concern,* Janet told herself firmly. She, Janet, was not one to butt into things that were none of her business. No sir.

Janet's heart was beating uncomfortably fast by the time she came within view of the vine-sheltered seats that overlooked the valley. She slowed to a nonchalant stroll and, without looking into either of the secluded alcoves, stood at the hill's crest and gazed out at the valley below. Only after a few moments did she casually glance at the stone seats. A tiny breath of disappointment escaped her. One of the alcoves was occupied, but it wasn't Frank sitting there. Janet gave what she hoped was a pleasant smile.

"Hello Birgit," she said. She came to the bench and sat beside her. "I've missed going to class with you since you started coming on your own. How is Shoma doing?"

"She's fine, thank you. You're doing very well, aren't you, Shoma?" she addressed the large rabbit beside her. It rose on its hind legs, nuzzled Birgit's cheek, and jumped from the bench to the grass at her feet.

Janet looked at Birgit sharply. Where had that impeccable English come from? And what had happened to the short, squat girl from the gardens who never looked at you directly? The young woman next to her, clad in draped aqua that fell in folds around a slender body, seemed, though shy, wholly composed. Yet undeniably it was Birgit.

"The thing you're wearing is really lovely—it's a sari, isn't it?" Janet asked uncertainly. She wanted to ask more about this astonishing transformation, but somehow couldn't quite find the words.

"Yes. I found it in my closet this morning," Birgit said, smiling shyly. She smoothed the silk over her knees. "I think it's because I've been paying attention to my lessons."

Janet thought of the silent girl she had walked to that first class. Birgit's reluctance had been painfully obvious as she slipped into a seat at the back of the room, and though Birgit had come by herself a few times after that, she seldom spoke and never took part in the discussions. Was the girl coming to classes? When was the last time she'd seen her? "You know," she said, "I don't recall seeing you recently."

"Hannah said I do not need to go to classes any more," Birgit said happily. Then she caught the look on Janet's face and a shadow crossed her own. "Perhaps it is because I am not smart enough to be taught with everyone else," she said.

"Oh I'm sure that's not it," Janet said, though fairly certain that this was exactly the reason for Hannah's suggestion.

"I said I would not mind having a—what do they call them?—a tutor, so they gave me one," Birgit said.

"Really?" *They could have asked me about tutoring,* Janet thought. She'd have been more than happy to coach the girl. After all, she already did know quite a bit about what they were hearing in class and she had been the one to encourage Birgit to participate in the first place. "Who's this tutor?"

"Her name is Cara. We talk. She makes everything clear to me. She tells me what heaven is like."

"Cara is an angel?" Janet whispered it.

"Yes."

Janet's cheeks burned. So much for her tutoring Birgit. She cleared her throat. "What sort of things do you talk about beside heaven?"

Something flickered in Birgit's eyes. "She shows me my life."

Janet flinched. "I suppose you mean your Book of Life."

Birgit frowned in momentary incomprehension and then said, "That is the name for the record of all the choices I made, all the things I did? Yes, that is what I mean."

Janet found she could not meet the younger woman's eyes. "Do you see everything—every one of the things you did on earth?"

"Oh no. Only a few things, and not all at once. Some of the times were not good," Birgit said, her voice lowered. Her hands clasped each other tightly. "But when I see them with Cara, I can bear it. The bad things don't hurt so much and I can see the good that came, even in the bad times. I saw it was good that I did what I could."

"What did you do?" Janet asked despite herself.

"I held the little girls who had been sold."

Janet's throat closed. "What girls?" she said when she could speak.

Birgit looked at Janet, her dark eyes liquid. "The house in the city where I lived bought children," she explained. "Most of them came from the country, as I had. They did not last very long, not nearly as long as I did. Because I was an ugly child, not many men wanted me. Not if they could afford better. When I was older, they kept me and gave me food because I was strong and could work. I dug weeds in the garden and cleaned the rooms. It was when I cleaned the rooms that I comforted the children—after they were left alone. At first it was only the girls. I never spoke to the boys. Then one day there was a little boy; he was crying so hard it hurt my heart. I dried his tears and washed him clean and held him. After that I gave what help I could to any child who was kept in those rooms. Those who wept and those who had no more tears to weep."

Birgit leaned to stroke the large rabbit nibbling at the grass by her feet. "Cara told me I had done well. She said that when I was comforting the children I was allowing God to use me to console them." Her face brightened. "And what is wonderful, it wasn't only them—Cara says that those times when I held a weeping child, I was letting God make me into someone who can be happy in heaven."

"Oh Birgit." Janet made a little movement to touch the girl's shoulder, but withdrew her hand. "Oh my dear, I'm sure you will be happy in heaven. And I am so sorry for what you've had to endure." She started to say more, but sat back and looked over the valley, her eyes bleak. Then she rubbed her forehead. "You'll probably be leaving soon. Did Cara tell you when?"

"Not for a while. She said there is more I must know before I find my home. I had no idea of God. Now I do, but I have much to learn. And did you know," Birgit said, her tone wondering, "that I will keep on learning when I find my home? That I will keep on learning forever?"

Janet nodded. Her arms crossed tight on her chest; her hands clasped her shoulders.

"Cara says there are other people here besides the teachers who can help me and people that I might be able to help too! She said I should be on the lookout for them." Birgit looked at Janet and her eyes widened. "Do you suppose you are one of those who can help me?"

"Me?" Janet gave a bitter laugh. "I don't think so. Not that I wouldn't like to," she added hastily, "but you are so far ahead of me, Birgit; I, I don't think I'd be able to teach you much."

"Oh yes, you know so much more than I do, and yet you're kind," Birgit said. "I was a little afraid of you at first, but you were the one who walked me to class when I was afraid to go," she confided. "And when you listened to me just now, I felt you were listening with your heart. I felt your heart hurt for me."

"It did," Janet said quietly. And this time she did reach out to gently touch Birgit's sari-clad shoulder.

"I never talked with anyone before, but now I have found three people who I can talk to," Birgit said. "Do you think that's what I am supposed to do? Learn to talk to others so I can find the ones who will help me and the ones who I can help?"

"I think so." Janet smiled as she rose from the bench. "And I'm really glad you talked to me, more than you realize, but I'd better get to class." She took a few steps, then turned back. "You know, Birgit, I think you've just fulfilled one of your assignments."

The young woman looked at Janet, mystified. "What assignment?"

"You were told to find others who needed your help. Well, I think you've just met your first case—and helped her."

"But how?"

"You've shown me what a heaven-bound person looks like. It's something very different—" Janet swallowed. "Let's just say it has given me a lot to think about." She touched her hand to her forehead in an awkward little salute and walked down the path toward the campus.

Frank eased himself onto the large, jutting rock beneath the tree. Was it a live oak? Looked like it. Anyway, he was grateful for the dappled shade its small, sparse leaves provided. He surveyed the desert landscape. *I'm ready. Show me whatever it is I need to see. Or am I here to think about my life? Been doing a lot of that lately.* The niggling objection came to him that if thinking was what was in order, why did it have to be out here in the desert? Why not back in the comfort of the Academy gardens? No, he wouldn't second guess. Frank shifted to a more comfortable position on the hard rock, content to wait.

His thoughts strayed to Janet. Interesting woman when she wasn't sniveling. When was it they'd talked? A week ago? Two weeks? Did it matter? For someone who claimed to know so much about this new world, she was unaccountably vague about a lot of things. She sure hadn't been in a hurry to meet any of her high-powered clergy relatives. Well, he wouldn't be too anxious to look up folks like that either, not that there'd been any high-powered people in his family, let alone clergy. His family. Not a lot to shout about there. Except Ben, of course. Nine out of ten of 'em had been more like Dad, and Frank sure didn't need to run into him again. There was Mom, of course. Frank realized with a pang that he hadn't thought of his mother since he'd arrived. Of course, he'd never really known the woman who'd died when he was three.

Frank picked up a thorny twig and twirled it. Surely his mother was aware that her son had come to this world. Hadn't she wanted to see him? Perhaps her new life did not include memories of him.

Frank wasn't really surprised to see the woman coming toward him across the desert. Yes, she looked like the pictures he'd seen. A large woman with a firm chin—his chin. He got to his feet. "Mom?" he said uncertainly.

"So you're Frank," she said as she drew closer. She stopped just outside the shadow of the live oak and looked him over, her eyes cautious.

Frank's heart sank. It wasn't that the woman before him was bad-looking; she wasn't. But the long hair that fell unevenly about her face was lank and her clothes were worn and unkempt. When she gained enough confidence to take a few steps toward him Frank was conscious of a slightly sour odor.

"You're a big guy, aren't you? Take after your dad." Her lips pushed out in a grimace. "You seen the bastard?"

Frank had to make an effort to breathe evenly. "Not since back when I was wandering. I ran into him then. He was heading some sort of quasi-official motorcycle pack rounding up people who were making trouble."

"That's him. He really gets his kicks outta the bounty hunter routine. Always did like throwing his weight around, but I guess you grew up knowing that, didn't you?"

"You knew about it? The beatings?"

"Didn't know about you; I knew firsthand." She touched her cheek. "Figured he wouldn't change."

"The beatings stopped when I got just about as big as he was." Frank's reflexive gesture was uncannily like his mother's, except that his hand found his jaw rather than his cheek. "He just about killed me before I got away."

She laughed, showing a missing tooth. "Lemme tell you, if he gets too nasty with the fake police stuff now, if he roughs up anyone, including his prisoners, he finds himself at the other end of the stick. Last time he landed in jail I hear he got shaved—hooboy. He's so vain he stayed out of sight 'til that beard of his grew again." She looked Frank over. "So what did you do after you took off?"

"Went into the army. Then I did a lot of things; ended up as a cop."

"Like him! What d'you know?" Her eyes were suddenly sly. "Hey, you're not one of those real police here, are you? The ones who can make that bastard behave?"

"No, I've been here a while but basically I'm a newcomer."

"But you'll be heading out of here. I can tell. I bet if you wanted you could walk out of the Trackless Parts right now and go back where you come from."

Frank felt a trickle of sweat thread beneath his arms as he considered the implications of his mother's comment. *Would he continue to be able to travel back and forth?* "You can't leave?" he forced himself to ask.

"Not 'less I get permission," she said. Then she brightened. "But I got a real nice place of my own."

"You live here?"

"Well, I was here a while when I first came, no, wait, I was in another place first. It had lots of trees and flowers and stuff. Nice, but boring. Then I came here and after a while I went to the place where I am now. It's down the road a ways."

Frank hesitated. "Are you happy?"

"Happy?" His mother considered. "Well sure, I guess. I get to live the way I want with the kind of people I like. They're a great bunch; they'd do anything for me. I could do with a better job though. You think you could help get them to give me something that takes up less of my day and doesn't interfere with my other, uh, commitments?"

"Commitments?"

She grinned. "That would be telling, wouldn't it? Let's just say I got me some interesting hobbies."

Weariness descended on Frank, wrapping itself around him like a heavy blanket. "I don't have any pull, Mom. I told you I'm a newcomer; I'm just learning."

"But you're headed out. Like I said, I can tell." The apprehensive look returned to her face. "You're going to be one of them."

"Why do you think so?"

"Your face. The way you talk. Everything about you." For a moment her eyes softened. "You've grown up to be a real good-looking guy."

"Did you know you have a grandson?" Frank said quietly. "You want to see good-looking, you should see him. His name is Ben, or at least it was when he was with us."

She picked a thread from the many hanging from her frayed shirt. "A grandson? No kidding."

Frank continued despite her obvious disinterest, "He came here when he was a toddler. I've been allowed to meet him a couple of times, and talking with someone like him, so wise and good, makes you realize what heaven must be like. He is an 'usher,' and while I don't know exactly what that entails, it's obvious he loves being one." Frank stopped. The woman who had been his mother had half-turned away, now no more than a misty figure.

"Mom!"

She quickly turned back again. "Sorry, thought someone was calling me. Look, I've really liked talkin' to you, but I gotta go. Some time when I don't have so much to do maybe you and me can get together and you can tell me about your kid. But how 'bout you wait until I give you a call, okay?"

Frank smiled wryly. "Got it," he said.

His mother was already fading, and a moment later she disappeared completely.

Frank shoved his hands in his pockets and looked out over the empty, sere landscape. The two people who had brought him into the world sure weren't anything to boast about. And neither of them seemed to have the slightest consciousness of having chosen a life in hell. Apparently it didn't seem all that bad to them. He hoped not. *What does it mean when both your parents chose to live in hell?* In class he'd learned that everyone was born with evil inclinations, proclivities toward certain evils from his or her forebears; did this mean that as this couple's son he had inherited so many evil inclinations he had no chance but to be like them?

Frank sat down on the rock, his head in his hands. "Oh God!"

The inclination toward an evil doesn't condemn a person. The thought came like a cooling shower. That's right. It was only when you actually did that evil and thought there was nothing wrong with it that you made it a part of you. He'd had the freedom to choose to live a life unlike either of his parents.

And I did, Frank thought thankfully. *Yes, I did. I took the wrong path sometimes, made mistakes, but when I realized I'd done something wrong, I tried to correct it, tried not to do it again.* A searing thought pierced these comforting musings. *What about Kate?* His fixation on Kate was more than just mooning over something he couldn't have; it had become an obsession. He knew it was wrong, yet he hadn't put her out of his thoughts. Frank pulled away his hands from his face and stared at them. With good reason. He couldn't. He had tried; God, he'd tried, but he couldn't. Frank sank to his knees and clasped his hands together.

My Lord and my God, I can't do this. He took a deep breath. *I can't, but you can. Please help me, help me obey your commandment.* That was all. He remained on his knees, his head bowed, and waited. He didn't expect to hear anything and he didn't, but a sense of peace and well-being flooded him as it had when he'd prayed in the sandy woods by the lake. Would the feeling last this time? Would he be given the strength for which he had prayed or would he find himself back on his knees once again, having failed miserably? "I'm going to do my part best I can," he muttered, "so now let's see you do yours."

Frank thought he heard the faint sound of an amused

chuckle. Of course it had been his imagination, but as Frank got to his feet and strode off in the direction of the Academy he allowed himself a small grin.

It was still there. Kate reached for the small volume on the shelf. Her hands shook. What was inside, the poems or blank pages? She took a quick breath and opened the little book at random.

"... filigreed and chancelled with flavor of blood oranges, fashioned from moonlight; yarn, nacre, cordite," she read. Yes, Campbell McGrath's poem was still here. They all were. Kate closed her eyes. "Thank you," she whispered.

She opened her eyes.

She was in Howard's study. Howard was at his desk, bent over a book. Copying another poem for the anthology? Kate did not approach the desk, but remained where she was by the lamp in the corner, simply grateful to be near him. After a moment she realized Howard was not copying a poem or studying a text. He wasn't doing anything but riffling the pages of a book, turning to one page and then another. He looked up at the flowered wallpaper, his eyes unseeing, then back at the opened book, frowning confusion on his face as he studied the printed words.

What's the matter? Is there something wrong with his eyes? Kate watched in growing dismay as she realized the confusion on her husband's face was mirrored in his mind like a hideous miasma encircling and clouding it. She knew then. Howard could not understand the printed symbols on the paper before him.

Howard blinked. Kate could feel him concentrating fiercely, could see a sliver of comprehension penetrate the mist of confusion as he managed to read two lines, said them aloud and tried to make sense of them.

Kate's hand went to her mouth. *Oh, my love.*

Howard swore long and fluently. *Nothing wrong with his vocabulary.* And as the angry words echoed in the silent room, Kate saw the confusion lift, saw comprehension return.

Howard surveyed the printed words again. "That's better," he growled. He reached for the canes that leaned against the desk. "Brain freeze," he muttered. "That's what the kids call it. That's all it is. Got to get up, do some exercise, get the systems going." He lurched to his feet and propelled himself from the room.

Kate watched him leave. Though he tilted forward on his canes, he held his back ramrod straight. But Kate had seen the look on her husband's face. It was one of utter devastation.

12

"Did I have anything to do with it?" Kate said, her words choked. "Is it because of something I did, something I thought?"

"Oh Kate, Kate, that's not the way it works," Hannah said gently. She put her briefcase on the ground. She was tempted to ask whether Kate had paid any attention when they'd discussed this in class, but found she couldn't add to Kate's distress. "The Lord doesn't cause illness or disease," she reminded Kate, "though he allows these things so that human beings can be free. It's true that if there was no evil in the world there would be no ill health, but an individual doesn't cause his own illness—unless he abuses his body—and one person's thoughts don't cause another's disease." Hannah waited until she saw some of the misery leave Kate's eyes. "I don't know why your husband has this illness, Kate, but I do know it will not affect his eternal life."

"But what about right now?" Kate wailed. "I know Howard. He won't make an appointment with a doctor to find out what's wrong. He'll ignore things until they get so bad someone notices. And who's going to take care of him then?" She was silent, her mind working furiously. Who was there to notice? Howard was a loner; their friends had been mostly hers. There were his colleagues, of course, and his students. His students. How was he managing his classes? Were the lectures continuing to come from some undamaged part of his brain?

"And another thing. He seemed to be in a lot of pain, more than usual, but thank goodness he can still get around." She paused. "Wait a minute. His hair, what there is of it, isn't brown and gray anymore, it's grayish white." She stared at Hannah. "How long has it been since I've seen him?" she asked in a whisper.

Hannah merely looked at Kate, her eyes soft.

"When I came here Howard wasn't due to retire for several years," Kate continued. "And don't tell me that days and months are merely states of mind here," she said fiercely. "I know that! But it hasn't been just states for Howard. It must have taken a lot of time for him to get to this. Why has it been so long since I've been with him? And why, why haven't I known about it?"

"Does it matter?" Hannah saw that it did. "You've both been busy, my dear," she said. "You here and he on earth, each progressing in your own way. Perhaps, after a period of grieving, Howard began to get on with his life and had less need of your presence."

Kate's arms clutched her stomach as though she felt a sudden cramp. "Is that how it works? We touch the lives of those we love only now and then? If they forget us, we forget them?" The idea pierced her like a dart to her heart. Had Howard found someone else to share his life during the time they'd been apart? Was that why she'd been unaware of his illness and its progression? No. More likely it was as Hannah had said. It was easy to imagine Howard being able to compartmentalize his grief and give himself to his work so completely that he seldom thought of anything else.

Kate straightened. No matter. Whatever had happened, Howard was her partner, her friend and lover. Had been almost since the first day they'd met at the faculty meeting where he'd seen Kate's glazed boredom and given her a sardonic glance of complete understanding.

Hannah broke into Kate's reverie. "Perhaps it might help if I told you something about my own experience," she said. "Gregory has told me that he was with me during much of the time I thought we were apart, although he wasn't always conscious of it."

"Gregory was your husband—before?"

"We had only a short time together on earth, but oh, how I loved him. I wanted to lie down and die too when they told me he was among the missing." Hannah's eyes filled with remembered grief. "Of course I didn't know that what I so mourned was not a death but a rebirth."

"You said he was with you," Kate prompted.

"He was there when I received the terrible news; he was with me during those first sleepless nights and often as I raised our children from babyhood to adults. But as I say, it was more of a generalized 'being there' at those times. He was, however, quite definitely with me when I was a blind, deaf old woman trying to hear the voices of grandchildren I could not see. Perhaps it will be this way with Howard and you."

"You were old," Kate said, bemused, "and of course you grew young here."

"As we all do."

"Were you often aware that Gregory was with you?"

"Only in the sense that a feeling of comfort would sometimes envelop me when I thought of him. But there were a couple of times—when I awoke in the middle of the night and realized he was gone—when I cried out for him. I felt his love then. It was as strong as if he was there next to me." Hannah smiled. "Which he was."

Kate was silent a long moment and then gave a sigh that came from deep within her. "All right," she said. "It's not my call. I know Howard is in the Lord's hands, that he's cared for." But as quickly as her acceptance had come, it was washed away in a tidal wave of rebellion. "But I want to be the one to help him," she cried in anguish. "I want to be the one to comfort him—even if he doesn't remember me."

She pressed her hands against her mouth. "Sorry," she muttered, "I didn't mean—well, I guess I did, but I shouldn't have said it."

"Don't forget the Lord sends angels to be with your Howard." Hannah smiled at her. "And those angels are with him every moment of every moment."

"I know," Kate said again, and this time remorse tinged her words. "I know Howard is not my responsibility. But I," she stopped to blow her nose, "I still feel I should have been with him."

"You were. Your love was with him all the 'time,' if you will, that you were going about your business here, learning what you need to know. And all during that 'time' Howard has been living on earth going about his business. He's been learning, growing, and now he has reached another phase of his life."

"One where he can't read his own notes," Kate said, her eyes morose. "Why?" she whispered. "What possible use could it be to have his wonderful mind disintegrate?"

"I don't know," Hannah said quietly.

"You keep saying that," said Kate. She shivered as a fresh breeze from the hills blew over the garden. "I thought an angel would understand why something like that happens."

"There's a lot I don't understand. Gregory either." Hannah smiled. "Many angels know more than we do. Angels in different heavens than ours don't have to be taught things; they perceive them." She shrugged off her light wool sweater and placed it around Kate's shoulders. "They know immediately whether or not something is true; they intuit the reason for things without being told."

"Thanks," Kate said absently as she shoved her arms through the sweater's sleeves. "But there's so much you do know. Can you tell me what I can do to help him?"

"You can continue to prepare so that when you meet him again you can help him learn about this world," Hannah suggested.

"When we meet . . ." Kate's taut muscles relaxed. She took a deep breath. "Yes, there is that. We will be together, won't we? I just have to be patient," she smiled wryly, "and patience is not a particularly characteristic attribute of mine." She folded the cuff of her sleeve. "But you're right; I have to pay attention to the here and now. I've got to see how I can help the people around me, and I am trying. There's Janet. And Dan," she stopped. "Dan gave me short shrift when I ran across him and his wheelbarrow. Do you think I should stay clear until he calls me?"

"Try checking in on him from time to time. Don't push yourself on him if he doesn't want you with him," Hannah said, "just keep testing the water to see if he's willing to allow you to help him."

Kate nodded and began to turn up the cuff on her other sleeve. "Thanks, Hannah. Thanks for everything. I do feel better . . ." Kate stopped and looked from her arm to her companion. "Oh Hannah, I'm so sorry. You've given me your sweater and I didn't even notice!" She began to take it off.

"No, no. Keep it." Hannah smoothed the sweater about Kate and gave her a hug. "Being able to help you, to see you smile again, warms me more than any sweater could." She picked up her briefcase. "I'd better be going. I have a loaded conference schedule to attend to before afternoon break. And by the way," she said, indicating the dog at Kate's side, "I'm glad to see Buster is back on duty." She turned away and was gone.

Kate pulled the thin wool about her. A soft, wet nose pushed against her hand. "Yes, Buster. I know," she said. "It isn't just getting a handle on knowing what I should do, it's doing it," she paused, "and when it comes to Dan, it's if he'll let me."

Frank shook his head to clear it. No question about it—he was back on campus. Last thing he remembered was walking through dusty wasteland, but over there were Birgit's roses, the new scarlet climber she'd added clinging to the rear brick wall like an espaliered tree. Must be a reason he found himself here. Frank had the unsettling feeling he was here to meet someone. He looked about, but Birgit was nowhere to be seen. If it wasn't Birgit, who was it? Dan? Had Kate's nephew finished hauling bricks, or was he still stubbornly unwilling to absorb what he so obviously needed to learn?

Frank saw the shadow of a figure and took a startled half step backward, barely avoiding the large, coffee-colored man who suddenly stood before him.

"You're interested in Dan?" the man asked.

Frank stared at the stranger. The man topped Frank's six-two by half a head. An incredulous grin spread across Frank's face. "Perce? That you, Perce?"

Percy checked the motion of his outstretched hand. "Frank?" he said. "Frank!" He clapped the detective on the back. "I can't believe it!"

Frank flinched. "Damn it, Perce, you'll break my neck." He shook the big man's hand. "Man, it's good to see you." He hesitated.

It was Percy who broke the awkward pause. "It's okay, Frank. I don't mind talking about it." He cracked the knuckles of his hand. "I never really told you how much I appreciated your visiting me. It took balls to do that. Y'know, you were the only one on the force who came to see me. Bet it let you in for plenty of trouble."

Frank waved this aside. "I knew you weren't part of the games those buddies of yours were playing. I knew you didn't get anything out of it."

"I didn't turn them in. And I did more than look the other way; I let them use my place at the lake to store their stuff."

Percy's eyes were haunted. "I did it to myself. I turned in my uniform for a convict's jumpsuit." He let out a breath. "But I'm past that now. I was past it while I was still in the slammer." His grin returned. "So what's happenin' back at the station?"

"I retired, so I'm not up on things. Riley's still there, a commander now, Rios too. Jackson was with us until just before I went on sick leave. He tangled with a bad guy, took a slug in the gut and was in the hospital for four, five days before he died."

"Yeah. I saw Jackson when he first got here. Didn't have much luck with him; he wasn't interested in hearing what any of us had to say. Haven't seen him since."

Frank briefly considered asking what had happened to Jackson, but decided not to pursue it. "What are you doing here, Perce? You in charge of this kid, Dan?"

"I work with security here, sort of a junior-grade assistant at that. One of my jobs was helping the kid's aunt get him out of the Trackless Parts. Lately I've been trying to help him come to terms with why he opted to blow himself away. Give him a chance to find out what he's really about."

"Yeah, I've tried my hand at that too. I wouldn't call that three-day session he had with the lady who shanghaied him anything like finding out about himself, but from what I hear, he nearly busted a gut doing the research."

"Tell me about it." Percy looked at Frank. "Say, are you the one who got him to admit some of the stuff he's been avoiding? Got him to the point where he doesn't have that Baby Browning plastered on him all the time?"

"I did have a talk with him one day while he was hauling bricks," Frank admitted.

"Hey, good going. Maybe you should be the one working with security."

"It was a lucky shot. Listen, Perce, who are you?" Frank paused. "I mean are you—an angel?"

The big man smiled. "Not yet."

"But you will be, right? You're what they call a 'good spirit,' aren't you?"

Percy's beaming grin broadened. "Guess so. Leastwise that's what they tell me."

Frank punched the big man's massive arm. "Who'd of thunk it? Perce with wings and a harp."

"Come on, Frank. You've been here long enough to know that's a bunch of crock."

"I know." Frank sobered. "I'm not surprised you're going to make it, Perce. Not surprised at all." He gazed at Birgit's roses, his look reflective.

Percy slapped Frank's back again, this time gently. "Hey, let's skip all this talk about me and get on with the subject we're supposed to be dealin' with."

Frank nodded. "The kid?"

"Got it in one."

"How did we get so lucky?"

"You and me, we're privileged we have the opportunity to help someone," Percy said, a touch of reproach in his voice. "Or are you just dissin' me?"

"Dissin'. But I am beginning to learn that I'm here to help the people around me as well as being helped myself." Frank took a seat on the wooden bench beside the path, one that had not been there, he noted absently, a moment ago. He motioned to the big man to sit. "Okay Perce, bring me up to speed."

Janet speared two pineapple slices, put them on her plate, and slid her tray down the buffet line.

"It's stupid," the woman behind her muttered, "absolutely incomprehensible."

"Were you speaking to me?" Janet said.

"I was saying I find it incomprehensible that adults aren't

free to even mention important philosophical concepts around here, let alone discuss them." The woman reached across her tray and held out a hand. "I'm Pegeen, by the way."

"Janet." Janet took the outstretched hand briefly.

"Yes, I've seen you around," Pegeen nodded and continued her aggrieved complaint. "For a place that touts academic freedom it's ironic that they won't allow you to talk about ideas so vital to a person's well-being."

Janet looked at her blankly. "Come again?"

Pegeen made an annoyed tisk. "I had a little cadre of students here who were interested in discussing my ideas, things I've studied for years. And these aren't just my opinions, mind you; they're hard facts I've researched, facts that can't be refuted. But now they tell me I can't meet with my group any more. It's like I'm some kind of intellectual Mata Hari." Pegeen grinned at the thought and flung back her head, her mane of chestnut hair swinging free of her bare shoulders.

"You're a teacher?" said Janet, wide-eyed.

"I did teach," Pegeen gave a dismissive wave of her hand, "but I've become involved with larger issues, and it's not a part of my life at the moment. When I first came here I asked about teaching some of their classes and you might think I suggested I blow up the buildings. I only offered to help out because it's obvious they need a broader spectrum of ideas here. They said if I liked I could attend classes! And in spite of the insult, I have—now and again. Obviously they didn't have the faintest idea who I was and had never read any of my articles. Anyway, now I'm not allowed to get together with my group. What's wrong with discussing things like the fact that for the past several thousand years women have allowed men to restrict them? And we're not just talking burkhas and chadors here. Women find checks and curbs everywhere, even today, even in our 'enlightened' culture."

"That's pretty much of a given," Janet said. "I can't imagine why you aren't allowed to discuss something that's historical fact." She frowned. "I don't think I've seen you in class."

"As I said, I only attend now and again. I can't believe they expect me to sit there and listen to them spiel that unsubstantiated garbage." Pegeen looked about and lowered her voice. "Got to watch it; they're absurdly sensitive about the stuff they give out as gospel."

Janet had reached the end of the buffet. *The woman's a nut case.* Giving her a brief nod, Janet escaped to the far corner of the great dining hall and took a seat at one of the small tables. To Janet's dismay, Pegeen followed and put her tray on Janet's table.

"Mind if I join you?"

Unwillingly Janet gestured to the seat across from her.

Pegeen plunked herself down. "It's the whole subject of marriage that they're so sticky about here," she said. "Their views are so one-sided. I've always maintained that it's completely against nature to restrict a woman's sexual contact to one person. Limiting herself by saying a few words and signing a document is simply something that's been foisted on her by any number of male-driven cultures. Not that she'd have been able to sign her name in most of them."

Janet looked at her in amazement. "Do you attend any of the classes on marriage?"

"Not if I can help it." Pegeen said it with such simple candor that Janet couldn't help smiling. "I did go to one or two," Pegeen continued, "but it confused me. And that's not something I ordinarily like to admit, but there you go, it did. Couldn't get a handle on what the teacher thought was so great about two people living their life as one. One what? Come on. The poor woman obviously needs a reality check."

"So what are you doing here?" Janet asked, fascinated. "Most people think it's a privilege to have made it to the Academy, but apparently you're not impressed."

"Well, yes and no. I have to say I've liked being here—off and on. It's safe and it's comfortable." A mischievous gleam lit Pegeen's eyes and she added, "Though unsafe and uncomfortable can be interesting once in a while." She shook her glorious head of reddish-brown hair over her shoulders again. "Now and again I'd like to be able to believe what they say in these classes, but then I stop and realize I don't really believe in Tinker Bell." She took a spoonful of soup. "Look, there's something I wanted to ask. Have you ever been outside the grounds here?"

Janet's attention sharpened. Was this why Pegeen had waylaid her? What was the woman's agenda? "No, can't say I have."

"You don't ever have the urge to explore, to see what's out there?"

"We do plenty of exploring in our classes," Janet said, adding wryly, "and then there's the exploring we do on our own. But you don't have to go outside the grounds for that."

Pegeen didn't ask for an explanation, but pressed ahead. "I've been outside and it's," she grinned, "well, let's say it's quite interesting. I got a kid to go with me last time and we had a great few days—until he got cold feet," she sniffed, "among other things. Anyway, I wondered whether maybe a group of us might go exploring." Pegeen blinked, and Janet had the feeling she was trying for an earnest expression. If so, it didn't quite work. "I thought I'd start by asking you," Pegeen finished.

"Why me?" Janet asked.

Pegeen waved a slim hand. "The people here are such stick-in-the-muds. I know they're going to make a fuss if I take off on my own, and since they won't let me have any contact with my little cadre of students, I figured I'd get a few other folks to go with me. I haven't been what you'd call a regular at attending classes, so I don't know all that many people, and, well, I notice you don't hang around much with anyone either, so I thought I'd start with you," her voice trailed off and she looked at Janet hopefully.

Janet stared at her. Her mouth tightened. The gall of the woman! She might as well have said that she'd chosen to invite Janet along because, like Pegeen, Janet had no friends. The prospect of going anywhere with this harridan had less than no appeal.

Janet caught herself. *Harridan? Where did that thought come from?* Pegeen might be irritating and completely self-absorbed, but the gorgeous twenty-something sitting across from her could by no means be termed a harridan. Or was she as young as she seemed? Janet studied her. There was something about her that made Janet wonder. And what about the years Pegeen said she'd spent researching her "ideas"? Of course, like everyone here, she'd become younger since she'd arrived.

Pegeen frowned at Janet. "What?"

"I was wondering how old you were when you came here," Janet said baldly.

Pegeen stiffened. "That's a hell of a strange thing to ask," she said.

"I don't think so. It's true we don't usually talk about our lives before we came here, but you brought up all the years you spent doing research, and I wondered—" Janet cocked an eyebrow, leaving her question unfinished.

"Umm," Pegeen said. She took a huge bite of her club sandwich and chewed.

Janet remained silent.

Pegeen swallowed and tossed the rest of her sandwich on the plate. "Oh, all right. I was sixty-nine when I came here."

"You're kidding! That's older than me!"

"In a couple of weeks I'd have been seventy," Pegeen said glumly.

Janet choked back a laugh. "I'm sorry," she gasped, "I don't mean to be rude, but the thought of you—"

"Oh, I know. It's a hoot to think of me pushing a walker—not that I ever did," Pegeen said. "But walker or no, let me tell you, my life was no picnic. I've always been a realist. I knew I had brains, but I was a homely girl who grew to be an unattractive woman, and looks count for one hell of a lot where we came from. Always did, always will." She blinked rapidly. "Then I came here and it seemed each day I got younger and prettier. It, it was like every day I looked in the mirror I'd been given the present I'd always wanted. Men looked at me the way I'd seen them look at other women." She looked down at her clasped hands. "I always said I didn't care about looks, but oh, it's so wonderful being beautiful."

Janet sat quiet, moved despite her antagonism. Pegeen's unabashed joy in her unexpected gift was touching, and in spite of the woman's ridiculous theories and ranting foolishness, there was something about her honesty that was oddly appealing.

"How about you?" Pegeen said. "Isn't it a buzz being attractive?"

Janet looked her in surprise. "Who, me?"

"Oh come on, don't tell me you haven't noticed," Pegeen said impatiently. She pointed to the mirror on the wall opposite them. "You don't look a day older than I do."

Janet followed her gaze. The women reflected in the mirror did seem the same age, and they were both . . . Janet blinked. While the chestnut-haired one was undoubtedly gorgeous, the slender, brown-haired woman beside her was quite pretty, too. Janet flushed. How long had this been going on? She'd never been particularly conscious of her looks. She'd always taken care to be neatly and appropriately dressed and each morning she'd applied the obligatory cream to her acne-pitted skin and the lipstick and blusher her sallow complexion required, but she hadn't bothered about makeup since she'd been here. The reflection in the mirror, however, showed a woman with full, red lips and unblemished skin.

"Goodness!" she said.

"Nice, isn't it?" Pegeen observed. Then, her attention caught by something across the dining hall, her eyes narrowed. "Well, well, well. Look who's coming to dinner. Haven't seen Danny boy since our verbal spanking by the powers that be."

Janet looked over to see Kate's nephew enter the dining hall. Dan looked self-conscious, keeping his head down as he took a tray from the rack and pushed it along the nearly empty line.

"Hope you don't mind if I invite him to join us," said Pegeen. She was on her feet, waving and yoo-hooing before Janet could say anything.

Janet couldn't have replied anyway. She was staring at two large men who had come in behind the boy and were getting trays. She didn't know one of them, but she certainly knew the other. The man who had just put a large piece of cake on his tray was Frank Chambers.

13

At Pegeen's trilling yoo-hoo Dan stiffened like a trapped animal. He hesitated for a moment, then trudged over to the table holding his tray before him as though it could somehow protect him from whatever was in store.

"Well hello, lover," Pegeen said, her throaty voice descending an octave lower. "Come sit over here."

Dan cast an anguished look behind him. The two men who stood taking in the scene with their trays in hand exchanged glances and followed him to the table.

"Nice to see you, Janet," Frank said. "This is my friend Percy."

"Hello, Percy." Janet found she could not meet Frank's eyes.

"Would you introduce us to your friend?" Frank prodded politely.

Janet blushed. She hadn't missed the surprise on Frank's face when he'd seen her sitting with Pegeen. She did not want to be here. She did not want to introduce her new acquaintance to these men. And she certainly didn't want Frank to think Pegeen was her friend. "Of course," she mumbled. She nodded to the still-standing Pegeen. "This is Pegeen."

Pegeen gave the men a full-wattage smile. "Hi there!" she said. Hands on hips, she inspected them, eyebrows arched. "My, but you're big—both of you. Big, big, big," she said with a giggle that somehow managed to make the statement slightly obscene.

Percy seemed unmoved, but Frank was plainly annoyed. "You called Dan over because you wanted to ask him something?" he said to Pegeen.

"Thought we might chat, talk about our adventures on the, uh, outside." Pegeen flicked a glance at Dan, who had taken a seat and sat hunched miserably over his tray, and then back at Frank and Percy. She took in Percy's bulging biceps. "But you make it hard to concentrate on the boy. I mean, it's difficult when there are real men around," she purred. "Especially men like you," she said, slowly lifting her eyes to Percy's face.

Percy met her look with a level stare. "I wouldn't try to go there, ma'am," he said.

"Why not, big man, you in training?"

"Not interested."

Not at all discomfited, Pegeen's gaze swept from Percy to Frank. For a moment it looked as though she would attempt a secondary assault, but then she shrugged and slid into her chair. "Well I suppose now that you're here, you might as well sit down and join us. Janet and I have been having an interesting discussion about sex and the role of women and we've been longing for some input from the masculine point of view, haven't we, Janet?"

Janet gave her head a little shake. "Sorry, but I really can't stay," she said quietly. She gathered her plate and silverware and put them on her tray. "I have things—things I have to do." She rose from the table and, not looking at anyone, skittered across the floor.

"I'll get back to you on that trip we were talking about," Pegeen called after her.

Janet, desperate to be gone, did not reply. It was as she pushed her dishes and tray onto the revolving counter sliding into the kitchen that Janet looked at the mirror on the wall above the narrow opening. She gasped. Reflected behind her was the group she'd left at the table. Or was it? Sitting beside Dan and across from Frank and his friend Percy was a woman Janet had never seen before. Even from this distance Janet could see that her face was mottled and scabbed, the flesh hanging in folds about her neck and chin. But it was her hair that made Janet shudder. Surely it was illusion, but it looked as though the woman's hair was coiled into a nest of tiny snakes that swung and writhed about her face.

Janet made herself turn and face the group. There they were. Dan sat slumped over his soup, Percy and Frank had their backs to her, and Pegeen—Pegeen was chatting animatedly, gesturing with those long-fingered hands, her lovely dark-red hair falling to smooth, bare shoulders. Janet closed her eyes and opened them again. Yes, there she was, looking quite normal. Janet felt a chill. She darted toward the big double doors of the dining hall. She did not look at the mirror as she passed.

"If I've said it once, I've said it a hundred times; I believe in meaningful relationships," Pegeen flashed another megawatt smile at the men opposite her. "I don't know where the people at the Academy get the idea I go around preaching unbridled sex."

"I'm not in any position of authority at the Academy and don't have anything to say about what you do or don't advocate," Percy said to her. "We're just concerned about your interest in Dan."

"I simply called him over to renew our rather abruptly abbreviated acquaintance. You don't have to worry; I'm not going to shanghai your little charge. Not that I ever did. You came with me willingly enough, didn't you, Danny boy? In fact you were more than eager." Her mouth hardened. "But here's another thing I've always maintained. Any relationship has to have a degree of commitment to survive. And I'd say running away doesn't show a great deal of commitment, does it, sweetie?"

Dan looked up from his soup and darted a quick glance at Pegeen. "You didn't say anything about commitment when we were together," he mumbled.

"Didn't give me much of a chance, did you?" Pegeen's lips curved in a fleeting smile, but her eyes glittered. "I don't like having someone run out on me. Don't like it at all." She collected herself and batted her eyes. "But I'm more than willing to let bygones be bygones."

Dan swallowed. "Didn't think you'd mind. I mean, you said all that stuff about being free to do what we liked—that is, I thought—"

"Let's face it, sweetie, you weren't doing much thinking. You were too busy with—other things."

"Okay troops, maybe we could call this a draw." Percy laid a hand flat on the table. "Dan, why don't you apologize to the lady, and if she accepts it, we can all get on with our business."

"Whoa there, big man." Pegeen leaned toward Percy. "If there's need for an apology, I'll be the one to ask for it. I said I just wanted us to have a chance to renew our acquaintance, and that's exactly what we'll do. I may have a few things I'd like to talk to Danny about, but I'm not going to boil him in oil. So why don't you gentlemen leave us to chat?" She looked Percy straight in the eye and added, "No one tells me what to do. I call the shots."

"Not here, you don't."

The four at the table turned as one at the quietly spoken words. The slim officer before them was the same one who had interrupted Pegeen's discussion with her group the first time Dan had seen her. His khaki uniform with an arm patch that showed a jagged bolt of lightning across a blue cloud was the same, and he stood, feet spread wide, thumbs in his side pockets, casually commanding their attention.

Pegeen was the first to recover. Thrusting out a pugnacious lower lip, she pushed away from the table and stood. "Not you again! I wasn't aware that anyone asked you to join the conversation," she said.

The man turned his pale-blue gaze on her and Pegeen took a hasty step back. "What I meant was, ah, we're having a private discussion," she said.

He ignored her. "How's it going, Percy?" he said. "Need a little help?"

Percy raised a hand in greeting. "Yo, Jerry. I was hoping one of you guys would come by. I'm not exactly sure how to handle things here."

Jerry smiled. "Like this." He turned to Pegeen. "What you choose to do in the Trackless Parts is up to you, but you may not exhibit this kind of behavior on Academy grounds and you may not harass any student."

"Harass? Harass?" Pegeen said indignantly. She pointed to Dan. "This young man and I were just about to have a chat when these two bozos butted in." But she didn't meet the uniformed man's eyes, and when he remained silent, she continued more mildly, "I don't know what 'behavior' you're talking about; I've just been stating my opinions."

"The relationships you talk about are nothing but dry, wasted couplings that harm the very fabric of a person's being." Jerry took the seat beside Percy and looked at Pegeen amiably. "You are free to promote your ideas elsewhere," he said. "Not here."

Pegeen lifted an eyebrow and with a flip of her hand, tossed a thick lock of her magnificent hair over her shoulder. "Dear, dear. I'm sorry my views shock you. But I'm even more sorry, no, I'm amazed that you feel it's your job to run around annoying people." She eyed him shrewdly. "Or were you called here?" She rounded on Frank and Percy. "Were you big, brave men so shocked by little me you had to call the campus police to the rescue?"

Since neither Frank nor Percy rose to the bait, Pegeen's

belligerent gaze shifted to Dan, who was watching his fingers tap the tabletop in a nervous little jig. He looked up for a brief second. "Not me," he said.

She looked at the policeman, who returned her look calmly. Perhaps it was the pity in the uniformed man's light-blue eyes that made Pegeen catch her lip in her teeth. "Okay, okay," she said, "if I'm not welcome I'll go elsewhere."

She reached out to stroke Dan's shoulder. "I didn't mean to scold you, sweet-pie. I was only teasing, but it wasn't nice of Pegeen to make you feel uncomfortable." Her voice went lower, huskier. "Feel like coming with me? I have to go to the library," Pegeen gave an artful flutter of her eyelashes that somehow wasn't quite as successful as her earlier attempts, "and I need someone to carry my books."

"No, Pegeen." The policeman's quiet words were not much louder than Pegeen's, but they cut the air like a whip.

Pegeen recoiled, but only for a moment. Her chin went up. "You don't have to put it in writing," she snarled. "I'm out of here." But before she flounced from the table, she paused to say, "Maybe I'll see you later, Danny; you might be surprised to discover we have lots to talk about." She turned to face the policeman, though she didn't seem able to look above his sleeve patch. "Don't worry, I'm not going to harass or subvert the boy." Then, her high heels clicking an angry punctuation, Pegeen made her exit from the dining hall.

The men looked at each other. "When she said she was out of here, did she mean she's leaving the Academy?" Frank asked Jerry.

"'Fraid not. She can stay as long as she adheres to the ground rules. She's on some sort of errand, and the folks here want to give her the chance to decide whether or not to go through with it."

Percy had been silent since he'd first greeted the policeman. Now he said, "You know what her errand is, Jerry?"

"I have a good idea, but it's best we don't go into that just now. As usual, it's the small matter of leaving people free to make their choice." Jerry's smile enveloped them all, but he spoke to Dan. "You have anything in mind you'd like to do now that you're out of the brick-hauling business? Have any questions Percy and Frank haven't answered?"

Percy exchanged a look with Frank. "Dan hasn't had all that many questions and we didn't want to push it."

"You're just not interested enough in your new life to ask questions about it?" Jerry's eyebrows raised.

Dan shifted in his chair. "I do ask questions. I asked if I had to go to school, and when they said I didn't, I asked what I'm supposed to do here." He turned to Percy and Frank, an aggrieved expression on his young face. "You guys didn't exactly come out with any great game plan except to suggest some kind of 'tutoring' with Aunt Kate that sounded pretty much like school to me."

At the look on Jerry's face, he continued, "Okay, so I'll ask you; what should I be doing?"

Jerry didn't seem to mind the boy's belligerent tone. "I'm not surprised that you're finding this world somewhat confusing. Some newcomers do. What I'd advise is something that seems to help most everyone, and that is to reach out to your fellow arrivals and try to help them."

Dan frowned. "Me—help? Like who?"

"Can't you think of anyone?" Jerry asked.

Dan thought, and then brightened. "I can. I definitely can."

"All right, have at it then."

Jerry watched, amused, as Dan got to his feet and scrambled off. Then he turned to Percy. "I have to hand it to your young friend. He gives new meaning to the word obtuse."

"You know where he's going?" Percy's eyes glinted with amusement.

"Sure. He's heading for someone who needs his help right

now as much as a hole in the head." Jerry shook his head in mock despair.

"Well, you just said it yourself. He's young. Very young."

"Yeah. Nineteen when he came here, but nineteen years should be enough to develop some insight."

Frank looked at Jerry, surprised. Jerry saw the look and drawled, "Whasamatta, you think I'm too hard on the kid?"

"Well, you're an angel, right? I thought an angel would be more, ah, more—" Frank hesitated.

"Charitable?" Percy offered it with a grin.

"Perce knows I want more than anything for the kid to be able to accept what he's being offered here," Jerry said to Frank. "But you're correct. I should watch my thoughts, because right now I want to wring his neck."

"Why?" Frank said, smiling himself.

"Away the kid goes, charging off to where he figures he can get some sympathy and score some points, but he doesn't have a clue that he wants ego stroking way more than he wants to help her." He shook his head. "All we can hope is that those good impulses he has, and he does have them, are stronger than the ingrained idea that Dan is the most, if not the only, important being in the universe." The campus policeman hesitated and then said, "I didn't want to mention it when you asked about Pegeen's errand a while back, but now that the kid's gone, there's something it might be good if you knew."

His listeners were still, quietly attentive.

"There may be trouble in that quarter. It seems she's hooked up with one of the more dicey characters in the Trackless Parts. We don't know how deep she's in—could be she's just testing the waters, but if she is scouting the folks here with the idea of coaxing some of them to join the group in the town there, we could have a situation."

"Who's the dicey character?" Frank asked.

"Now that he's in the Trackless Parts he calls himself

Zaroth, though that wasn't his name when he was here." Jerry's lips thinned into a grim line. "He may be trolling for disciples; if it's Pegeen, that's one thing, but if it's Dan, that's another story. The kid hasn't had enough of a chance to see what he's made of his life."

"So what's the program?" Percy asked slowly. "Sounds like we should keep an eye on the kid but let him go his own way."

"You got it." Jerry got up. He clapped Percy on the shoulder, his joviality returning. "By the way, I hear congratulations are in order. Good going, Novitiate."

Percy ducked his head. He seemed oddly shy as he stood and took Jerry's outstretched hand. "Thanks," he said.

"We're all happy about it." Jerry waved a quick salute to them both. "You might consider hanging around with our Perce for a while," he said to Frank. "I know he's a friend of yours and you helped him through a rough time at one period of his life on earth. Could be he might return the favor." And with that enigmatic statement, the policeman gave a brisk nod and was gone.

Frank waited for his friend to comment. After a moment Percy rubbed his ear and said, "You're going to ask what's with the 'Novitiate' business, right?"

"Among other things," Frank said dryly.

"It looks like I'm going to be allowed to join one of the forces—don't know which one yet," Percy said. "I've enjoyed being with newcomers, but I wondered whether I'd ever be allowed to get back what I threw away." He looked down at the table. "What I really want is to be like Jerry. I want to be someone who assures that order is preserved and the innocent protected." He cracked his huge knuckles and looked up. "Does that sound as syrupy as I think it did?"

"No," Frank said quietly. "No it doesn't." He toyed his fork. "About Jerry, I know he's a cop—you could tell that without the uniform. But he's a completely different type from some I came across here before I came to the Academy. Those guys sort of had the feel of cops, but the bad ones you see every now and then, into bullying and throwing their weight around."

"Oh, those. The dudes you're talking about think of themselves as cops but they're not. Different line of work altogether. They are useful, but it's the usefulness of vultures who clear the streets of roadkill. Long as they stick to what they're supposed to do and don't get too rough with their charges they're allowed to wander the Trackless Parts, but if they get out of line, they're out of there."

Frank nodded. "That's what someone said to me a while ago." He put his fork down. "Are you going to stay here, or does this Novitiate thing mean you're going to be stationed elsewhere?" He hoped it didn't sound too pleading, but the thought of losing his friend was unsettling. Jerry's suggestion that he could learn from Percy seemed oddly right and somehow comforting. Frank remembered the last time he'd seen Percy. His friend had been sitting behind reinforced glass in prison overalls. Percy, careful to give no indication of anything that might be seen as vulnerability, had sat immobile, eyes hooded, expression unreadable. Yet there had been a moment when Percy thanked Frank for coming when Frank had seen, despite the dignity of his old friend's bearing, a glimpse of his misery and desperation. How strange that Percy should be the one able to guide him through the snarls and tangles in which Frank now found himself.

"I'll be here, at least for a while," Percy assured him. "I'll be finding my home soon," his face lit as he said these last words, "but that won't have any effect on where I'll be carrying out my duties."

"Your home?"

"My community, or what will be my community. I've seen

it." Percy's eyes focused on a point behind Frank as though seeing it again, and Frank realized with a jolt that he probably was doing just that—looking at what would be his "community."

"It's the kind of place I've always dreamed of having," Percy continued, "right by a lake, not too big, but real pretty. Near enough to the city to go there if we want."

"And it's just given to you? It's yours?"

"Ours. It will be my wife's and mine." Percy said it softly.

"You have a wife?" Frank remembered Percy's former wife, a thin, angular woman who had left Percy for another man years before, at the beginning of Percy's time in jail.

"No. I will one day, but I haven't met her yet."

Frank stared at him. "You haven't met her!"

Percy nodded.

"Care to tell me how that's going to work?"

"There's going to be a meeting of Novitiates from other academies; I'm pretty sure she'll be there," Percy said.

"You're going to be given a slip of paper with her name on it?"

"I'll look around. I'll know."

"Sounds like something out of the Psychic Hour by way of the Dating Game." Frank hadn't meant to make the jeering comment, but it emerged of its own volition. And worse than the words was the note of naked envy Frank heard in his own voice. "Damn it, Perce, I'm sorry," Frank said, a catch in his throat.

The look of understanding on Percy's face made Frank flinch. "You'll be given it too, Frank, if you really want it," he said. "Everyone who asks forgiveness when he does wrong, if he stops doing it, everyone who obeys his conscience to the best of his ability during his life on earth, receives the gift of a true marriage love."

"I made so many wrong decisions in my life." Frank did not look at Percy. "And I'm afraid I've continued to make them here."

"You made a lot of right ones, pal." Percy put a hand on Frank's shoulder. "Some I know about personally. Not just the times you visited me. You were one of only two cops who came to my funeral. You were the only one who offered to help my mom and sister afterwards. Yeah, I knew about that. I was there."

Frank raised his head. "Maybe I did do some stuff right—some of the time. But were there enough of those choices?"

"Come on, Frank, you've been here long enough to know it's not like there's a scale where you weigh up the good choices against the bad ones," Percy said. "What matters is what you've grown to love, what makes you the real *you*."

Frank managed a grim smile. "I've been told that before; we all have. Many times. Doesn't make me feel much better."

"Feeling better about yourself may not be what you need right now, friend. How 'bout we stop concentrating on how you feel and pay attention to the job we've been given?"

"We?"

"You heard Jerry. He thinks we should hang around together for a while." Percy drew a big hand over his face. "I'd sure like to know more about this Zaroth character. He sounds lethal—at least for Dan. What do you think, should we let Kate know what her nephew might be headin' for?"

Frank looked at his friend in surprise. "You're asking my opinion?"

"No, I'm just jerking your chain. Of course I am, stupid; you're not some junior-grade rookie." Percy gave Frank's arm a playful punch that almost sent Frank off his chair.

"You keep doing that and I'm going to have to take you on," Frank said, rubbing his bicep.

"You just try it, friend," Percy said with a grin. "I seem to remember a couple of sessions in the gym way back when we were rookies where the results were pretty one-sided."

"I've bulked up since then." Frank got up and put the dishes on his tray. "As for my opinion, yes, I think Kate should be in the picture. And do me a favor, will you? You be the one to tell her."

14

Dan carefully brought the orange rose to his nose and sniffed. "Nice smell," he said to no one in particular. He bent the stem a fraction and then hesitated, as though considering whether to snap it.

"Oh don't!" The wail came from the depths of the garden.

"Like I would." Dan dropped his hand and grinned at the girl who rose from behind the tall flowers that grew against the rear brick wall. "But how else do I get your attention when I come looking for you and find you're hiding out—as usual?"

Birgit made her way onto the grass, a large rabbit hopping behind her. She stopped to stand a circumspect five feet from Dan and awkwardly hitched her sarong-like skirt about her.

Dan looked at her. Birgit seemed taller. Taller and some-how slimmer. Yes, Birgit had definitely lost weight. "Come on," he coaxed, "sit and let's talk."

At first he thought she might turn away, but then the girl smiled shyly and took a seat on the iron bench he'd indicated.

"Nice outfit," he said as he sat beside her. "New?"

Birgit smoothed the silken material. "It was in my closet this morning, like the one I wore yesterday. I wasn't going to wear this one, not to work in the garden, but Hannah said I could. She said it wouldn't tear or get dirty. She said the saris are presents."

It was the wonder in her voice when she said the word

"presents" that caught Dan. "You haven't had many presents," he said.

"Never before."

"How come Hannah gave them to you?"

"Oh, they were not from Hannah; they are from God." Birgit said it as easily as if she'd announced the weather.

"He's giving out presents?" Dan said, trying to sound casual as she.

"He gives us all we have. Everything." Birgit's gesture took in the blue sky, the gardens, the buildings beyond.

"Yeah. But somehow I don't picture him handing out dresses."

"You are making fun," Birgit said uncertainly.

"Yes I am," Dan's voice was gentle. "But you deserve your presents, Birgit. You deserve a closet full of dresses."

"I think it is like my rabbit. When I found Shoma I didn't realize she was a gift, but now I know she is." She reached down to stroke the rabbit's downy back. "When I thought something bad she was taken away, but when I was sorry she came back. And now I try not to think bad things." She leaned toward Dan and confided in a whisper, "I don't want my lovely clothes to go away."

Dan felt something, he didn't know quite what, loosen in his chest. And when he saw the glint of moisture in Birgit's dark eyes, the tightness that had been there ever since the embarrassing session in the dining hall left completely. *What a sweetie.* It was nice to be with someone who didn't judge you, who was grateful for your attention and didn't expect anything from you. Dan extended his legs before him and leaned back on the bench. He hadn't felt this good in—well, he couldn't remember feeling this good. Birgit was the kind of girl he could find himself getting interested in. Dan took in the way the patterned silk fell in folds about Birgit's slim body. With a little help, a little coaching, she could become a person he might be glad to have around for a while—maybe permanently.

He noticed that Birgit was looking past him, her forehead creased in a frown.

"What is it?" Dan whipped about to look behind him and then back at Birgit, who was still staring into space. "It's that, that thing, isn't it?"

"I thought perhaps," Birgit pointed to a dark patch of shrubbery, "but it was only a shadow."

Dan shivered. "You thought you saw the wolf?"

Birgit nodded. "I thought so, but it is gone now. You do not need to be afraid."

"Who's afraid?" Dan leaned back again and kicked at the grass with the heel of his sneaker.

"You are," Birgit said. "I do not want you to be afraid, but I think perhaps it is a good thing. It means you do not want the wolf thing to be with you." She looked at him. "You do not wish it, do you?"

"Like I'd want something like what you saw anywhere near me." Dan hesitated and then asked, "You think it appears because something in me wants it to?"

Birgit flushed. "I am not smart, but since I have been here I find I know things. Some things. I don't know why a thing is, I just know it." She looked uncertain. "At least I think I do."

"Hey, there's some weird stuff here. Don't let it throw you. I don't." Dan wiped his face with the edge of his T-shirt, exposing his stomach. "Man, it's hot." He saw Birgit looking at his hard abdomen and straightened. "Get a load of these abs," he said, patting them. "Been working out with that brick-hauling, but not enough to make these babies."

Birgit's mouth curved in what might have been a smile. "Maybe they are your present?"

Dan gave a hoot of laughter. "I can't believe it." He thrust out his lower lip and growled, "You are making fun."

"No, no." But her smile widened.

"Yes, yes." Dan bounced to his feet. "Hey look, why don't we go for a walk? Where do you want to go?"

Birgit considered and then brightened. "Why don't you come with me to visit one of the communities nearby? Hannah said it's time I began looking for my home, that I should spend some afternoons visiting some of the societies that I'll find near here and see if I feel comfortable."

"Communities?" Dan said cautiously. "Out in the Trackless Parts?"

"I do not think it is called that. They are in heaven." Birgit looked at him from beneath lowered lids. "I have not gone yet because I have been a little bit scared. It would be nice to be able to go with someone."

"You sure it's all right for me to go?" he asked. "Isn't this something you're supposed to do by yourself?"

"Hannah said that the communities welcome visitors. If they welcome me, why would they not welcome you?"

"Good question." Dan shifted his stance, thinking. Then he said, "Why not? They don't want me roaming the Trackless Parts, but nobody could object to my keeping you company while you trot around heaven."

"Then you will come with me?" Birgit's dark eyes glowed.

He hesitated only a moment. "Sure, kid, let me get my track shoes and we'll go."

Janet closed the door behind her and inspected her living room. She usually relished this moment of entering her apartment with its white, unadorned walls, this room with its tall French windows open to the sunny balcony. She always took pleasure in being surrounded by the things she'd chosen—the soft, white leather couch and matching reclining chair with the tubular reading light adjusted just as she liked, the bright red and orange pillows and multicolored striped rugs scattered about. It was all so different from the chintz-covered furniture she'd lived with over the years. She'd never realized how much she disliked those puffy chairs and insipid pastels until Hannah had asked whether she would like to decorate her rooms. Would she? She'd been almost disappointed that it was all done so quickly, and she never tired of returning to this safe haven.

Except that right now it didn't feel like a safe haven. All she felt was anger, anger and shame. Why had she allowed that freak of a woman to sit with her? Why had she listened to her spew her ridiculous theories? *What must Frank think?* Janet's cheeks burned. His look of surprise gnawed at her. Why hadn't she responded to that mild questioning look? Why hadn't she told him she hadn't even known the woman until moments before? Why had she sat there tongue-tied instead of denouncing Pegeen's spiel? Why had she fled like a guilty teenager?

Janet threw herself on the couch and covered her head with her arms. She almost didn't hear the tap at the door. When it came again she sat up but remained on the couch. At the third tap she pushed herself off the couch and yanked open the door.

The man standing at the doorstep seemed far too young for his white hair. Or was his hair white? It might have been so blond it looked white. Janet's hand tightened on the doorknob. The man standing before her was an angel. She didn't know how she knew it, but she did. Janet cleared her throat. "Please come in," she said.

He smiled at her. "If you're sure you'd like me to."

"Yes, of course." She stepped back. "I, that is, I thought angels just appeared."

"Sometimes. But when we come to a person's home, we prefer to wait until we're invited in."

Janet led the way to the couch and took a chair from the dining table for herself. "Um, is there anything I can get you?"

What could she offer an angel? *Tea? Coffee? Water! Yes, water stands for truth*, she thought. But so did wine. The whole thing was ridiculous. How could she offer an angel truth?

"Nothing, thank you, but it's kind of you to ask." His smile was so gentle that Janet's tensed shoulders relaxed. "My name is Walter. I've come to see you because you're so upset about a number of things."

"That horrible woman intimated that she was my friend, but she isn't," Janet said in a rush. "Believe me, I never even spoke to her before today."

"Why would I not believe you?" Walter said mildly. "No, I haven't come because of that poor, misguided woman. It's because of you. You seem to be having a difficult time processing your life on earth. Perhaps I can help you."

Janet eyed him warily. "What do you mean, 'process'?"

"You haven't been dealing with some of the things you've done, the decisions you made." He sounded regretful. "Matter of fact, you've been avoiding any thought about them."

"I, I'm trying to live in the here and now," Janet said. "I thought that's what we're supposed to do."

"We have an internal and an external memory, Janet. The external one you used on earth along with the facts you learned does not come with you when you transition, that is, it's not in the forefront. It's not part of your life here, but everything in that external memory is within your internal memory and can be accessed when needed. The memories there are sometimes called your 'Book of Life,' and most of our students find that they must do a fair amount of looking back on their lives to gain insights into why they made the decisions they did and how it relates to what they're learning here." His eyes were kind. "You need to look over your Book of Life, but you've been avoiding it, my dear. Perhaps you need help." He looked at her hopefully. "Would you like me to help you look at it?"

"Not really," Janet said quickly. "I mean, I'm obliged to you, but maybe another time—" She stopped. Walter looked so disappointed she couldn't go on. "Oh, if you really think . . ."

"I do."

Janet had no sooner given an acquiescent sigh than the living room of a small house appeared before her. It was filled with familiar chintz-covered chairs and a long sofa that was too big for the little room. It was her house. And there she was, a younger Janet, curled up on the sofa, a telephone cradled at her neck as she filed her nails.

"I'm sorry, but I'm not going to sit by and not say anything," Janet heard her younger self say. "There they were, the two of them in the darkest corner of Schappio's, him with his arm around her and her crying and carrying on. And don't tell me he was just doing his job. There was a whole lot more than family counseling going on." Janet put down the nail file and moved to a more comfortable position as she listened to the person on the other end.

"Yes, it makes my blood boil too," she said after a few minutes. "Frankly, it would serve him right if someone told Fanny." She made a moue of distaste. "Me? Oh no, I couldn't tell her; Fanny is one of my best friends." For the first time a look of uneasiness crossed the young Janet's face. "Well you have to do what you think you should, but I'm not sure—" She twisted the phone cord around her finger. "No, no, we can't just ignore it. A note left on her desk? Well, that would be one way, I suppose," she said uncomfortably. "If you think so, but I wouldn't want anyone to think it came from me . . ."

The light in the little room faded. Janet bowed her head and covered her face with shaking hands. "No! Please, no more."

"What happened?" Walter asked gently.

Janet took her hands from her face but did not look up. "His wife Fanny left him," she said, her voice dull. "None of us knew she'd been depressed for months, that she would leap on this to prove her suspicions. She got up at a town meeting that was being held on water rights and out of the blue accused Peter of unprofessional conduct and outright philandering. Peter's clients left in droves." Janet lifted her head, her eyes haunted. "I've always been afraid that perhaps I was wrong. Perhaps what I saw had a simple explanation. Because I never saw Peter and the woman together after that."

"Is that the only reason you found this scene difficult to witness?"

"No." It was a whisper. "When I was watching I saw how pleased I was to be passing on such an exciting tidbit. I felt the spark of the glee I'd experienced when I told my friend. I felt the cowardice that kept me from objecting when she said she was going to put the note on Fanny's desk."

Walter nodded. "You did learn from that, but at a great cost to Fanny and Peter. Perhaps we should look at something else."

"Please no."

Walter merely waited, his fingertips resting on his knees.

"Must I?" Janet whimpered.

"I think you should, my dear," said Walter.

Unwillingly, Janet looked up to see a whirling kaleidoscope of pictures that slowed to show an older Janet sitting in that same living room, a book in her lap. ". . .if you forgive men their trespasses, your heavenly Father will also forgive you," the woman read. She closed the book and gazed at a point in mid-air, her eyes unfocused. "Marcia's review is tomorrow," she murmured. "I suppose I shouldn't bring up our quarrel to the committee; the fact that she doesn't like me has nothing to do with how she's doing her job." A rueful grimace curved her lips. "And she's doing it well, darn it."

The Janet sitting with Walter felt the woman's struggle, her reluctant acquiescence to the passage she'd just read, her twinge of regret at the thought of giving up the anticipated disclosure of Marcia's intemperate remarks. She wondered if Walter felt the swirling emotions too.

Walter was watching her. "Did you speak of the quarrel at the review?" he said.

Janet shook her head. "I wanted to, though."

"But you didn't. You paid attention; you learned."

"So one time I got it right," Janet said glumly.

Walter chuckled. "Ready to go on, my dear?"

"There's more?" Janet said, appalled.

"You don't have to do this all at once, but you've made a good start. How about revisiting another memory with me? Just one more and I think you'll find you're able to do it on your own."

Janet locked her hands together so tightly the laced fingers showed white. She sat silent a long moment, her head bowed. "Okay," she said, the word not more than an exhaled breath. "Let's go."

Dan pulled off his loafers and put on an athletic shoe, resting his foot on his knee to lace it up. His head snapped up at the feathery knock on the door. "Yeah?" he called out. "Who's there?"

"Kate," came the reply as his aunt let herself into the cabin.

Dan swore under his breath.

"I hope you don't mind, but I thought I'd drop by—see if we could talk."

"Gee, I'm sorry, Aunt Kate," he said, putting on the other shoe, "but I was about to go out."

Kate simply looked at him.

"For a walk. With Birgit."

Kate's carefully neutral look relaxed. "Really? With Birgit?"

"Yeah, she's checking out some place she's heard about and wanted company."

"And you volunteered to go along. How nice."

"That's me, all heart."

Uninvited, Kate sat down on the couch beside him. "Dan, we really have to talk. I've been hearing some things about your little adventure, and it scares me." She saw the look on his face and said hastily, "Sorry, I didn't mean to come across like a disapproving chaperone. It's just that I think Pegeen may be really dangerous."

"Trust me, Aunt Kate, the farther away Pegeen stays the happier I'll be."

"I'm glad to hear it. But if you feel that way about her, why don't you tell her?"

Dan got to his feet and paced about the room. "I don't know why you think you have the right to ask me that, but, okay, to tell you the truth it was a blast while it lasted. What I learned about Pegeen when we were together, well, let's just say I don't want to cross her. And you can relax; I'm not about to go trekking out to the Trackless Parts anytime soon, but frankly it didn't seem all that bad." He glanced over at her. "At least nobody's checking up on you all the time."

Brat. Had she said that aloud? No, fortunately she hadn't. "You do realize your time here is supposed to be for the purpose of discovering who you really are? You're supposed to be doing some thinking here at the Academy, Dan, some digging into why you did the things you did." She tried to keep the exasperation from her voice. "You seem to need some help with that, but you haven't allowed anyone to get near enough to do it." In spite of herself, her tone sharpened. "And now you're talking about the Trackless Parts as though in spite of everything, you rather liked the place."

"Oh, come on, Aunt Kate," Dan protested. "Give me a break. I only said it wasn't as bad as everyone makes out."

She got up. "Look, if you don't want me to butt in, let me take you to someone else, someone who might help you sort things out." She saw the look on his face and said quickly, "Oh, not now. I know you're heading off to Birgit. But later?"

"I don't want to talk to anyone." The set of his mouth was mulish. "Don't you understand? I don't particularly want to leave here. But there's stuff, things I don't want to be reminded of. Let it alone, will you?" He flung this last at her as he strode out the door.

Birgit pulled aside a branch to disclose a path leading upward through dense undergrowth. "This must be it." She began climbing.

"How do you know?" Dan said, digging into the dirt trail with his thick walking stick.

"I don't, but it feels right to go this way." Birgit put Shoma down so the rabbit could scamper up the steep incline. "Are you feeling better?" she said, looking at him closely. "You looked so angry when you came back."

"Enough already, Birgit. I'm fine." He grabbed a vine and pulled himself along the slanting trail.

Birgit accepted this without comment. "Hannah said I'd know when I was going in the right direction." She picked up the pace, placing one sure-footed step in front of the other, until she well ahead of Dan.

"I hope you're right about them welcoming guests," Dan panted, clambering after her. "Hey, have a heart," he called out a moment later. "Let's rest."

She stopped, drew her gauzy scarf over her head, and waited for him to catch up.

"I thought I was supposed to be the athlete," he said, dropping to a mound of soft pine needles. "How come you're not even winded and I'm dying here?"

"I am sorry," Birgit said at once. "It is only that I feel there is something wonderful ahead. I want to hurry."

"Yeah, right," he murmured. "Can't say that I feel much of anything but exhaustion."

"Come," she said, holding out a hand. "You'll see."

He took it and hoisted himself to his feet. "I can't believe you're rocketing up this eighty-degree track like some gazelle," he grumbled as she scampered ahead.

It was only moments later that Birgit gave a small cry and Dan looked up to see her hurrying to an opening in the forest foliage ahead.

"Hold on," Dan said, scrambling up the slope. "Wait for me!" He reached her just as Birgit stepped into a slanting grassy meadow sprinkled with small, brilliant blue flowers. Dan edged into the sunshine after her. On the crest of the hill ahead, outlined against the azure sky, he saw a village of small cottages and several impressive houses. The cottages and houses were all shades of the same warm, tawny stone, as were the paved streets between the houses. Geraniums and begonias spilled from window boxes, and riotous flower gardens, some small, some large, filled each front yard. Ivy and blooming clematis clung to the stone doorways and the wrought-iron gates that stood open before the village.

"Oh how lovely," Birgit breathed. "What should we do? Wait here or go in?"

"You're asking me?" Dan sidled closer to her.

Birgit took his hand, but before they got more than a few steps across the grassy meadow, a young man came out from between the open gates. "Good morning," he called to them. "You've come to see if Caritas is your home?"

"I have," Birgit said shyly. "And my friend here has come with me to keep me company."

The young man's expression changed subtly as he looked at Dan. "Perhaps your friend might find it more comfortable if he waited here while you visit us?" he suggested.

Before Birgit could say anything Dan shrugged and said, "Sure. Fine by me."

"You won't mind waiting?" Birgit asked him uncertainly.

Dan took a deep breath and then another quick one in an effort to fill his lungs. "Not at all. Go for it."

Birgit hesitated, but when Dan brusquely motioned her to leave she followed the young guard through the gates, her face alight and Shoma hopping beside her.

By the time Birgit had stepped inside the gates she'd forgotten Dan, forgotten everything but the beauty of the gardens she and her guide passed and the fragrance of the flowers that was overlaid by the faint but pervasive scent of lavender. At the end of the street they entered a square where, among young trees and newly mown grass, grape arbors shaded groupings of glass-topped, wrought-iron tables and comfortable cushioned chairs.

"Where I live now they have something they call picnics," Birgit said. "Do you use these tables for picnics?"

"We don't call them that, but we often eat our midday meal here," her companion said. He smiled at her. "I see you like it here in Caritas."

"Oh yes," she said simply.

"Then perhaps you will be one of our community," he said, looking pleased at the thought.

"Do you think so?" Birgit's face glowed.

"I'm not the one to say. Partly it's how you feel about being here, but it's really up to the magistrate."

Birgit stopped so suddenly she nearly stepped on Shoma. "Magistrate?"

"Don't worry, you'll like her. She's very nice." He took Birgit's elbow to guide her to one of the larger buildings on the square. "That's her office over there."

The woman who rose from behind the carved desk came round it to greet Birgit with a shining smile. Her chestnut hair was caught up into a loose chignon that allowed curling wisps to escape and frame her smooth-planed face. Birgit felt a small dart of pleasure as she noticed that the woman's dress, flowing to her sandaled feet in soft aquamarine folds, was not unlike Birgit's sari. When she drew near Birgit was aware of the same lavender fragrance she'd noticed throughout the village, stronger in this enclosed space, but still light and lovely.

"So you've brought us a visitor, Peter," the woman said. "Two," she added, catching sight of Shoma. She looked into Birgit's face, her green eyes searching. "I see you seek your home, my dear," she said, "and I see it won't be long before you will be ready to join us."

Birgit took a quick breath. "This is my home?"

"No." The magistrate smiled at her. "I was using the word in the generic sense. I'll consult my husband, but I think Caritas is not right for you. I would not be surprised, however, to learn your home is not far from us."

"Oh." Birgit tried to swallow. But then she thought of her walk through the little village with Peter. She'd loved the quiet beauty of the village, its peacefulness and lovely gardens, but she hadn't imagined herself living here.

The magistrate went to her desk and, flicking on a small, metal console, spoke in low tones to the man who appeared on the screen.

"Who is her husband?" Birgit whispered to Peter.

"The co-magistrate," he whispered back. "He usually talks to the men who come to visit and she questions the women."

Her conversation finished, the magistrate turned to Birgit. "It's as I thought. Another community awaits your visit."

"You said you thought it might be nearby." Birgit fingered the folds of her sari. "Can you tell me where it is?"

"That is something you must discover for yourself," the woman said gently. "But since you're here, would you like to share our midday meal? Peter's wife Claudia continually surprises us with her menus; I know she'd love to have a visitor sample her cooking."

The young man beside her had a wife? "I, I think I must go back," Birgit said.

"She has a friend waiting for her outside the gate," Peter explained.

The magistrate looked at him in surprise, but reading his look, she simply nodded, gathered up her papers, and placed them in a leather folder. "Well then, there are things I must attend to, but if you'd like, Peter can show you the rest of our village before he takes you to the gate."

"I'd like that," Birgit said shyly.

The older woman came round her desk again and placed a light hand on Birgit's shoulder. "You have things to learn before you find your home," she said, "but know that the Lord is with you on your journey every step of the way."

Birgit did not know why tears sprung to her eyes; she only knew she wanted to throw her arms about this woman and weep. "Thank you for letting me visit," she managed to say.

She'd wiped her nose with the back of her hand before she realized Peter was holding out a handkerchief. Birgit accepted the linen square with a watery smile and wiped her face. "I do not know why I cry," she said sheepishly. "I never cry."

"When your heart is touched it is natural to do so," Peter said simply. "There is no shame in it."

By the time Birgit had seen the rest of the village, people were beginning to come out of the little cottages and stood conversing in small groups. "Where was everyone when I first came?" she asked Peter.

"Working," he explained. "We all work in the mornings. Most finish by noon and have the afternoon to do whatever they wish—hobbies, sports." He glanced at Shoma and grinned. "Walking their pets."

They came to the gate, where Birgit thanked her guide and

said a hurried goodbye as she scanned the meadow for Dan. "I don't see—"

"Over there," Peter said, pointing to the far end of the sloping meadow. "And now I must return to the village."

Birgit wasn't listening. She ran to Dan, who was slumped on the grass, rocking back and forth as he held his hands to his chest. "What is it?" she cried. "What is wrong?"

"What does it look like?" he gasped. "I'm having a heart attack."

"Oh no!" She knelt beside him. "When did it happen?"

"After you left. Chest pains. Not bad at first, then worse."

"I'll get help." Birgit looked back at the entrance to the village where Peter had been standing moments before. He was no longer there. The gates were shut.

"Hey, it's better." Dan sat up straight, a surprised look on his face. He moved his shoulders, stretched his legs and pulled his arms back. "The pain. It's gone." His face darkened. "I could have gone into full cardiac arrest while you and your rabbit were up there having your tour or whatever it was you were doing."

Birgit pressed her palms together. "I was asked to stay for a meal but I refused because I did not want to leave you alone," she offered softly.

"I'm supposed to be grateful because you didn't forget about me completely?" Dan took an exploratory breath, then a deep one that filled his lungs. "Much better." He smiled at her. "Hey, don't look like that. Seems like I'm good as new."

"It was wrong of me to bring you," Birgit said unhappily. "I did not know you would be hurt."

"What's that supposed to mean?" he said, his voice sharp. "I can't manage the same rarified atmospheres as you?"

"No, no, I did not mean that."

Dan got to his feet. "I just charged up here way too fast; must have got my heart rate out of kilter. At least the way back has to be easier. Look, I've got stuff to do. I'll go ahead and you can take your time coming back." He headed for the trees. "See you later," he said, and loped to the opening in the foliage.

Birgit looked after him. After a long moment she followed. Head down, she trudged to where the trail snaked down the mountain. She should have been more considerate. Perhaps he hadn't wanted her to see him make his way down the mountain. Just because she'd had no problem climbing or descending the path didn't mean others wouldn't.

Had Dan's heart hurt because she'd left him alone? But it had stopped hurting when she'd come back to him. Birgit brightened at the thought and caught a vine to ease her way down the dirt trail. But he'd been very angry with her. Would he still be angry when he got back to the Academy? Did this mean he wouldn't seek her out, wouldn't tease her anymore?

Birgit told herself she didn't care.

15

Kate gathered her books from the bench beneath the arbor and turned away from the view of the orchards below. It hadn't worked. Trying to help Dan had failed miserably. She'd probably come across as an old lady school teacher. What could she have done differently? After a lifetime of teaching young adults, was she now that out of touch with them?

I tried to be patient. Please help me learn to meet Dan's needs. Help me be the mother Ann would be if she could. But Ann hadn't been able to help her son during the last year of his life. Maybe she hadn't been able to help him for longer than that. Howard would know. He must have been in contact with his sister in the time since Dan's coming here. But was Howard in any condition to get in touch with Ann now?

Kate dropped her head to her clenched fists until faint sounds made her look up. The air around her shimmered, the morning light lessened, and Kate saw a man sitting on the floor, propped by pillows piled around him. *Howard!* The sounds she heard came from the television he was watching. Where were his canes? How would he be able to get up from the floor by himself? And Howard never watched TV. Ever. Kate teased him about it, calling it an affectation, like the reverse snobbery of his refusing to answer to "Doctor" Douglas because he claimed he wasn't a pill pusher. But here he sat, watching a large pink bear dance across the screen and sing a song about washing your hands before every meal.

Kate crossed her arms tight about her chest. Obviously, the canes were no longer an option. The disease had progressed to the extent that they didn't matter. Without volition she took a step closer to the man on the floor. What was left of his thin hair was now snow white. The lean planes of his face had filled out and an unhealthy puffiness ballooned his cheeks. But it wasn't so much Howard's physical decay that caused Kate to suck in her breath; it was his slack mouth, the vacuous expression in his eyes.

Two men in blue smocks, one tall, the other pudgy, appeared through the door behind Howard. They were joking about something and did not halt their conversation as they leaned over, gripped Howard beneath his arms, and hauled him upright. Howard yelped in pain and the tall attendant interrupted his story to say, "Sorry fella, didn't mean to hurt you," before he jerked open a wheelchair. While the pudgy attendant held Howard, the tall one slid the wheelchair underneath Howard's sagging body. Howard's arms and legs retracted against the sudden movement. His head flailed back and forth and he uttered a series of mewling cries.

"Relax, Howard," the tall one said as he tied the tapes attached to Howard's webbed vest to the back of the chair. "Yellin' at us won't do no good. You keep this up, you gonna hurt yourself."

A chill settled in Kate's chest; tears filled her eyes. She knew Howard. It wasn't that he was hurt or feared being hurt, he was furious. Her beloved scholar had come to this, forced into a wheelchair, a contraption he'd always refused to consider, not even able to protest or articulate his rage. Kate blinked, willing her tears not to fall. "Howard, I'm here. My love, I'm here."

Howard's hands stopped plucking at the tapes that bound him and for an instant there seemed a look of inquiry in his eyes. The look faded, but the fear and anger did too. He gazed about distractedly, moving his head from side to side as though searching for something. Her hand? Her presence?

"There, there, my love," Kate crooned. She held out her hands, palms upturned and felt a current flow from her fingers. A bright shaft of something luminous bridged the gap between Kate and the man in the wheelchair and Howard sighed like a tired child. He leaned his head back and closed his eyes. "There, there," Kate whispered again.

"Now what do you s'pose that's all about?" the lanky attendant said to his companion. "Not like this one to calm down so quick. Thought we were going to have one of his tantrums."

"Don't know, don't care, as long as he's quiet," said the pudgy one. "Come on, we got seven more to get to the dining room." He kicked aside the pillows and wheeled the chair to the door.

Kate gazed at the bougainvillea-covered garden trellis that gradually came into focus before her. "Thank you," she whispered. "Thank you for letting me comfort him," she stopped herself and finished, "Thank you for using me to comfort him."

It would be all right. Howard's unhappiness would end. They would be together. *Concentrate on those thoughts. Don't think of Howard propped against pillows on the floor. Watching a children's program. Alone.* No. He was not alone—never alone. God was with him even now. Perhaps especially now. *Stay with that thought. Stay with the thought that Howard would come here, would be whole and well again.* The tears that she'd refused to shed when she'd been with Howard suddenly released and streamed down her face. Her tongue flicked at the salty, fluid warmth that gathered at the corners of her mouth and slowly a measure of solace eased her pain.

Kate felt a nudging pressure against her knee and looked down to see Buster. Her hand went to the great, flat head and stroked it. She knelt down and pressed her face against the dog's rough coat. "It hurts, Buster. Even though I realize it's his eternal welfare that's important, not what's happening at the moment." She gave a shaky laugh. "I know the words, but I guess I haven't quite gotten the music. But I'm learning."

Buster's brown eyes regarded her, unblinking.

Kate thought of Howard's expression as he watched the dancing bear. His bemused half-smile. "And I guess he's not unhappy all the time," she said to the dog. "His angels were with him when he was watching the TV, weren't they? They're with him now."

Kate smoothed her cheeks with her palms, wiped her hands on her slacks and got to her feet. "But oh, how he hates to be helpless," she sighed.

We're all helpless, whether we admit it or not. Perhaps Howard's present vulnerability might make it easier for him to realize that fact when he arrives here. Perhaps his helplessness and vulnerability make it easier for his angels to be near him. She didn't know where these thoughts came from. Perhaps something she'd heard in class? But there it was, as clear in her head as if the words had been spoken.

She fished a handkerchief from her pocket and wiped her nose. "Think you can stick around this time if we go for a walk, fella?"

They followed the winding pathway down to the orchard valley, Buster wandering off from time to time to investigate enticing scents among the flowering orange, apple, and peach trees. Kate didn't notice the girl beneath the peach tree until she was almost upon her. The girl knelt, a statue staring trance-like into the distance, her lovely aqua sari falling in folds about her slim form. Kate looked more closely. *Birgit?* It couldn't be. It was. Kate halted, wondering whether to interrupt the girl's absorption or pass by unnoticed. Birgit's dark eyes flickered. She looked in Kate's direction and sank back to sit on the grass. "Oh, hello," she said.

"I didn't mean to disturb you." Kate couldn't help feeling large and intrusive as she approached the kneeling girl.

Birgit calmly regarded Kate and the dog that gamboled behind her, neither indicating that Kate and Buster had disturbed her nor inviting them to stay. Buster padded up to the brown rabbit crouched at Birgit's side and lowered his great head to touch his huge wet nose to its small pink one.

"Would you like us to leave?" Kate said gently.

"I don't know." Birgit cradled her rabbit's head in one hand and patted Buster with the other. "I think perhaps I would like to talk to someone about a thing I have been wondering, but I have never done that. All my life I trust myself to see what I must do, not others." She sat back on her heels. "It is difficult."

Kate squatted on the grass beside the girl. "Why don't you try? I've had some experience with listening to young people's problems. Could be I happened along for a reason, you know."

Birgit looked at her uncomprehendingly. "I don't have a problem. I just don't know what to do."

"Try me," Kate said again.

"I visited heaven this morning," Birgit said, "—a heaven," she amended. "Not the one where I will live, but it is a lovely place." Her face lit at the remembrance.

"That's right, my nephew told me he was going for a walk with you. I didn't know it was to heaven."

"I didn't know he was your nephew," Birgit said. "Yes, he went with me, but he didn't go into the heaven," she continued. "I think maybe he couldn't. He had very bad pains—in his chest."

Kate's eyes widened. "Dan had chest pains?"

Birgit nodded. Once again her eyes focused on something in the distance. "He was very angry when I returned from my visit. He was still angry when he left me." Her gaze returned to Kate. "But when I came back and was with him his chest did not hurt anymore. That must mean that I can help him, don't you think? It must mean that he needs me?"

"Do you want him to need you?" Kate said cautiously.

"Oh yes."

Oh, dear. Who was she to be offering advice to the lovelorn? And what was Dan thinking? Birgit was delightful, but quite simple really, an uneducated country girl. *Still, better Birgit than that Pegeen.* Kate looked at the girl before her and took a breath. "Have you prayed about it?" She felt a blush heat her cheeks as she spoke the words. Who was Kate Douglas to ask people whether they prayed?

But Birgit did not seem to take it amiss. "I had not thought of that; sometimes I forget. Hannah says I am praying even when I am not saying any words, that I pray with my life." She twisted the sheer scarf in her fingers. "But she says I must also learn to go to God each day with my thoughts."

"Sounds like a plan," said Kate. "How about trying it out when I leave?"

Birgit nodded unenthusiastically.

"Well then, I think Buster and I should be on our way." Kate got up. "And they always tell me not to forget the listening part. I'm sure Hannah told you about that."

"Yes," Birgit said in a small voice.

Kate stood looking at Birgit's bowed head, at the black cap of thick, straight hair that had grown to a lustrous sweep that fell to her shoulders. No wonder Dan was enamored. "If you'd like someone to visit and don't have anything better to do, perhaps sometime you could come to my rooms and have a cup of tea with me?" she said gently.

The girl looked up. "Oh yes, I would like that." She smiled at Kate. It was a smile of pure joy.

Kate felt a stab of shame. "Anytime." She whistled Buster to her and strode up the path. The shame did not leave her. Kate touched her flushed cheeks. Birgit, about whom she'd just been having such patronizing thoughts and spoken flippantly of her "having anything better to do," had been invited to visit heaven. Birgit, whom she'd been lecturing about prayer, lived a life that, according to Hannah, was prayer. The "simple, uneducated country girl" was surely what they called a good spirit—all but an angel. And who was Kate Douglas? Someone who, despite her erudition, only now was learning how to pray, someone who, if she'd accompanied Birgit on her recent visit, would probably be outside with Dan having chest pains.

The chuckle that rose in Kate's throat at the thought escaped in a guffaw. "Oh my," she gasped. She grasped Buster's heavy coat and let him help pull her up the steep path. "Buster, your mistress may be educated, but sometimes she's a purely egocentric fool." He stopped and looked back at her. Kate smacked his large rump. "Get going, you big old thing, and stop looking at me as though you agree."

At the top of the hill Kate cast a quick glance at the iron bench beneath the arbor where not long ago she'd been with Howard. She took a deep breath. *Thank you,* she said silently. *Thank you for letting me be with Howard, thank you for guiding me to Birgit. Help me to be more understanding with Dan, and please, please help me to do your will.*

"Let me tell you, it wasn't easy getting out of that place without alerting anyone." Pegeen stopped at the sight before them, causing Zaroth to halt, too. "I thought you said this was a village."

Zaroth smiled. "What do you see?"

"Same thing you see—a city," Pegeen said promptly. "Well, maybe a town, but it certainly isn't just a village. The lakefront is lovely; it could be a miniature Toronto or Lake Shore Drive in Chicago."

"I knew you were a singular woman; some misguided people see something quite different. Remind me to talk to you about coming here to teach. I can tell you there's been an interest from several quarters in hearing you lecture."

"Really?"

Pegeen flushed with pleasure, but before she could pursue the subject Zaroth tucked her hand in his foreclaw. "Come, I've ordered tea for us at a little place near here."

Pegeen raised an eyebrow at the antiquated idea of tea, but allowed her companion to lead her down a side street whose timbered buildings overhung a scattering of outdoor cafés. The one to which Zaroth guided her had only a few tables set out on the cobblestones, but the tablecloths were linen and the waiter who bowed them to their table was attired in scarlet and black doublet and hose.

"You've got some sort of medieval festival going here?" Pegeen settled herself in the wicker wingback chair and smoothed a white linen napkin in her lap.

"We have all sorts of festivals here," Zaroth said easily. He handed her a plate of open-faced sandwiches. "Try one of these; I think you'll find them excellent."

Pegeen ate the little round hors d'oeuvre in two dainty bites. "Delicious," she said, taking another. "I'm going to have to watch it or my waistline will be a thing of the past."

"The more of you to enjoy," Zaroth said.

"What bull." Pegeen helped herself to two more. "But go ahead, I'm beginning to enjoy it." She touched the napkin to her lips. "Anchovy paste, my favorite." She took a sip of the tea Zaroth had poured into her gold-leaf-decorated teacup and looked up, startled. "Single malt scotch! In a teacup? What is this, Prohibition?"

"I like to have it served like this sometimes, just for old times' sake."

"Hey, it's all right with me. Personally, I've never gone for the tea and crumpets routine." Pegeen took another sip and set her cup on the saucer. "Now let's get down to business. There's a reason I came here instead of phoning, Zaroth. I hate to admit it, but I'm afraid I may have screwed up." She gave a defensive little laugh and flicked her hair over her shoulder.

Zaroth lifted an eyebrow, or the retracting scales where an eyebrow would have been, but waited without comment.

"Getting him to come here with a group should have been a snap, but it's going to be trickier than I thought. For one thing, I'm pretty sure they think I'm up to something because they're watching me like hawks, and for another, the kid is reacting to me as though I have some disease. I tried the come-hither routine, but found myself wanting to smack his silly face." Pegeen collected herself and took another dainty bite of sandwich. "Since I couldn't very well do that with everyone around, I'm afraid I got my jollies by making him quiver in his boots. He practically hid beneath the table. So as I said, I have a feeling there's not much chance of coaxing him to come away."

Zaroth did not look pleased. "You're sure you can't give it another go? See if you can't, ah, revitalize his interest and convince him to visit the Parts?"

"I'll try, but if there's another way you could work it, maybe you'd better consider it." She smiled, relieved to have the confession off her chest.

That it was an effort to return her smile was evident, but Zaroth waved a negligent, multiple-jointed finger in the air. "Too true. There will be other times, other ways." Zaroth put his claw over her hand and pressed it gently. "But we've had enough of business for a while. Let's enjoy this little get-together," he said. "Why not take our time and—" his voice deepened, "—get to know each other."

Pegeen's breath quickened. "What do you mean?"

"Just what you think."

Pegeen removed her hand from beneath his, took a sip from her cup, and carefully patted her mouth with her napkin. "Slow down there, friend," she said when she looked up. I don't mind taking the fast track, but only if I'm the one in charge and giving the signals."

Zaroth shook his leathery-spiked head. "That's going to be difficult, my dear. You see, around here I'm the one in charge."

Pegeen felt a small shiver at his tone, a pleasurable shiver, but a shiver nonetheless. She looked about for something to comment on, and for the first time took note of the surrounding streets. "Why is everything so empty?" she said. "There's hardly anyone around."

Zaroth's yellow eyes glinted, but he made no mention of the rapid change of subject. "I gave orders before you came that no one is to bother us until and unless I wish to introduce you to the citizens here."

Pegeen had been reaching for the teapot but her hand stilled at the calmly spoken statement. "I heard that there were people I should talk to if I wanted to teach here," she said, "people with power, and I know you're one of them. But exactly where do you stand in the hierarchy of this place? Just who are you?"

"Let's say I'm a fairly important person. There was another who shared the honors in this little town of ours, but lately I seem to have it all to myself." Zaroth smoothed the scales back from his high forehead. "And I must say I like it that way." He lowered his voice. "I have plans, you see, plans you, my dear, may well become a part of, an important part. I know you're interested in teaching here, and I think I may say you won't be disappointed if you come here, for part of my plans, and only a small part, is my intention to have our university become a worldwide seat of learning."

Pegeen's breath caught. "You're making me an offer to teach?"

"I don't usually bother myself with such minutia, but I

made the staff aware of your presence at the Academy and of course they, ah, value my opinion." He took a sip from his cup. "Evidently your reputation has preceded you; the consortium is all atwitter. They were quite impressed by the breadth of your research and the conclusions you drew from it. One of them gave me a couple of your more recent articles." His eye slits narrowed. "Let's see if I remember. Ah yes, you felt the perceived need for a child to be raised in the traditional family has been greatly overrated. As long as the child has a responsible caretaker there is really no particular need for a father or even a mother to be part of his or her social construct." He cocked his head. "Do I have it right? The paper was a trifle emotionally overcharged and in my opinion, if not the consortium's, it is lacking enough concrete evidence to back up your theories. But withal, the article makes a valuable contribution and of course I agree with its basic thrust."

Pegeen's eyes flashed, but she calmly refilled her cup. "I can assure you that these 'theories,' as you call them, are the result of carefully researched studies. Perhaps I made my points more forcefully than needed, but I'm not ashamed to say I feel deeply about the matter. Anyway, I think if you'd taken time to read the body of my work rather than an isolated piece, you might have a better idea of what I'm getting at."

"I love it when you're angry," Zaroth purred, "just love it." He leaned across the table and looked into her eyes. "Enough of this silly sparring. I didn't bring you here to argue. I chose this particular café because it is also an inn. Upstairs rooms. Discreet staff." His narrow red tongue flicked out, then disappeared between thin lips. "Would you consider moving our tête-à-tête indoors?"

Pegeen's pulse quickened. Her breathing came fast and shallow, and she found it hard to swallow. When she replaced the teacup her hand shook so that the cup danced against the saucer. Hadn't she told him that she was the one who called the shots? Pegeen cleared her throat to remind him of this, but found she had difficulty speaking.

Zaroth's smile widened; he sat patiently waiting.

Pegeen took a quick breath and nodded. Zaroth gave her an answering nod and, tossing his napkin aside, rose from the table. He did not look back to see whether Pegeen followed him inside.

But of course she did.

16

Frank bounded up the stairwell into the hall and let himself into the sunlit classroom. He glanced around the empty room. He'd half-hoped to find Percy slouched in one of the chairs set in a semicircle around the raised dais. The Novitiate meeting must have taken place by now, and he couldn't help wondering if Percy had met his future wife. But more important, now that Percy had made Kate aware of Dan's situation, had she been able to get the kid to let someone help him?

But Percy wasn't here. So if it wasn't to meet Percy, why had he experienced the distinct sense that he should come here? It hadn't been a voice or a summons, just a gut feeling he should head over. And by now Frank had learned enough to obey gut feelings. He slid into one of the blond wooden seats and waited, idly picking up a pencil and tapping a drum roll on the desktop.

"Frank! What are you doing here?"

The pencil jumped from Frank's fingers and rolled across the tiled floor.

"Kate!" Frank stood up. The dog beside Kate padded over and leaned against his knee so that Frank could rub his ears. "And this is Buster, isn't it?"

"Buster, you hardly know the man; have you no sense of loyalty?" She looked at Frank. "Where have you been, Frank? I haven't seen you in ages."

Frank stooped to pick up the pencil. "Around," he said. "I

guess you're here because of Dan? Percy said he was going to talk to you."

"He did. And I talked to Dan, but I don't think I made any headway at all. He stomped off to go on a walk with Birgit. I had hopes she'd be what he needed to come around, but apparently he ended up picking a fight with her too. Can you imagine anyone arguing with Birgit?" Kate sat down in the chair next to the one he'd vacated. "No, I had no particular reason to come here—I just felt, somehow, I should." She smiled at him. "I've missed you, Frank," she said. "What have you been doing?"

"Been checking out the Trackless Parts some." Frank gingerly reclaimed his seat.

"Oh? I know the place seem to hold a certain fascination for Dan, but I'm surprised you would go there."

"Not all of the Parts are like the places your nephew explored," Frank said. "I've been allowed to leave the campus at will to—well, to think things out. I take my Wanderer's pass just in case."

"You still have your pass? I have no idea where mine is or even if I still have it."

"That's because you don't need it." Frank made a visible effort to relax his stiffly held shoulders. "So. Why do you think we're here?"

"Of course there's some reason." Kate looked around. "Any idea what it is?"

Frank wasn't going to go there. "What have you been learning while I've been away?"

"What haven't we been learning? I think I could take a pop quiz on Heaven 101." Kate sobered. "Of course what really keeps me glued to my seat and paying attention is I know it's a chance to prepare myself for when Howard comes. There's so much I want to learn so that I can share it . . ." She turned and looked away.

"What happened?" Frank rasped the question.

"Howard is ill," she said, her voice hollow. "Alzheimer's or something like it. I know I shouldn't let it distress me, and really, most of the time I realize his angels are especially near him now. I know he'll be fine when he comes here." Kate turned back and managed a smile, but it wavered.

"Of course it hurts," Frank said, his voice still rough. "You love him."

Kate's eyes held the suspicion of tears. "You understand."

Frank reached toward her, then stopped. "You know God is looking out for Howard's eternal life, not just the few years he spends on earth. I guess that's what you have to hold onto right now."

Kate nodded. When she trusted herself to speak, she murmured, "Thanks, Frank. I do know, but it helps to hear someone else say it."

They were silent; then Kate glanced over at the big man. "By the way, I see you've gotten to know my friend Janet."

"She's a friend of yours?" Frank said, surprised.

"I've gotten to know her. She . . . she's a nice woman."

"Well, yes." Frank hesitated. "But not all the people she hangs around with are, ah, particularly agreeable. Last time I saw her she was with Dan's, quote unquote, friend Pegeen."

"Where was this?"

"The dining hall. She and Pegeen were having lunch together."

"That means they're friends? Who's to say the woman didn't just plunk herself down beside Janet?"

Frank considered this. "Guess she could have."

"I'd say you shouldn't jump to conclusions," Kate said. "Janet told me you'd helped her, Frank." She crossed her arms against her chest. "Your taking the time to listen to her, to talk with her, made a real difference."

Buster had left Frank and returned to Kate. She patted the

dog's head absently and then took a quick breath. "You know, I think I may have an inkling why we're here. Remember back when we were Wanderers, Frank, and I very clumsily tried to clear up a misunderstanding between us?"

Frank's newfound composure evaporated. "Damn it, Kate!"

"No, let me finish. I meant every word when I told you how much I love Howard and that all I want is to be with him." A tic contracted Kate's lean cheek. "But I was flattered by your attention. And after we came to the Academy and I saw that you were still—interested—I was, stupidly, flattered. It felt good to have someone think I was special."

"Kate, stop!" Frank's hands balled into fists. "It wasn't your fault. When you first told me about Howard that should have taken care of it. But I just couldn't, I can't seem to—"

"You'd have had an easier time of it if I'd been honest and faced my silly gratification at your interest. It was wrong of me, terribly wrong."

Frank's mouth curved in a slight smile. "Listen to you," he said. "You might think you'd broken all Ten Commandments, some of them twice."

"Don't talk me out of it, Frank. I need to say this."

"Okay, you've said it. What about me? I've been stumbling around for the last forever like a heartsick teenager in need of a swift kick." Frank smiled. "You think maybe the Lord got us here to give us a chance to laugh at ourselves?"

"Laugh?" Kate said. She didn't look entirely pleased.

"I think so. I think maybe laughter is what's needed here. Maybe we shouldn't be taking ourselves so seriously. And, y'know, it's working." Frank held out his hands to her. "See that? Steady. No shaking. No perspiring."

Kate raised an eyebrow. "Congratulations are in order? Just like that?"

"I think it's gone," he told her simply. "I think maybe I'm over it." He gave Kate a rueful grin. "Over you."

"Great." Kate gave him an unwilling smile. "I think."

"I'm not about to try to prove I can handle things on my own," Frank continued. "I know this is a gift. It's one I've prayed for, that I could be around you and not feel like, like Buster here eyeing a bone."

"I guess we have to say thanks for small blessings." The asperity in Kate's voice did not hide her own amusement.

"You want to hear about blessings?" Frank said. "Back there when you were talking about how much you wanted to prepare for Howard coming here, I felt your joy at the thought of being with him." Frank stretched out his hands again, fingers splayed as he struggled to explain. "I know I'm not saying it right, but I felt your happiness like it was my own."

She nodded slowly. "We've been learning about that— feeling another person's joy as one's own."

"Whatever. But it wasn't only that. When you told me about Howard's illness, I felt a tremendous pain; it was like a wave emanating from you." He thought. "Maybe that was the first step in this little recovery program of mine. Feeling your hurt." Frank thrust his hands in his jeans front pockets, thumbs spread across his flat stomach. "I only hope someday I'll be able to have what's been given you and Howard."

Compassion put a catch in Kate's voice. "You will, Frank," she said. "You will." She held out a hand.

"Thanks." Frank took the hand, then released it with a wry smile. "I really am fine, but let's not push it, okay?" he said.

Awareness replaced Kate's look of incomprehension. "Gotcha," she said. She got up. When she reached the door, she turned with a smile. "Thanks for being such a good friend, Frank."

He nodded. "Where you headed?"

"I think I'll check on how that nephew of mine is doing. If he's still feeling sorry for himself and Pegeen is on the prowl, he may need a little help."

Pegeen tossed her head and ran her fingers through her heavy chestnut locks. "So this is where you work?" she said. Her gaze swept over the book-lined walls and the opulent oriental carpet on the polished floor and came to rest on the massive walnut desk through which Zaroth was rummaging with increasing impatience.

"Only when I can find where the incompetent idiot who runs this office puts my files." He slammed the top drawer shut.

Pegeen did not envy whoever ran the office.

Zaroth recollected himself and flashed her a sharp-toothed smile. "A moment more, my love, and if I can't find what I'm looking for, I'll save it for another day and walk you partway back to that campus of yours and its constipated constituents." He tugged open the lower drawer and looked up, annoyed, as a timid tap sounded on the office door.

"Come!" Zaroth snapped.

The door inched open and the stick-thin woman whose desk guarded Zaroth's office peered in. "Someone to see you," she quavered. "He says he knew you—before."

"Didn't I tell you I'm not to be disturbed?" Zaroth snarled.

But a rotund little man had already pushed past the woman and rushed to grasp Zaroth's hand. "John! It is you! I can't believe it. They told me you were here; said I could see you if I wanted to. If I wanted! Can you imagine my not wanting to see you!" For a moment it looked as though he might kiss the hand he clutched, but Zaroth snatched it away.

"Who are you?"

"Don't you know me, John?" the little man asked, dismayed.

Zaroth's yellow eyes narrowed; he sniffed the air about his guest. "Peter?" he said at last. "Peter Cadmium?"

"Your most devoted follower." Cadmium beamed his pleasure at Zaroth. "I can't tell you how excited I am to finally be here. I've prayed you'd somehow know that I spent my life spreading your message—though of course I couldn't do it nearly as well as you." He clasped his hands together. "Oh John, everything has been simply marvelous since I've come here. I woke up feeling wonderful and with the nicest people around me. I've been traveling quite a bit since, stayed in several places, some more appealing than others, to be sure, but all very interesting. I was certain one or two must be heaven, but it seems not." Cadmium paused, as though at some less than pleasurable memory, but regained his sunny jocularity. "For some reason I hadn't recollected that of course you'd be here too, but when I did, I simply thought about how I wanted so much to see you and," he paused as though for a drum roll, "here I am." He spread his arms wide and took a step toward Zaroth, who quickly retreated behind his desk.

Pegeen, who had been watching the scene wide-eyed, gave a discreet cough.

"Ah, yes, Pegeen," Zaroth said hastily. His greenish scales showed a blush of puce. "Where are my manners? Pegeen, I would like to introduce the Reverend Peter Cadmium. Peter is—was—my assistant, my right-hand man. Peter, Pegeen is a brilliant academician who, if she accepts our invitation, will soon be one of our instructors here."

Pegeen's jaw dropped. "Reverend Cadmium—your assistant?" She stared at Zaroth. "Do you mean to tell me you're a preacher?"

"A minister of God, ma'am," Peter Cadmium said reprovingly. "John is a religious leader whose name still echoes in the halls of religious learning and philosophical thought, one whose accomplishments are regarded with awe by the worldwide religious community."

"Enough, Peter," Zaroth said modestly. "We don't need to talk of that."

"A minister?" Pegeen said, still stunned.

"Yes indeed," Cadmium assured her. "A great one whom I had the privilege to assist for only a few years, alas, a few short years at the beginning of my career." He turned to Zaroth, a dampness about his eyes. "I remember—how could I ever forget—the day a ruptured appendix took you from us so suddenly. You in your prime, I, a young acolyte. Like every one of your followers, I was devastated."

"It wasn't the highlight of my life either." Zaroth examined a long fingernail and tapped it on the desk's polished wood. "Tell me, Peter, what happened to my belongings? The things at headquarters, in my home?"

Cadmium frowned. "That was strange. Of course, it was my job as your assistant to clear things up, but by the time I got to your office, someone had ransacked your files. Apparently they went through your office at home, too. No one ever found out who took your things, or if, indeed, anything was missing."

"An unsolved mystery, eh?" Zaroth did not hide his relief.

A shadow crossed Cadmium's round face. "Well, there were rumors about what might have been taken, some quite nasty. But of course I didn't pay attention to such scurrilous gossip." He regarded Zaroth earnestly. "To my thinking, if a man has a few private peccadilloes that remain unnamed and unknown, so be it. He should be remembered for the good he gave the world. And you gave it much." Cadmium regained his momentum. "I never again heard sermons like yours, John, never again saw homilies affect people the way yours did. We should all be thankful for your brilliantly honed skills."

A throaty chuckle erupted from Pegeen. "Ah yes, those brilliantly honed skills. Tell me, um, John, did you hone the skills we've both enjoyed just recently, before or after you gave those marvelous sermons?"

Zaroth's lipless mouth curved. "Any of that type of thing was performed well away from the pulpit."

Cadmium's head swiveled from Pegeen to Zaroth. "I don't understand," he said.

"Miss Pegeen is just teasing," Zaroth said, his tone indulgent. "The young lady enjoys being naughty, very naughty indeed." He dipped his head in a small bow to the laughing Pegeen. "As Peter can testify, my conduct was nothing if not circumspect."

"And I bet there was a lot to be circumspect about," said Pegeen. She shook her head. "I still can't believe you were a clergyman." Her eyes widened. "Don't tell me you were one of those televangelists!"

Zaroth looked pained. "Can you imagine me bellowing into the camera asking for funds like one of those sweating, frenetic dolts?"

"No," Pegeen admitted, "not in my wildest dreams. But then my wildest dreams wouldn't have included you in a pulpit."

Zaroth smiled and resumed his search of the desk drawers. A moment later he gave an exultant cry and held up a sheaf of papers. "Well, finally!" He turned to Cadmium. "Now if you'll excuse me, Peter, as delightful as it has been to see you, I'm afraid you'll have to leave. As you can see, I'm extremely busy."

The little man's face crumpled. "Can't I stay? I don't want to put you out, of course, but I'd be quite happy to wait here until you've finished your business. I, I would like very much to stay here with you—if you'll have me."

Zaroth shook his head in a brisk refusal, but then paused to give Cadmium a considering look. "Why yes," he said at last. "If you'd like to stay, I think it might be arranged. As a matter of fact, it might be possible for you to become one of us." He indicated the papers in his hand. "I must take these to be processed, but I'll be back shortly. Meanwhile, why don't you and Pegeen keep each other company?" He directed a lipless smile at Pegeen. "I'm sure my good friend here would be happy to tell you about her theories. I guarantee you'll find them fascinating."

"I'm sure I will," Cadmium beamed. "And thank you, John," he said to Zaroth's departing back.

"A clergyman," Pegeen muttered, shaking her head again as she rounded the desk and settled herself in the leather swivel chair behind it. "So you knew Za—John," she said. "Do sit down and tell me about him." She nodded graciously to one of the damask wingback chairs in front of the desk.

Cadmium took a seat and, crossing one short leg over the other, beamed at her. "What can I say? That it was the greatest privilege of my life to have worked with John? That I admired him more than any man I've ever met?" Cadmium leaned forward. "You should have seen him, my dear, you should have heard his sermons. His preaching made wrongdoers tremble." The earnest little man's voice softened. "But he could be gentle, too. He was so kind to me, but then he was kind to everyone. That's why they all wanted to be around him, why everyone flocked to him. Especially women." He looked at Pegeen. "That's probably what gave rise to the rumors, don't you think?"

Pegeen's mouth quirked. "Possibly," she agreed.

"Ah well, that's all in the past." Cadmium's brow cleared. "I always said that John was the first person I wanted to meet when I got to this world. For some reason he wasn't, but at least I'm here now. If I understand correctly there's no 'past' or 'future' here, only now. And I feel so very, very fortunate that my 'now' is being here with John."

"So you're planning to take up where you left off? As his assistant?"

"Oh, yes. If he'll have me," he said earnestly.

"That's something I'd like to see," Pegeen said, her voice dry. "And if I accept this teaching position, maybe I will."

"Yes, you're an academic, aren't you?" Cadmium said. "And indeed, from what John said, one of some prominence."

"Some might agree with you," said Pegeen.

"And what is your field, my dear?"

"I've spent my life in gender studies as it relates to cultural mores. My research has been called cutting edge, and it's probably because of that that I've been at the center of so many controversies throughout my career. You've probably read about them."

"I'm sure I must have," said Cadmium. "Stupid of me, but I'm afraid I can't remember an academic with the unusual first name of Pegeen, and I don't believe John mentioned your last?" he said in gentle inquiry.

A startled look flashed across Pegeen's face. "Actually my name isn't Pegeen. That is, that's what it is now, but it wasn't then. And my surname, ah—" For a moment she seemed panicked, but quickly recovered. "What do names matter? The important thing is my work, my theories." Pegeen sat back and swung the chair around like a child on a merry-go-round and came to rest to face Cadmium. "While we're waiting for Za—your friend to return, Reverend Cadmium, sit back and I'll be happy to tell you all about them." The smile she gave him wasn't particularly nice.

17

Dan ducked under a low-hanging branch and patted the back pocket of his jeans. No, it wasn't there. Not that he'd done anything to make the damned pistol reappear. But there had been those chest pains. Hadn't done anything to deserve them, either. The remembered horror of the pain, of being unable to breathe, brought a spike of anger. What had that been all about? After all, Birgit had asked him to come with her. He'd slogged up that mountain out of simple kindheartedness and then sat and waited the whole time she went visiting. Dan swung the stick he was carrying at one of the tree's flowering branches, causing a shower of pink blossoms to drift toward the grass.

Wasn't there anything to do around here besides wander through gardens and orchards trying to stay out of the way of well-meaning advice-givers? It was better than hauling bricks, but it was getting boring not having anyone to hang out with except people who didn't have a clue how he felt. Or much care. Except for Birgit, of course. She was different, definitely not boring, and she did care. Shouldn't have gotten ticked and yelled at her. Shouldn't have left her to come back alone.

Dan slumped to the ground and sat with his back propped against the knobby tree trunk. He'd avoided Percy and Frank since that episode in the dining hall. Dan's jaw twitched at the thought of Pegeen's mocking jibes. She was probably still sniggering about how she'd made Dan look like a wimp. Percy and

Frank probably were, too. Who cared? Not Dan. Why should he? After all, no one cared about him, about how he felt. No one around here really cared, not anyone.

Dan jabbed the stick into the green grass carpet.

"Don't!"

Dan's head snapped up.

"You're hurting the grass." The boy standing in front of him pointed the gouge of black earth. "And look." The boy, a skinny little kid who looked about five or six, stretched an accusatory finger at the blossoms littering the ground. "You hit my tree, didn't you?"

"Your tree? You own it?" Dan said, amused.

"'Course not, the Lord does. But I take care of it, so it's sort of mine." The child stared at Dan, his blue eyes somber. "I don't like any of the trees to be hurt, but especially not this one."

"You wouldn't happen to be related to a person named Birgit, would you?"

"No." The child frowned at Dan.

"She feels the same way about her flowers." Dan sighed and patted the uprooted grass over the scarred earth. "Okay, is that better?"

"I guess." But the child's lower lip thrust out as he squatted and began raking a pile of pink blossoms together with his fingers.

"I haven't seen any kids your age around. You live near here?"

"He does, and then again, he doesn't." The pleasantly deep voice came from a man standing beside them.

Dan shielded his eyes against a sudden shaft of sunlight that surrounded the man who had spoken. Had he been there a moment ago? Dan got to his feet. The man's shorts and white T-shirt showed an athletic build, and the sweat on his face and the fact that his short, curly hair was plastered to his head indicated he'd been running. He seemed about Dan's age. Or maybe not. The eyes that met Dan's gaze looked as though they'd seen a lot more, lived more, than anyone Dan had ever known.

"I'm Joe," he said. "And this is Charlie, who should not be here." He stooped to ruffle the boy's hair. "Why did you wander off, Charlie?"

"He hit my tree." Charlie scowled at Dan. "And dug up the grass."

"A, that's not your tree. It's like your tree, but yours is in your garden just like always. And B, accusing someone else of something doesn't distract me in the least from the fact that you haven't answered my question." He put a finger beneath Charlie's chin and raised it. "Why did you wander off?"

The boy lowered his eyes, avoiding the man's smiling gaze. "Wanted to," he said.

"Not good enough. Lunch is on the table and Mama and the rest are waiting for you." He patted the boy's sharp shoulder blade. "Scoot."

Charlie turned away, but before his small figure had done more than fade a bit, he turned back again. "He did whack the tree and it does look like mine."

"Scoot!"

Charlie glowered but turned away again. This time he disappeared.

Dan looked at Charlie's—what? Father? Teacher? Mentor? "Didn't mean to upset the kid. Does he really think trees have feelings?"

"Just about everything around the children here seems alive to them," Joe said. "Just as it often seems to the littlest ones on earth."

"Looks like you've got a real rebel on your hands."

"Charlie? During the short time he lived on earth he suffered some pretty incredible abuse from every adult he ever knew. He's come here with a lot of baggage, and we try to let him go his own way. He has to discover things by himself and learn that he won't be punished for disagreeing with adults, even those he's learning to love." Joe studied Dan. "What was your childhood like?"

Dan looked away. "I guess my mom and Phil gave me what I wanted, mostly. They were pretty low key." He picked up the stick and swung it against his knee. "Of course, giving a kid what he wants isn't the be-all and end-all."

"No beatings, no starvation, neglect?"

"'Course not." Dan's tone betrayed his annoyance. "But I guess you probably knew that already."

"Yes, but I wanted to give you a chance to say it."

"Okay, I've said it. Everyone around here seems to think I'm stupid. I'm not. I know it sounds like I was a pampered subur-ban kid, but you don't know the pressures—at school, at home."

"Really?" Joe looked interested.

"Why didn't I return any of the applications stuffed in our mailbox? Why didn't I want to apply to any of the colleges? Why didn't I at least try to have an idea of what I wanted to do with my life? I had to take off to get away from it all. Even then, there were the phone calls." Dan's voice mimicked a falsetto whine, "'Son, you don't know what you're doing to your mother. You're breaking her heart.' Had to change my cell phone, get a new number." Dan reached for his stick. "Guess I shouldn't have done that," he admitted. He began to jab the stick into the earth, but halted before its tip hit the grass. "Oops." He gave a lopsided smile and looked up at Joe in apology, but Joe wasn't there. Two misty figures appeared beneath the tree where Joe had stood. Dan squinted, and they came into focus. One was crying; the other leaned over to comfort her. The crying woman was his mother; the broad back belonged to Phil.

"I can't help thinking that there was something I could

have done," his mother sobbed, "I can't help wondering if there was some way we failed him."

"Oh no!" Dan flung away the stick. "I'm not gonna go there; you can't make me, you hear?" The figures vanished as suddenly as they had appeared and Dan bolted through the orchard and up the path toward the Academy buildings. "Not gonna do the guilt thing," he muttered through gritted teeth. "The past is over; it's so over."

He took the long way to the far campus building, avoiding Birgit's rose garden, and by the time he reached the quadrangle, with its great trees shading groups of chatting students, he had recovered his equanimity. Until he saw a familiar face that challenged that newfound composure. Dan changed direction, but the woman, what was her name—Janet?—was looking right at him. Not only looking at him; she seemed to be pointing him out to the rotund little man in a shabby black suit next to her.

The little man nodded and puffed his way across the quadrangle to Dan. "I understand you're the very person I've been hoping to meet," he said. He pumped Dan's hand, a megawatt smile lighting his round face. "That kind young woman back there tells me you are Dan, lately from Chicago?"

Dan snatched his hand from the man's soft, damp one and took a step back. "What's it to you?"

"We haven't met 'til now, and I'm sure the loss is mine. I'm Peter Cadmium. Very glad to meet you; it's a real pleasure." He reached out his hand again but, at the look on Dan's face, gave a little flapping wave instead of trying for another handshake.

"How come you're looking for me?"

"I come bearing a message, sir."

"From who?"

"Well, I don't think you know him, either; his name is John, ah, John, ah, well—never mind." Cadmium paused. His pudgy hands fluttered about his waistcoat, and for the first time he seemed uncertain. "John is a friend of mine from, ah, long ago. I assure you I can vouch for him."

"So what does he want?"

"Well, let's see. He asked me to tell you that there is something you need to know." Cadmium blinked earnestly. "Information has come into his hands that he feels honor-bound to pass on to you. And again, I can assure you if John says this information is important, it is. You may not know it, but John was one of the world's foremost authorities in matters of religion; today he would be called a megastar. And apparently he is also," Cadmium raised a wispy eyebrow, "a person of some importance here."

The little man took a breath, but before he could continue the litany of praise that threatened to go on indefinitely, Dan said, "Okay, what is it he thinks I should know?"

"Well, ah, I must confess I am not privy to that information. Evidently John considers it necessary to tell you about it himself. The matter is, I gather, too sensitive to put in writing, and since John is a very busy man he sent me to ask that you come to him—at your convenience, of course." Cadmium lowered his voice. "But he told me to tell you he hoped you would not delay too long, because the matter is of the utmost importance."

"If it's so important, why didn't he tell you about it?"

Cadmium was beginning to look harassed. "I would no more ask that he confide the information to which he alludes to me than I would presume to question his decision to hire or fire. I wish I could tell you more, but I can't. As I said, he deems it necessary to give you the information himself." Cadmium wiped his forehead. "I take it as a real privilege that John gave me the task of bringing you this message."

"You expect me to leave here and go find him? Where is he?"

"John resides a short way from here, in the western division of what I believe they call the Trackless Parts, though why they call it that I don't know; there are tracks and paths and roads all over it." Cadmium cocked his head like a puppy hoping for a treat. "I'd be happy to take you there."

Is the guy for real? Is any of this for real? Dan shook his head. "I'm going to take off with you to a place I don't know anything about to find out quote, unquote, information that I have no interest in hearing about from a person I don't know and frankly don't give a damn about?"

Cadmium looked crestfallen, but not surprised. "John told me this might be difficult," he murmured. "He said if you proved, ah, uncooperative, I was to tell you that the message contains knowledge about a person who is searching for you. John says he can and will provide for your safety from this person should you wish it. He says he is the only one who can do so and that it would behoove you to come to him as soon as possible."

Dan's cheeks whitened; his cockiness disappeared like a floating bubble catching on concrete. "Did he say who is looking for me?"

"I don't know. Only that John said to tell you the person's initial is 'T.'"

It was a moment before Dan could talk. He swallowed. "It's safe here," he said, his voice barely audible. "Nothing that can hurt us is allowed on campus." He did not sound convinced.

"I wouldn't know about that," Cadmium pulled at a frayed sleeve. "This seems a remarkably nice place to be sure, lovely surroundings, very pleasant people, but I can only repeat what my friend told me. Apparently you are in danger, but John is certain he can protect you." Cadmium clasped his hands before him. "My dear sir, I can't tell you how many people John helped when I worked with him. People like you, people who have perhaps made a mistake or two—"

"What mistake? What the hell does he know about me?" Dan lashed out at the little man. "What do you know about me?"

Cadmium crumpled. "Oh dear, why do I always make a mess of things?" he moaned. "And this, my first commission from John. Please, please don't tell John I've set you against him. I promise you he told me nothing about you or your problem. I simply inferred from the fact that he was prepared to provide you with sanctuary that you had done something unlawful—as had many of those he helped when I was with him." The little man looked as though he might blubber into the handkerchief with which he was wiping his hands. "There is one thing more John said I might tell you if you were having a difficult time deciding to come." He stood on his tiptoes and whispered something in the vicinity of Dan's ear.

For a moment the panic left Dan's face and he gazed at Cadmium, slack-jawed. "I don't believe it. Couldn't happen."

"I don't know anything about it. I'm just repeating what I was told," Cadmium said. "Please do come. I don't know what I'm going to tell John if I come back without you."

"Oh for Pete's sake, stop with the whimpering," Dan snapped. He rubbed his forehead. "Look, how far away is this place of yours?"

Cadmium brightened. "Not far, not far at all." He stuffed his handkerchief back in his pocket. "You'll come? I promise you if my friend tells you he can give you safe haven, he will do so. He is a man of his word. And you can always come back here if you like." He looked at Dan hopefully.

Dan frowned. The bell for classes had rung while he and Cadmium had been talking and most of the students had gone into the buildings, leaving the quadrangle nearly empty. If he went with the little man, how long before they'd miss him? And so what if they missed him? He could go see what this John person knew, what kind of security he promised. If it seemed inadequate, it would be easy enough to come back here, tell them he'd made a mistake. *If you admit making a mistake they fall all over themselves forgiving you here.*

He absently wiped away a bead of sweat that had formed at his hairline. "Yeah, I'll go see your friend," he said. It wasn't as though he was going off campus with someone like Pegeen. He was going with a clergyman, for Pete's sake.

"I'm so glad," Cadmium beamed at him. "I promise you won't regret it."

18

"So there you are, Perce." Frank lowered his bulk and slid across the booth's leather seat. "I was beginning to think you'd deserted us for higher places."

"Don't I wish." Percy seemed intent on the blueberry muffin before him. He gave Frank an absent nod. "How's it going?"

"Good." Frank rested his palms on the rounded edge of table. "Better than good. I want to talk to you about our recalcitrant young charge, but first, I think I may have a handle on that problem of mine we were talking about—or maybe I should say I've been given a handle on it."

Percy looked up at that, his eyes sharp. "I see," he said after a moment. "Yeah, I guess you have." His lips curved in a slow smile.

A waitress, one of the students by the look of her, took Frank's order and returned a moment later with a cup of coffee and a steaming pot that she set on the table. "You ever get to that Novitiate's meeting?" Frank asked.

A shadow washed his friend's blunt features. "Yeah."

"Anything interesting happen?"

"Sure. I learned a lot. And it looks like I have a good chance of joining Jerry's organization."

"Congratulations."

"Thanks."

"She wasn't there?" Frank said quietly.

Percy gave an infinitesimal shrug.

"Sorry. I shouldn't have mentioned it."

Percy's smile was a tight-lipped grimace. "Hey, I'm not about to question what happens or when it does. I'll meet her when it's right." He broke off a piece of muffin and crumbled it onto his plate. "So you have something to tell me about Dan?"

"I ran into Jerry and he mentioned that the kid's taken off with someone for the Trackless Parts again. Can you believe it? Thought I'd see if I can find where he's gone; wanted to ask if you'd like to come with."

"You think he's gotten himself into trouble?"

"I have no idea, but he doesn't have a great track record, does he?" A frown creased Frank's forehead. "Think I should ask Jerry before we go looking?"

It seemed an effort for Percy to drag himself from wherever his thoughts had gone. "Jerry should probably be left out of this," he said. "You see, Jerry's in charge of campus protocol and behavior. His job is to protect students from whatever or whoever might harm them—but if anyone wants to leave here, they can. It's the old freedom thing. But I'm not restricted to what's happening on campus, and since you've been wandering the Trackless Parts pretty much at will with no bad results, there seems no reason you shouldn't go see if you can find him." Percy shoved his plate away. "Sure, I'll come with. If we can head someone off at the pass when they're about to be entrapped, it's worth a try." But he didn't get up. Instead, he sat back and rested his head against the booth's high back, his eyes closed.

Frank studied him. "Glad you're so enthusiastic. I have another question for you. When I decided to check on Dan, I concentrated on wanting to see him and nothing happened. Wouldn't just thinking about him bring his presence?"

Percy did not open his eyes. "Not if he doesn't want it. This isn't heaven or hell; he's free to wander where he wants to, to answer a call or not."

Frank drained his coffee cup, stood up, and considered the somnolent Percy. "Okay, I think I'll go see if I can find out where the kid is and what he's up to."

Percy roused himself. "I thought you came to enlist me in your posse?"

"Yeah, I did. But right now I'm thinking maybe I should leave you here to do whatever it is you have to do to shake you out of this."

Percy sat up. "And what's that supposed to mean?"

"Maybe you should try some heavy-duty thinking? The same kind of thing you advised me to do a while back?"

Percy stood up slowly. He stood eye to eye with Frank. "Suppose you explain," he said, his tone even. "Suppose you pretend like I'm not all that smart. Use small words, not more than two syllables."

"You may not know it, bro, but you're in the middle of a funk the likes of which I've seldom seen. I know you're supposed to be one step from heaven, but I gotta tell ya, you looked better in prison." Frank cut off Percy's startled denial. "Yeah, Perce. If I showed someone a picture of you sitting there and told them that you were on your way to that heavenly home of yours, they'd wonder if maybe I hadn't made a mistake, that you really chose hell." Frank placed a hand on his friend's shoulder and lowered his voice. "You talk a good line about how you're willing to trust as to how and when you'll meet this lady of yours, but you don't sound very convincing. Not that I'm anyone to judge, but have you thought that maybe there are things you need to work on before she comes into your life?" He let his arm drop. "Anyway, I figured it wouldn't hurt if I went looking for Dan and left you to figure things out."

Percy's fists unclenched and he looked away. When he

looked back Frank saw ruefulness behind the pain in the big man's brown eyes. "Could be you're right," he said at last.

Frank felt himself relax. "For a moment there I figured you might belt me."

"I considered it." Percy rubbed his jaw. "Out of the mouths of babes," he muttered, shaking his head.

"First time I've been called a babe."

"You are when it comes to living here." Percy swallowed. "Okay, I admit I was ticked when the meeting ended. I'd sat there waiting, and, and nothing happened. Guess I'm still bummed. I know I have no right to be, but I am. I wanted it to happen, thought about it so much I figured it had to happen." He looked away again. "Y'see, in jail I protected myself by living in my head. Did whatever I was told to do, took whatever I had to take, but I was the one in control of what went on in my head. Anytime anyone tried to make me think one way, inside my head I'd go the opposite. I knew what I knew and no one was going to change my mind. Got to be a habit, that control thing, and it probably saved my sanity. Hasn't been the easiest thing to let loose of, though." He sat back down in the booth and lowered his head into his hands. "Thought I'd progressed further than this," he said, his voice muffled. "Thought I'd learned that real freedom was to be able to trust the Lord, to give myself into his hands. Oh God!"

Frank flinched, wishing his friend's anguish could be less public, only to realize that they had separated from the rest of the restaurant. It wasn't that the waitress and the other patrons had disappeared. Though barely visible, they were there, but a kind of golden scrim hung between them and Frank and Percy that protected the two men from the restaurant's sights and sounds.

Percy raised his head and managed a wry smile. "Cool, isn't it?" he said. "You don't have to worry about having a private conversation in this place. If it doesn't concern others they don't hear it." He took a deep breath and let it out. Then he reached for the remaining hunk of muffin on the plate he'd pushed aside, popped it into his mouth, and chewed. "Thanks, Frank. I think I'll take you up on that suggestion. Any ideas about where you're going to look for the kid?"

"I figured I'd start with Birgit."

Percy raised an eyebrow.

"Dan has been hanging around her a lot lately," Frank explained. "Kate says he chewed her out last time they were together, but if he's told anyone about where he went, I have a hunch it's her."

"What does that sweet-faced little girl see in him? I haven't talked to her, but I can tell you she's about ten phases ahead of that dude."

"You think that would stop our Dan?" Frank gave Percy's shoulder a friendly clip. He turned to leave, and as he did, the golden scrim parted, then dissolved, and immediately voices and the clatter of dishes filled the air.

Percy watched his friend depart. Then he closed his eyes, laced his hands, and placed them on the booth's table. A passerby might have thought the big man was praying. The passerby would have been correct.

"Just why was Frank sent to look for the boy?" Hannah cocked her head, her dark blond hair illuminated by a ray of streaming sunshine as she leaned back from her desk and regarded her husband.

"Dan's not a boy," Gregory said.

"I know, darling, and I know some of the students have to learn things they couldn't experience on campus, but Dan is stretching the limits and Frank has spent enough time away from us already, don't you think?"

"If anyone is able to collar Dan and bring him around, it would be Frank. Of course, Percy could do it too, but Percy has enough on his plate right now."

"I can't believe Dan decided to take off, that he swallowed Zaroth's claim to be able to protect him. The whole thing is, well, it's worrisome," Hannah finished lamely.

"And you know you shouldn't be worried, but you are," Gregory finished for her. He rose from his desk, moved over to where she sat behind hers, and rested his hand on her shoulder. "Tell me."

Hannah leaned her head against his hand and sighed. "There are changes coming, Greg, states ending and new ones beginning. I can feel it."

"States are always changing, m'love. Things begin to come out that people have spent a lifetime hiding, or else the good things they've loved and let be a part of their life become stronger and come to the forefront. You know that's the natural order of things. And it isn't unusual to have several people's states changing at the same time." Gregory's knuckles lightly touched his wife's cheek. "But I trust your feelings," he said as he went back to his desk. "If you're uneasy, there's reason to be concerned."

Hannah swung her chair so that she faced the curved, white balcony that opened onto a garden of varying shades of blue, purple, and lavender flowers. "And there's another thing," she said, musing. "Why is Zaroth still here? Why hasn't he discovered his home? He's been here far longer than other, less insidious spirits."

"I'd guess it's precisely because he is insidious. But then, he wouldn't still be in the Trackless Parts unless there's a reason, unless he performs some use. As he did when he was with us. Remember when he was at the Academy?"

"How could I forget?"

"In the beginning he seemed to absorb everything he

heard, giving back brilliant insights that amazed us all. But of course that was all part of his external persona; we had some ugly previews of what he was really like when what was inside showed itself."

"As it did on more than one occasion until he chose to leave us." Hannah shivered, remembering. "But you're right, his presence gave those around him a chance to refuse to be like him—or to listen to him. And a few of them did listen." She sighed. "I thought when he left us he'd find a comfort zone that would be simply a short-term way station on his journey to his home."

Gregory shrugged. "It's not always that simple. The man's a mass of contradictions. He actually did a lot of good during his life on earth, you know, and not just because of the adulation and accolades given him, though he thoroughly relished them. He really enjoyed the teaching part of his ministry, especially helping people. His tragedy is that he thought the rules, the commandments, didn't apply to him. They were valuable tools to live by, but in his case—oh, let's see—" Gregory held up his fingers in succession as he counted off the points, "His job was a gargantuan one and he needed respite from it; he had tremendous natural appetites that had to be fed; he could skirt issues of honesty because he was able to judge the essential truth of a matter better than others. There were as many excuses as there were incidents." He shook his head. "Given that Zaroth became such a mixture of good and evil, it's not surprising it has been difficult to separate those loves. They must be separated, and the good that was in him but did not truly become a part of him dissipated, before he will decide to leave the Trackless Parts for his final home."

"Because he is evil."

"Make no mistake, he is that. And the part of him that loves evil is becoming stronger. Zaroth may be serving a use in that quasi-intellectual community of his, but from the way you're reacting to Dan heading out there I'd guess this is nearing the end of the line for Zaroth there."

Hannah gripped the arms of her chair. "There will be danger. I feel it."

"For Dan?"

"Not just Dan. Others will go there."

Gregory got up again and went to her. "Darling, this isn't like you. You know the Lord guards and protects all of us, wherever we make our home."

"Oh I do know. I do. But it makes me so unhappy to see those who are choosing hell try to bring others with them."

Her husband gently pulled Hannah from her chair and drew her out onto the balcony. He gestured to the symphony of flowers below. "Remember, my dear, that evil has no power here," he said. "Ultimately Zaroth will prove to have no power."

Hannah wrapped his arms about her waist and nestled against him. "I know," she said again. After a moment she turned to face him. "What about the little minister?"

"Cadmium? Don't know how that's going to play out. Cadmium relished being in his mentor's reflected glory, and for years after 'John' came here Cadmium lived off his association with the man. Looks as though Cadmium was blind to any faults he may have seen during their friendship; if he continues to willfully look the other way he'll be in real trouble."

Hannah trailed a finger along the railing and turned to her husband. "I know enough not to interfere with another's process or his journey; I know my job is to offer help so that the person can come to see what he has loved and made his own," she said. "You'd think by now I wouldn't need you to remind me, but there it is, I guess I'm a slow learner."

"Slow learner?" Gregory gave her a quick kiss. "I don't think so."

A soft bell sounded and Hannah leaned over to look at a

small, clock-like instrument on her desk. "That's Kate," she said. "I'd better see what she needs."

Gregory nodded and went to his desk. "Let me know if there's anything I can do to help."

Hannah regarded Kate. "I see you're concerned about Dan. He's off campus at the moment." Hannah tilted her head. "How did you fare with your latest attempts to help him?"

Kate looked away to hide her discomfort. "I'm afraid I made rather a botch of it. Matter of fact, I don't think I've done all that well with anyone I've tried to help. Janet. Birgit. Maybe I should go back to square one and see if I can do a little better."

Hannah looked sympathetic, but said nothing.

Kate raised her head and caught Hannah's look. Her eyes narrowed. "Is that why I've been given all these little assignments, Hannah?" She bit her lip. "Is it to give me a chance to learn something about someone other than myself, to concentrate on other people's problems and care about them?"

"You care very much about some people," Hannah said calmly.

"Howard."

"Yes, of course Howard. And your students. You cared about them."

"I did."

"But you're right, you know. You could use a little practice thinking about other people's problems."

"You've just said I cared about my students; that covers a lot of people."

"Sure. But they were your students. Anything they did, what they became, reflected on you."

Kate's jaw tightened. "You're saying my main interest in them was how their success reflected on me?"

"Kate, you're a lovely person. You are kind to others and

you did care about whomever came within your little world, but it was a rather small world, wasn't it? You and Howard had a tendency to enclose yourselves in a cocoon that excluded the rest of the world. It may be something you want to work on, so I'm happy to hear you've decided to do so."

"I'm glad you're happy," Kate snapped. She mustered a smile. "Sorry. I'll do my best, but I have a feeling it won't be easy. And what about Howard? If I'm in need of a little mellowing, he'll have to take a graduate course." The mulish look on Kate's face was replaced by intense concentration. She gave a long drawn out "Oh!"

Hannah's face softened. "It's Howard, isn't it?" she said quietly. "Go on, child. Go."

The I.V. pole beside the hospital bed held two bags that emptied into the needle that probed Howard's stick-thin arms. A pump suctioned fluid directly from his stomach into a container hanging from the bed, its noise all but masking the labored rasp of his breathing. His eyes were closed, but his fingers plucked the blanket at his chest with little, ineffectual gropings.

Kate stood by the bed listening to the fragments and flutterings of her husband's damaged mind. *I want,* she heard. *I want—Who? Her. I want her. Where is she? I need. I need . . .*

"I'm here, Howard." Kate breathed the words. "I'm here, my love."

The slack face tightened; the deep-set eyes flickered open, but stared blankly at the area above the bed without focusing, then closed again.

A sudden contentment, an unexpected flood of golden happiness filled Kate at the thought that the man in the bed was about to make the transition to life and health and loving joy. *Thank you, Lord.* Kate caught her breath. *Thank you for this gift.*

Howard's eyes opened again. He looked at Kate, his gaze clear. "You're here," he said, his voice hoarse, unused. "Is it time?" he said. "Is it time to come to you?"

"Who you talkin' to, honey?" It was the nurse in the chair by the window. She heaved herself from the chair and came to the bed to check the I.V.

"She's here," Howard said. "My Kate is here."

"Uh-huh, sure she is." The nurse stilled Howard's twitching hands and took his pulse. She stiffened and drew the stethoscope from her neck, inserted the ear pieces, leaned over and pressed the stethoscope to Howard's chest, moving it from one area to another, finally pressing it to the base of Howard's neck. Wasting no motion, she pressed intercom above the bed and said, "Get the crash cart, Judy. And call the attending, I think it's Anderson; this one doesn't look good."

A sound caused her to look down at her patient. Howard lay still, his head awkwardly to one side, his hands at rest, no longer plucking the sheet.

The heavy woman swore and pushed the code blue button above the bed. Within seconds the room was filled with people, with doctors and nurses who came at a run, with lab technicians and aides and green-jacketed transporters who stationed themselves at the ready outside the door.

And after a while, in response to the frantic ministrations, Howard began to breathe again.

"Got it, he's back!" A young intern high-fived his companion in jubilation. "Attaboy, Howard."

A slight frown creased the forehead of the muscular nurse who had called the code. "Y'know, back before he crashed he seemed lucid; it's the only time I've heard him speak coherently since he came in." She gave a shrug. "Of course, he was talking to thin air."

"Anyone know why the old guy isn't DNR?" the resident asked.

The nurse looked annoyed. "He doesn't have any relatives to request a 'do not resuscitate' except some sister in another state who's got problems of her own. Since he's an Alzheimer's he sure can't do it himself and you know damn well the nursing home isn't going to—not while he's got the money for extended care."

"Too bad, Howard, old man," the resident said to the figure on the bed.

It was a long time before everyone left the room to the pulsing tubes and blinking monitors. Kate moved to stand beside the bed again. "There, there, my love," she crooned. "Don't fret, darling. We'll be together, but not just yet. Know that I love you, dearest. Know that I'm waiting for you."

Howard was busy breathing. He did not hear.

"Are you all right, Kate?" Hannah's voice seemed to come from a distance.

Kate blinked. "Yes," she said softly.

"Yes, I see you are," said Hannah. "You're beginning to have less trouble looking to what is eternal in all this. Well done, Kate." She began to turn away, but then paused. "And don't fret too much about whatever you decide to do about Dan, my dear. The important thing is that you reach out, that you try."

Janet adjusted her position on the warm stone of the balustrade that edged the flagstone patio outside the library. She flexed her hands experimentally above the open book that lay in her lap. She could hardly remember the way it had been before, the way pain shot through her fingers when she tried to straighten them. No more of that kind of pain. But there was pain. When she'd tumbled into bed last night she'd ached as if she'd been pummeled by baseball bats. Janet winced at the thought of yesterday's session with Walter.

Those pictures he'd shown her. Her weeping remorse couldn't change them. And with seeing the scenes, virtually living through them again, came the unwilling acknowledgement that she'd developed some pretty unpleasant attitudes during her life. Sure, it hadn't been all bad. There were those clips of when she'd tried to check her more ignoble impulses—though often with limited success. What remained with her, yesterday with Walter, last night before she finally fell asleep, this morning when the sun streamed in to awaken her, were the other scenes. She saw herself giving in to the urge to gossip, to shade the truth—okay, to lie—to take credit for things that others had done. She'd had to relive the time she'd accepted accolades for that after-school program when credit rightfully should have gone mostly to Charlotte. Charlotte, who was a shy young teacher while Janet, conveniently, was senior staff.

Janet pressed a hand against her eyelids, forcing back tears that threatened to slip down her cheeks.

"Enough."

Janet looked up, startled. Though she'd heard the word quite clearly, there was no one nearby who could have spoken it. The only other person on the patio was sitting at a table at the other end. Janet looked more closely at the sari-clad figure leaning over an open book. Birgit. Birgit, the innocent who had managed to care for others as damaged as she. Birgit reading a book? But Janet didn't pursue the thought, her attention flicking back to the word she'd heard spoken.

Enough. What did it mean? Janet frowned, puzzled, and then felt a jolt of comprehension. The beginnings of an unwilling smile curved her lips. What had Walter said when she'd sat wailing in despair after their session? "Don't, my dear, ignore the real progress you made in your attempts to obey the commandments. If you do, you are in danger of accepting all the evils that entered your mind as your own. They were not yours if you resisted them. They are not yours now. Don't clutch them to you."

At the time she'd not had the foggiest notion what that meant. Now, perhaps she did. Enough. Janet wiped her cheeks, closed the book in her lap with a snap, and got up. "Birgit," she called out, "would you like some company?"

"Oh yes. Please." Birgit placed a hand over her open book.

"What's that you're reading?" Janet said as she pulled over a cushioned, rush-backed chair.

Shyly Birgit removed her hand to show a watercolor illustration of a group of little children gathered about a bearded man. She pointed to a few lines in large print beneath the picture. "It is a very good story. It is about men who want to shoo some children away, but are told they must not, they should let the children stay," she said.

"Yes," Janet said, smiling. "I think I know that one." She sat down. "You're learning to read?"

Birgit's face lit. "I told the librarian I would like to know how to read and she gave me this book. She said to look at the pictures and see if I could read the printing beneath. And I can! It is wonderful. I look at the pictures and then at the words and I know what they say!" For a moment she looked doubtful. "At least I think I know what they say."

"That is wonderful." The warmth that filled Janet had nothing to do with the spring sunshine. "Tell you what, Birgit, I used to teach children to read. If you like I'll listen to you, and if there are any hard parts I'll give you a hand."

"You will?" Birgit's dark eyes glowed.

"Mind if I join you ladies?" Frank Chambers' large shadow crossed the webbed top of the iron table.

One of the seated women nodded shyly at Frank; the other flushed a bright, unbecoming red. Frank pulled over a chair and sat, seemingly oblivious to Janet's painful unease.

"I am learning to read," Birgit said. "Janet says she will help me."

"Good for you." Frank said. "And good for you, Janet," he added, including her in his smile.

Janet nodded abruptly. She would not simper. She would behave in a reserved, adult manner. She would—but Frank had turned away, unmindful of her mental ditherings.

"I wanted to ask whether you have any idea where Dan went," he said to Birgit. "And why he took himself off in the first place."

A flush crept across Birgit's face. A delicate hint of a blush, Janet noted, quite unlike the cherry crimson one she knew still stained her own cheeks.

"I do not know where he is. He is angry with me. I thought that perhaps I could help him, but when I went to my garden and thought of him he did not appear as he sometimes does. So I realized he is not here." Birgit paused, her small, full lips unsuccessfully trying to suppress a quiver. "Or perhaps he did not come because he does not wish to talk with me. Perhaps he is not angry anymore, but I am not interesting enough to talk to." She lifted her chin. "I decided I must do something, I must learn more, not just stay in the gardens and tend my roses. I decided I would learn to read."

"And so you did. An object lesson for all of us." Frank got to his feet. "Well, I'd better be going."

Janet cleared her throat. "I know where Dan went. Or at least who he left the campus with."

Frank looked at her in surprise.

"A clergyman, at least he was wearing a clergyman's collar, came here with a message for Dan, but he didn't know where Dan was or what he looked like. So I, I pointed him out." Janet bit her lip. "Did I do something wrong?"

"Of course not. They said nothing about where they were going?"

"I didn't hear their conversation. Just saw them walk off toward the gates."

Frank shook his head, exasperated. "Don't know what attraction the Trackless Parts has for the kid. You'd think by now he'd know it's dangerous."

"He looked scared," Janet said. "Actually, he seemed petrified."

Frank eyed her with interest. "This was after he'd heard the message?"

"Yes."

"He needs my help," Birgit said firmly. She got up, disturbing the large rabbit that had been hidden in the folds of her sari beneath the table. "I must go to him."

"Whoa, hold on there, young lady." Frank raised a large hand. "Don't you worry about this. Believe me, the Trackless Parts is no place for you. I'll go fetch him and bring him to you; that is, if he wants to come back."

Birgit remained standing, her eyes downcast. She said nothing, but the stubborn set of her chin must have warned Frank, for he put his hands on his hips and his voice deepened and took on a sterner tone. "I mean it. There's no way you'd be prepared for what lies out there."

When Birgit merely bowed her head and refused to meet his gaze, Frank turned to Janet. "You won't let her do anything foolish, will you?" he pleaded. "She shouldn't leave the Academy grounds."

"I'll try," Janet said dryly. "But if a Chicago cop can't scare her into compliance, I don't know what chance I have."

"I'm glad you find this amusing," Frank rasped. "I don't think you would if you had any idea what's out there."

"Don't get huffy on me," Janet said. "I'm just an innocent bystander."

"Sorry," Frank said stiffly. "I'm just trying to do a job I've been given."

"Well you'd better get going, because Birgit's not waiting for you." Janet looked across the table at the empty space where Birgit had stood moments ago.

"Oh for Pete's sake." Frank gave an angry shake of his head and strode off without another word.

Janet remained at the table, not unsatisfied with this last exchange. At least she hadn't acted like a complete idiot; she'd stood up to the big ex-cop. She might have annoyed him, but it was better than being ignored. She sat, waiting patiently, and sure enough, Birgit came walking up the steps to the patio. She gave Janet a small smile of complicity. "I don't like people to speak to me harshly," she said. She cocked her head. "How did you know I would come back?"

"Shoma is still here." Janet nodded at the large rabbit nibbling at the young grass between the flagstones. "I figured you couldn't be far away."

19

The auditorium was nearly full. A few latecomers bypassed phalanxes of knees and feet and slid into seats left empty in the middle of the rows, settling themselves as quickly and inconspicuously as possible.

A misty, sulfurous beam of light played on two maroon velvet chairs at the center of the stage. To the left of the chairs a polished black podium reflected the gleam of another spotlight. A rustling murmur swept through the audience as Zaroth emerged from the wings leading an auburn-haired woman in a low-necked, lime-green chiffon dress. The hem of the woman's dress brushed the top of her comely knees, swooping in the back to touch her high-heeled shoes. The end of the chiffon scarf draped about her neck wafted behind her as she walked.

His hand at her elbow, Zaroth escorted the woman to one of the chairs, then strode to the podium, where he stood looking out over the audience as though he'd just discovered it was there. "Good evening, friends," he said. Though he did not raise his voice and there was no visible microphone, his words reached every corner of the large, sloping hall. "We are here to listen to the Elida B. Mitchell memorial lecture, and may I say we are exceptionally fortunate today to have with us as a guest speaker a lady graced with the name of Pegeen, a lady who is a leading proponent of theories equally as daring and forward-looking as Ms. Elida Mitchell's, a speaker, moreover, whose views adherents of Ms. Mitchell's philosophy can not help but validate."

Pegeen smiled and began to rise from her chair, only to sink back as Zaroth rumbled on.

". . . views that by their very outspokenness and fearless candor have forced our speaker to bear the brunt of the world's pusillanimous harassment throughout her long and distinguished career."

Pegeen seemed slightly annoyed by the "long" part of her career's characterization but recovered immediately and inclined her head in a dignified nod. She cautiously sat forward in her chair but subsided once again as she realized Zaroth had not finished.

". . . a career that will resound in the annals of scholarship as one that embraced change, that did not shy from controversy, a career that will stand as a beacon for those who come after her—"

"*Sst*, Zaroth," Pegeen hissed.

Startled, Zaroth halted. A smile creased his lipless face, but his yellow eyes glittered as he looked over at Pegeen. "I see my colleague is anxious to address you," he said smoothly. "So without further ado, I give you an extraordinary scholar and my great and good friend, Pegeen." He held out an imperious claw and, when she came to the podium, took Pegeen's hand, not relinquishing it as both bowed to acknowledge the continuing applause. Under cover of the clapping Zaroth leaned close and whispered, "Don't ever interrupt me again, my dear."

Something flashed in Pegeen's eyes, but she did not reply. Instead, she gracefully extricated her hand and responded to the still-applauding audience with yet another bow. She stood waiting until Zaroth left to take his seat in one of the velvet chairs, then turned to the audience and in an elaborate pantomime, flexed the fingers of the hand Zaroth had been holding as though attempting to restore circulation. "My, I didn't know academics were so strong," she cooed.

The audience roared with laughter. Zaroth gave a small, pained smile. Pegeen carefully tucked the tail of her chiffon scarf into the belt at her waist and adjusted the papers on the podium before her. "When I accepted the invitation to speak to you at this great university," she began, "I had no idea there were so many distinguished scholars here, many of whom, I may say, inspired me in my own studies."

As Pegeen's well-modulated voice continued its measured cadence, two listeners standing at the rear of the hall scanned the audience. The large, shaven-headed man nudged his companion. "See him anywhere?"

"Can't see much of anything," said Frank. "You think they'll turn up the lights for the intermission? Or that there'll be an intermission?"

"Beats me." The other man glanced at Frank. "You sure you don't mind me deciding to horn in on this little expedition of yours?"

"I asked you, didn't I? Glad you got out of your blue funk and decided to come along. After all, Perce, he's your charge as well as mine."

An usher came up behind them. "You'll have to step outside if you're going to talk," he whispered.

The two looked at each other, shrugged, and followed the usher into the lobby.

Percy gestured to the heavy wooden doors. "Does everyone come out this way?"

"Yes, yes they do." The usher lowered his voice even more. "Crowd control, you know. You never can tell with these academics. You wouldn't think so, but the discussions get heated sometimes. Best to have just one way in and out."

"That makes it easier for us," Frank murmured to Percy.

"The guy who had this job before me said one time they all got so mad they tried to storm the stage," the usher said, warming to his story. "Had to rush the speaker out back."

"I thought you said this was the only exit."

"For the audience. 'Course the speakers have a backstage entrance."

A ripple of laughter came from the auditorium.

"Doesn't sound like there's any danger of rioting academics this evening," Frank said. He leaned against the unmanned refreshment counter and surveyed the empty lobby. "Since it looks like there's not going to be much in the way of interest in there, my friend and I will wait here until the program's over," he said to the usher.

"You don't want to hear the talk?"

"We've heard the lady's views before. I think we'll give this version a bye." Frank waited until the usher left to take up his post just inside the doors before continuing his conversation with Percy. "I'm not sure just why we came here anyway. What would the kid be doing in there? I can't believe our Dan would be interested in a lecture by a woman he's given every indication of wanting to avoid like the plague."

"Forget Pegeen, our Dan wouldn't willingly come to any lecture by any academic. I just thought he might have to be here because of Zaroth."

"He's the one Jerry talked about?"

Percy nodded. "Yeah, the one on stage with Pegeen."

"Strange-looking guy," Frank said.

Percy looked at him with interest. "Exactly what did he look like to you?"

"Weird," Frank said promptly. "There were scales on his hands and ones that covered his head and cheeks, sort of like a Greek helmet. And, let's see, a center line of spikes ran from the top of his forehead to the nape of his neck that seemed to raise and lower, kind of like the hair on a dog's back. We're talking more than weird."

"Um-hm. And how did Pegeen look?"

"You giving me a witness assessment test? She was about the same as when we saw her in the dining hall. No, wait, she seemed older; makeup laid on with a shovel, and she could have used some advice about that dress she was wearing. It didn't fit right, and even from where we were, it was pretty obvious both she and the dress could have used cleaning."

"I'm not surprised you saw them that way," Percy said, "But the fact is, I'm betting the audience saw something very different. I'm sure they thought their newest intellectual guru could give Miss America a run for her money. And as for Zaroth, the audience probably saw him as a handsome devil."

"Metaphorically speaking?" Frank said, grinning.

Percy did not smile. "Or not."

Frank sobered. "The audience was seeing an illusion and I saw Pegeen and Zaroth as they really are?"

"Uh-huh."

"That means—" Frank's jaw twitched, "—that means I'm not like them?"

"No, you're not like them, bro. You may have some baggage to contend with, but loving power and wanting to control other people isn't part of it. You took care of that stuff a long time ago, back when you were on the force."

Frank ducked his head in wry acknowledgement. "Let's leave that one alone." A short, sharp round of spontaneous applause came from the auditorium and Frank pushed away from the refreshment stand. "Seems our Pegeen's really wowing them," he said. "By the way, Perce, who is this Elida B. Mitchell?"

"Don't know, but we can find out." Percy unhooked a slim, wand-like instrument from his belt, spoke into it and then listened for a long moment. "Right. Thanks, Jerry." He reattached the wand to his belt. "Jerry says Elida was the star performer at this place until a little while ago. Evidently she had her very own secret society with ceremonies and stuff for the initiates. By the time she left she had quite a following here. Word is, Zaroth has taken her place."

"Why'd she leave?"

"The staged ceremonies got out of hand. Jerry says the final straw was stuff involving small animals being sacrificed to a pack of wild dogs."

Frank took a step back, as though to avoid the chill of a sudden draft. "Here? I mean, it isn't as if I haven't seen a hell of a lot worse, but I can't believe they'd let something like that happen here."

"'Here' is a place that's mighty close to a hell."

"A hell?"

"One of Elida B. Mitchell's own choosing. But if it makes you feel better, although her adherents saw all that stuff happen, it didn't."

Frank still looked uneasy. "Why would even the appearance of something like that be allowed?"

Percy shrugged. "It was what her followers wanted to see. Most of them, that is, though I'd guess it was a wake-up call for a few. And it would have allowed the last appearances of Ms. Mitchell's rationality to be stripped away and the real, unvarnished Elida B. to emerge." Percy looked over at Frank. "Gets your attention, doesn't it?"

"It's got mine." A crescendo of clapping came from the auditorium followed by the chatter of raised voices. "Here they come," Frank said.

"I'll take that side and you stay here," Percy said as the crowd surged from the auditorium and spilled into the lobby. "If our boy comes out, one of us can collar him."

"About time someone punctured both the matriarchal and

patriarchal systems," said a thin woman sprinting for the exit. "I've always said you don't need either conventional structure to raise children, but oh no, everyone thinks you have to have Mama and Papa on the scene."

"Too right," her companion twittered.

A ruddy-faced man behind them rumbled, "I liked that 'pair bonding' concept. Long-term bonds for those raising children, shorter ones if no kids are involved."

The first woman whipped about to face him, causing at least three people to bump into each other as they swerved to avoid her. "Yes, but what about her observation that a good percentage of pair bonding is the result of a woman being attracted to partners when she is ovulating, especially partners with robust genes?" she said. "That indicates humans have not yet evolved from the primary reason for sexual congress, which is, of course, the preservation of the speci—Ouch! Watch your elbow!" She winced as another rush of people poured from the auditorium, sweeping both her and her companion along.

There were more comments from the passing crowd, most favorable, but some mixed. "I miss Elida," a prim-looking woman sniffed. "This one wasn't nearly as good as our Elida."

A man hurrying along stopped to glare at her. "You didn't expect her to be, did you? How could anyone be as good as Elida?" He smirked. "And as one who is in a position to know, let me tell you Elida was good."

When at last the flow slowed to a trickle and Dan still hadn't appeared, Frank signaled Percy toward the open doors of the nearly empty auditorium. "How 'bout we check in there and then go see what this guy Zaroth can tell us?"

Percy shook his head. "We leave Zaroth alone; you only want to contact that dude as a last resort." He thought for a moment. "Y'know, if we haven't run across Dan it's probably because he doesn't want us to."

"Could be he's being held somewhere incommunicado—against his will."

"I guess it could seem that way," Percy said elliptically.

"Say again?"

Percy gave a last look into the auditorium and turned away. "I meant it may seem that way to him, but if the kid really wanted us, we'd be with him. Look, we've done what we can here. I think we should go back and talk to Jerry, see if he wants to involve one or more field agents in this."

Frank raised an eyebrow. "Field agents?"

"For the Trackless Parts. They keep an eye on the communities here; make sure things don't get completely out of hand." Percy headed for the entrance. "Let's go."

The rough brick of the garden wall tore at Birgit's sari as she pulled herself onto the wall's concrete cap. "Oh!" she cried, grimacing as she smoothed a two-inch rip in the fabric. Then she lifted her chin. "Are you coming with me?" she asked as she reached down to take Shoma from Janet's outstretched hands.

Janet waited a heartbeat, but found she couldn't ignore the plea in Birgit's dark eyes. "Yes," she said finally. "But are you sure you really need me? Mr. Cadmium will be with you to show you the way."

The perspiring little man standing beside her smiled uncertainly. "Does she expect me to climb that wall?" he said to Janet. "Can't we take a more, ah, more normal route from the campus?"

"If we go by the gate they'll try to stop us," Birgit said from above. "I know they will."

"No one has paid much attention to me so far," Cadmium objected mildly, "coming or going."

"Please. I will help you," Birgit said, holding out her hand to him. "Janet can push from behind."

Cadmium blanched at the thought. "I think I might be able to scale the wall with just your aid, Miss Birgit." He grasped one of the jutting bricks and put the toe of his shoe on another and scrambled up to take hold of Birgit's hand. "Ah ha!" he gasped as Birgit hauled him onto the top. "Well done." He paused, breathing heavily. "Think how delighted your friend Dan will be that you decided to join him."

"I was going to come help him even before you brought me the message from him," Birgit said. "But I've never been outside the Academy grounds. I didn't know which direction to go." She regarded Cadmium earnestly. "Did he say why he needs me?"

"Alas, I have no details. Other than my friend's assurance that your young man would like it very much if you cared to join him."

"Wait a minute!" a call came from behind them. Janet whipped about and the two on the wall clutched each other to keep from tumbling.

"Kate!" Janet gasped. "What are you doing here?"

"I came looking for Birgit; went to her rooms, but she wasn't there. I wanted to talk to her about Dan, so I simply wished to be in her presence. And here I am." She regarded Birgit on top of the wall. "Don't tell me; let me guess. You're up there in that ridiculous position because you're following Dan into the Trackless Parts." She shaded her eyes to take in Cadmium. "And you are?"

"Peter Cadmium, at your service," the little man said, bending from the waist to make an awkward bow that almost toppled him from the cap of the brick wall. "Haven't we met somewhere?"

"Not that I know of," Kate said shortly. "Why don't you both come down and we can all go through the gate like normal people?"

"Someone will stop us," Birgit said again. Her voice was barely audible, but her jaw was set.

"What do you mean, 'we can all go'?" Janet demanded.

"Just that," Kate said coolly. "I want to find Dan too. I'm afraid he may be in trouble. Why are you going?" she asked Janet as an afterthought.

"Birgit asked me." Janet's tone made it clear that should anyone assume she wasn't coming along, he or she had another think coming.

"All right," Kate sighed. She reached up, extending a hand to Birgit. "Come on down, Birgit," she coaxed. "Let's see if we can find a way out of here that doesn't entail climbing over walls."

Birgit took the proffered hand grudgingly. "You are sure they will let us go?"

"Absolutely," Kate said, hoping it was true. "Anyone can leave anytime she wants to."

Janet and Birgit and Kate all held up their arms to help the round little clergyman climb down the jutting bricks. "My, my," he puffed, "I do hope we won't have to do any more of this. I've been feeling quite spry lately, but I don't think I'd be up to much more."

The little group waited on the velvety grass beside the wall for Cadmium to catch his breath. A jasmine bush scented the air about them, and a line of flame-red and sunset-orange hibiscus tucked into the curve of the wall beyond. The air rang with warbling birdsong. Kate took it all in with a mixture of appreciation and mounting anxiety. "All right; everyone ready to leave?" she said. "The main gate's over there."

"Oh my dear," Hannah put a hand to her mouth. "Can you believe those children?"

"They're hardly children," Gregory said, smiling.

"Spiritually speaking, they're infants," his wife retorted. "And poor little Birgit. She truly cares for Dan, and I'm afraid he is not the person she thinks he is."

"Thinking has little to do with it."

"And Janet traipsing off too! You'd think she'd have more sense."

"Janet's only going because she saw how anxious Birgit was at the thought of leaving the safety of the Academy."

"Anxious? The girl's terrified—despite that stubborn determination."

"And Kate," Gregory continued, "We should know our Kate by now. Since you had that little talk with her, she's determined to do her best to help Dan and she's not going to let anything stop her." He turned from the open windows. "Janet's grown while she's been with us, hasn't she?"

"Kinder and gentler," Hannah agreed.

"It was there all along," Gregory mused. "There's no question she spent her life doing what she considered her duty. Of course the fact that she continually brought attention to it didn't endear her to others. She knew she was tolerated rather than liked, and it hurt, but she continued to try to do what she thought was right. What's surprising is that underneath her feisty, combative exterior, Janet became reasonably clear-eyed about her faults as she grew older—and tried to do something about them. And that's allowing the kinder, gentler Janet to blossom now."

He reached for a stack of papers. "The troops are gathering, aren't they? You were right about things coming to a head in the Trackless Parts." The phone on his belt beeped. Gregory answered it, listened a moment, and said, "Right. I'll be at the school office." He rose. "Jerry wants to talk to me, my love. After that, I want to go over some cases with you. We have some remarkable students entering next semester."

20

"I'm so glad you ladies decided to join us," Cadmium said to Kate and Janet between puffing breaths. "Your little friend seems in a great hurry. Anxious to meet up with her young man, I imagine." He looked ahead at Birgit, whose pace was rapidly distancing her from them.

"She'll wait for us if she gets too far away," said Janet, but she did not sound at all certain.

"I was most impressed when I first saw your campus the other day," Cadmium said, apparently determined to keep up a polite conversation despite his increasingly labored breathing. "Very impressive grounds."

"Yes, it's lovely," said Kate.

"Can anyone come to classes at the Academy?" he asked. "I mean to audit, of course. I wouldn't expect to be accepted as a student, not at my age, but I'd be very interested in attending some classes and learning just what they teach there."

Both women looked at him in surprise. "You've already been allowed to come on campus twice," said Janet. "I'd think that's a pretty good indication that you'd be allowed to attend classes if you want. Don't worry about being too old. I don't know how long you've been here, but you must have noticed you're becoming younger."

Cadmium stopped and looked at the backs of his hands, his ready smile widening. "Y'know, I did notice my knuckles don't hurt anymore; matter of fact, the arthritis seems to have disappeared altogether." He hurried to catch up. "And though I must confess these trips to the Academy leave me a bit winded, ordinarily I wouldn't be able to walk there and back once, let alone twice in a day." He looked about him. "Or has it been more than a day? I'm not quite sure." Cadmium's hand went to his cheek. "And as for how I look, I'm afraid I'm not one to spend much time with mirrors. Never been much to look at," he added sheepishly. "Hoped to meet someone who would look past my rather unprepossessing exterior, but that's another story. One that didn't happen." He ducked his head, embarrassed, and returned to firmer ground. "You said I'd be welcome to attend your classes," he said. "I'm not sure I agree. I was allowed to come on Academy grounds, but I wasn't exactly invited to make free with the place. There were guards this last time when I entered, and though they let me come in, they made it pretty clear that I wasn't to stay." The look he gave the women was troubled. "I didn't expect guards."

"I didn't even know we had them until Kate told me," said Janet. "But maybe that's because I've never gone off campus."

"Guards or not, you should at least ask about taking classes," Kate said, picking up the pace. "How far is this place we're headed for?" she asked Cadmium.

"Not too much further," Cadmium said, valiantly puffing behind her. "Might we perhaps slow down a bit?"

Kate looked at the little man's perspiring face and relented, slowing to match her step to his. "What happened when you took Dan to this village or city or whatever it is?"

"Well, I escorted him to J—Zaroth's office and left him there, but I didn't actually see him again after that. I imagine he has been engaged in all that's going on." He arched his wispy eyebrows at Kate. "It seems a very busy place, y'know. Zaroth did tell me about their conversation, however, and he said the young man expressed his gratitude for Zaroth's message and to me for bringing it to him. That's when Zaroth told me I could do the young man a further favor by asking the young lady ahead to come visit him."

Kate's lips compressed in a worried line, but she said nothing.

Janet spoke into the small silence. "So as a clergyman, what was it like to find yourself in a world you've spent most of your life preaching about?"

"I didn't preach about it," Cadmium said simply. "Except in generalities. How could I, or anyone else, for that matter, have known what it would be like? You could have knocked me over with a feather when I awoke in what I thought was my little house. I never expected things in heaven to be so similar to the world we came from. But of course it seems we're not in heaven. At least that's what the kind folk said when I asked." He looked at Janet for confirmation.

Janet surveyed the dry, cracked ground beneath the scrub pines that lined this section of the dirt road. "No, this certainly isn't heaven. I guess you could say we're sort of betwixt and between."

"Between? You mean between heaven and hell?" Cadmium's ruddy flush left his face, leaving irregular white splotches on his pudgy cheeks.

"You got it."

"Oh dear. I always said there wasn't any hell. I was so sure a merciful God wouldn't countenance one."

"Really? Did you ever consider what someone who actually enjoys doing evil and harming others would feel like if he found himself in heaven?"

"But he—ahem, or we might say she—could change."

"We might say it, but let's not," Janet said crisply. "Could he really change?" she continued. "If the person had spent his life thinking only about himself and loving only himself, he wouldn't want to change. If he suddenly was filled with the love that fills the heavens he wouldn't be the same person, would he? That person he knew and had thoroughly enjoyed becoming throughout his lifetime." Janet saw Cadmium's confusion and tried again. "Look at it this way. You could think of hell simply as a place where certain people want to be. Where they feel comfortable, where they're around others like themselves." Janet looked at the stunted trees and scrawny bushes growing beside the dusty road. "Frankly, I've always imagined hell would look a lot like this."

Cadmium bristled. "Oh I grant you this isn't as beautiful as your campus, but wait 'til you see our little city. It has some quite attractive gardens with well-appointed buildings and grounds and educational facilities—" he looked first at Janet and then Kate, "—but I'll let you ladies in on a little secret. It's not so much the surroundings that you'll find remarkable, it's who is there. I'm happy to say I will be able to introduce you to one of the foremost minds it has been my privilege to know." Cadmium had to stop and blink back his emotion before he could continue. "He is a man I am proud to call both teacher and friend. I can't imagine why it took me so long to remember him when I came here, but when I did finally recall him, there he was, or rather there I was with him. John, or Zaroth as he's known now, was just as I remember him—decisive, insightful, two steps ahead of everyone else, a giant among pygmies."

Kate looked less than impressed. "Birgit seems to have come to a crossroad," she said, pointing to Birgit, who had put Shoma down on the dusty road ahead and stood looking at a fork in the way. One branch went slightly downhill; the other continued on a level path.

"We take the fork down the incline to the left," Cadmium called out cheerily. "Watch out for the loose stones, they can be treacherous."

Birgit did not move in the direction he'd indicated, but stood twisting the torn skirt of her sari. For the first time since they'd left the Academy, she seemed uncertain.

Janet put a hand on the girl's shoulder. "Want to go back?" she said quietly. "If you do, say the word and we'll skedaddle."

Birgit looked at Janet, momentarily diverted. "What is this skedaddle?"

"Take off, vamoose, get the heck out of here."

Birgit flashed her a look of gratitude but shook her head. "I cannot. Dan wants me to come; I must help him if I can." She touched Janet's hand. "But I thank you, and you, Kate," she said, turning to the other woman. She took a quick breath, gathered her skirts, and began to pick her way down the rock-strewn road.

Janet looked down at her hand. "I don't think I've ever seen her voluntarily reach out to touch anyone or anything other than that rabbit and her roses," she murmured to Kate.

"I know," Kate said. "She's so vulnerable; it frightens me that we may not be able to protect her." She looked at the slender girl. "But we've got to try."

"Protect her from what? Dan? This Zaroth character?"

"I guess we'll have to find out," Kate said grimly.

"It's just around the next corner," Cadmium called out after they had stumbled a short distance down the stony track. "Yes, you see? There it is; there's the town."

Birgit halted, her eyes huge.

"Oh dear," said Janet.

Cadmium looked from one to the other. "What? What is it?"

"What do you see?" Janet asked Birgit.

Birgit clutched Shoma to her and shook her head.

"What?" Cadmium said again.

Kate frowned. "I saw a circle of huts with a big lodge of some sort in the center, but now it's changed. The air is still smoky and it's difficult to make out, but I can see the large buildings Mr. Cadmium was talking about, and streets and trees."

"Me too," said Janet. She studied Birgit. "What about you?"

The girl glanced at them and then back at the scene before her. She did not answer.

"I think Birgit still sees huts," Kate said quietly.

21

"Come here, my sweet." Zaroth patted the leather cushion beside him. "I must say I was quite pleased with your lecture; it went well, extremely well. In fact, I would term it a great success, my pet. A few more like that and I can see you easing into the void created by the departure of our late, lamented Elida B.; a position, I might add, that I considered filling myself."

"I'm not your sweet or your pet," Pegeen snapped. "And I'm not interested in becoming a second-rate Elida B. Mitchell. As for the lecture, yes it went well, but for a while there I was wondering whether I'd ever get to the podium to give it."

Zaroth's eye-slits narrowed, the dark, diamond-shaped pupils contracting to points of fire. Pegeen hastily sat down on the leather cushion. "Just teasing, darling," she said, snuggling next to his sinewy flank. "But what about that thing you promised?" She thrust out her lower lip in a beguiling pout.

"It's arranged, my sweet. At the moment, however, I'm using him for an interesting experiment—a test of methods, so to speak, mine against the Academy's. He seems to be particularly malleable, and I think I may have the upper hand. We'll see. But why is he so important to you? Why this callow youth?"

Pegeen's jaw clenched. For a moment the glittering anger that lit her eyes rivaled Zaroth at his most splenetic. Then she arched an eyebrow and said with a forced smile, "No one

241

walks out on Pegeen. And more important, no one makes Pegeen look ridiculous in front of an ersatz cop and a couple of muscle builders."

"Now, now, my little scorpion. You'll have him for your—amusement—after I've done with him."

Pegeen sank back against the leather cushion. She reached a hand to Zaroth's scaly cheek. "I don't know what's the matter with me," she murmured. "When I'm with you I find myself forgetting everything else and acting like a silly woman eager to please her lord and master instead of a responsible, independent scientist."

Zaroth gave a small, gratified hiss. He drew her to him, bending his crested head to hers. "That's because when you please me, I am likely to please you," his voice lowered, "as you well know."

They did not hear the knock on the door until the discreet tapping became several loud thumps.

"What is it?" Zaroth barked.

The door opened a few inches and the frizzled head of Zaroth's secretary peeked around it. She blinked rapidly. "I'm so sorry, sir. I wouldn't have interrupted, but Officer Frumel is on the phone. His guards have detained some people attempting to enter the city without passes."

Zaroth disentangled himself. He gave the woman a withering look but said nothing as she skittered across the room, holding out the cell phone she'd had clutched to her scrawny chest. Zaroth listened intently and gave a short, unpleasant laugh. "You imbecile, Frumel! Who told you to arrest them? That's Cadmium you have there, and presumably someone I sent him to retrieve. Let them go immediately." He listened again. "There are three women? Hm. Let's see." He lowered the phone to look at it, then showed it to Pegeen. "You know them?"

Pegeen studied the picture. "That's Janet, someone I met

at the Academy, and the other . . . oh yes, I know her. She's
Dan's aunt, a self-important busybody who taught at some
Midwestern school and thinks herself a scholar."

"Bring them to me immediately," Zaroth said into the
phone and snapped it shut. "Now where were we, my little
plumrose?"

The pencil-thin secretary was already at the door, but at
this she half-turned and shot an unreadable glance over her
shoulder. Perhaps it was because of her hurry to be gone that
she left the door open a few inches.

"'Pears you really do know the leader." The helmeted man
closed the phone and clipped it to his belt. "Got orders to
bring you to him. Didn't mean no harm, you know, but we
can't have just anyone coming into town, can we? Have to
make sure you're registered."

"But I wasn't questioned when I was here before," Peter
Cadmium protested. "Matter of fact, I'm not registered now
as far as I know and I've certainly never been aware of any
guards here."

"'At's as may be, but you're seein' one now, and you and
them best come along nice like and not give me no trouble."
He fingered the billy club dangling from his belt.

Cadmium twisted his pudgy hands. "These threats are
quite unnecessary, my good man. Of course we'll come with
you, but I'm sure John, I mean Zaroth, would want these
ladies extended every courtesy."

Their guard merely grunted.

"Don't worry; he doesn't bother us," Janet said, lifting her
chin. But she moved closer to Kate and Birgit. Birgit, who
had said not a word since they'd first seen the town in the distance, simply clutched Shoma to her.

The guard beside them, the little group trudged down an
incline into the town proper, where they traversed one twist-

ing street after another, the odd shopper gazing at them incuriously. The guard stopped in front of a large building at the center of town. Its dirty gray stone was chipped and defaced with graffiti, but it was an imposing structure for all that, with small, high windows that looked out on the street like staring, browless eyes.

"This here's it," the guard said. He gestured to steep stairs that fronted the building. "You go on up. I won't go with. But don't you try anything funny like tryin' to get away. They'll send me after you and you won't like that. Friends of the leader or not." He waited until they climbed the steps and then clumped off down the cobbled street.

Janet, Kate, and Cadmium stood before the great, copper door and looked at each other uneasily, Birgit a little to the side.

Cadmium gave a timid tap on the metal plate. "This isn't anything like it was before," he whispered. "It's all different somehow. I hardly recognize the town."

"How very pleasant to see you all."

They hadn't heard the door open, but there was Zaroth. "I'm so pleased you've come to visit us," he said, his voice velvet. "Do come in." He stepped aside, bowing them in, but the women made no move to enter. Cadmium dithered beside them, making little distressed noises.

"Come, come," Zaroth spoke to Cadmium. "Don't stand there looking like a hooked fish, man. Come in; they'll follow."

"Come, dear ladies," Cadmium coaxed, moving around them into the dark hallway. "I'm sure my friend John will explain everything." But his tone was dubious. "What's this all about, John?" he said, his voice low. "Why did that man accost us? He treated us as though we were criminals."

"He's a guard. Surely we are allowed guards. They have them."

"They?"

"The, ah, people at the place you've just come from. But, to coin a phrase, let's not make a mountain out of a mole-hill." He turned to Kate, who, staring at Zaroth, had nevertheless taken a few cautious steps into the hall. "I trust you ladies weren't put off by my guard's overzealous approach. If so, I do apologize." He extended a claw to Janet and Birgit, still on the doorstep. "Please come in, my dears." He smiled as they quickly crossed the threshold, Janet holding Birgit's hand. "May I make amends by inviting you to join us for a cup of tea?"

"Where is my nephew?" Kate said crisply. "I understand you persuaded Mr. Cadmium to get Dan to come here. Probably under false pretences."

"You think so?" Zaroth's smile was gleaming. "I'm sure you must have adequate grounds for making such an assumption; a brilliant academician like you would never make unsubstantiated charges." He responded to her startled look. "Yes, yes, your nephew has apprised me of your, ah, history." He turned to Birgit. "And he has spoken highly of you, my dear, most highly."

Birgit simply looked at him, dark eyes wide. Her grip on Shoma tightened until the rabbit gave a squeak. She quickly relaxed her hold and buried her face in Shoma's soft brown fur. Zaroth's lipless smile widened. He took her arm as he shut the door and led her further down the hallway. "Come. We have a nice fire to warm you."

Janet crossed her arms about her chest. "It is cold," she murmured to Kate. "When did that happen?"

Cadmium had been watching Zaroth throughout his exchange with Birgit and now said abruptly, "The temperature's been dropping since we came into the village." He put a light hand on Janet's arm. "I, I'm sure John can explain everything, but I can't help having a bad feeling about all this." He leaned closer to Janet and Kate. "If we should become separated and someone here tries anything ah, untoward with any of you ladies, I think you should, well, raise a fuss," he finished lamely.

Janet looked at him a long moment. "You have a bad feeling? I should hope to kiss a duck you do. And I'll tell you what—raising a fuss is the least of what we'll do the moment anyone tries anything, untoward or not."

"Why are you people lollygagging about?" Zaroth called from the curved entry of the large room to which he'd ushered Birgit. "Come join us; there's someone I think you'll want to meet."

Pegeen reclined rather than sat in a patterned satin chaise lounge before the hearth. The flickering fire seemed far too small for a fireplace that could have been used to roast an ox. "How nice of you to come visit me," she purred. Lifting her chin, she gave a regal shake of her head, flicking a lock of silvery white hair over her shoulder.

"Actually, I didn't come to visit anyone," said Janet. "The only reason I came along was to keep Birgit company. She heard that her friend might need some help and wanted to see her."

"Ah yes, that would be our Dan." Pegeen nodded sagely. "Yes, Dan has a problem."

Kate gave her a level look. "Where is he?"

"Now, now, let's not discuss what possibly might be a delicate matter until our guests have had some refreshments," Zartoth said. He went to the fireplace and jabbed the logs with an intricately molded iron poker. "I've ordered a variety of tea cakes, or you might prefer our chef's famous blueberry bombé. With ice cream."

Janet swallowed. She hadn't realized she was hungry, but she was suddenly ravenous. "I don't feel like sweets, but I could do with something a little more hearty," she heard herself saying.

Kate held up a hand like a traffic cop at a busy intersection.

"Wait just a minute," she said. "We have no intention of sitting here having high tea while my nephew is somewhere with what you call 'a problem.'"

For a moment Zaroth looked annoyed, but he recovered quickly and came to take Kate's upraised hand and, bending over, kissed her palm. "A thousand pardons," he said, taking no notice of either Kate's shudder of revulsion or that she snatched her hand from his. "I should have realized that you would want to see your nephew before partaking of our repast."

He jabbed at a button in the center of one of the carved wooden roses that decorated the mantle, and almost immediately a small door at the rear of the great room opened and his secretary appeared.

"Have Dr. Douglas taken to room 3B; she wishes to visit our guest," he said to her. "And you can tell the kitchen we'll have our tea now."

The harried, stick-thin woman bobbed her head and motioned Kate to follow her. Kate gave Zaroth a quick glance and left.

"Please," Birgit said, speaking for the first time, "please can I go too?"

"It's best that you don't all leave at once," Zaroth said genially. "Why don't you stay here with us until Dr. Douglas returns? We'll have just a small snack, something to stave off the hunger pangs until the banquet."

"Banquet? We're not staying for any banquet," said Janet. "We only came to make sure Dan is all right." Janet looked at Cadmium for support. "You didn't say anything about a banquet."

"You didn't mention this to me, John." The little man looked at his friend uneasily. "I'm sure you won't mind if these ladies leave after they talk to the young man."

"Peter, Peter, do you doubt my intentions? Of course they may leave whenever they wish. I wouldn't dream of forcing anyone to stay against her wishes." His head drooped. "It is, however, a bit disheartening to have one's attempt at hospitality tossed back in one's face."

"Oh I'm sure they don't mean to do anything of the sort," Cadmium began, but Zaroth interrupted him.

"A gathering of friends to share their bread is one of life's true delights. The words of the Good Book come to mind." Zaroth leaned his head back, preparing to declaim. "Ah . . ." He stopped. "Ah . . ." He frowned. A flicker of discomfort crossed his scaled face. "Well, never mind," he said abruptly. "Where is that tea?" He jabbed at the rose button again and a moment later his secretary opened a small door set in the great room's paneled wall. She carried a silver tray laden with a teapot, plates, cups, and an assortment of pastries and sandwiches to the sideboard, easing the heavy tray onto the linen runner. Then, with an awkward dip in Zaroth's direction that might have been a curtsey, she scuttled from the room.

Cadmium looked after her, his eyes round. "Your secretary seems to have a multitude of duties, John."

"What if she does?"

Cadmium swallowed. "Nothing," he said.

"Difficult to get decent help here," Zaroth grumbled. "If she doesn't mind doing a few extra tasks, who am I to complain?"

Birgit laced and unlaced her hands. "I don't want anything to eat."

Pegeen smiled. "How sweet, can't wait to see the boyfriend."

Birgit turned her dark eyes to Pegeen. "He said he needed my help. I must go help him if I can."

Pegeen rose. "I've been waiting to see him too," she said, giving Zaroth a cool look. "Why don't you have him brought up? His aunt can't have that much to say to him; you can have them both come up and we'll all be able to visit."

Zaroth took her hand in his claw. "You know that your wish is my command, my love, but at the moment that course of action would not, in its essence, be prudent."

"Oh Z, cut the blather. I've been here long enough to know you can do whatever you want." Pegeen gave him a honeyed smile. Then her veneer of politesse cracked to reveal an angry scowl. "If you don't want to bring him up, at least have these women go back where they came from."

"Now, now, dearest, we don't want to appear inhospitable. And anyway, I fear they can't leave now," Zaroth's voice was imperturbable. "If you look you'll note our little friend appears to have fainted."

"Birgit!" Janet ran to Birgit, almost colliding with Cadmium, who had already dropped to his knees beside Birgit's crumpled body.

"Stand aside," Zaroth said, kneeling to put a claw to the girl's neck. "Yes, just a faint," he said calmly as he lifted Birgit in his arms and headed for the hall. "We have plenty of rooms with made-up beds on the third floor. We'll put this little lady in one to let her rest and recover."

"Not without me, you won't," Janet said. She picked up the large brown rabbit and followed them.

Frank settled his large bulk into the dark-blue leather chair and listened as Percy, lounging in the matching leather chair beside him, and Jerry, sitting behind a neatly arranged desk, analyzed their trip to the Trackless Parts.

"It may look like you came up empty," Jerry said, twirling a spoon in his coffee mug, "but you might have found out more than you know. For one thing, Zaroth appears to have successfully taken over the city hierarchy and is thinking of Pegeen for the place Elida B. left vacant. If he's in charge now, he may be trying out his new powers. Which, in turn, may be why Zaroth decided to lure Dan to the Trackless Parts—to see if he can bring Dan under his influence the way he did with Pegeen. And if his megalomania has reached that point, things are going to get dicey in that particular city."

"Can't we find out what's going on in Zaroth's turf without anyone going there?" Frank asked. "I'd think you people would know just by, I don't know, thinking about it."

Jerry gave Frank a slight smile. "We don't run things, Frank. We don't always know what's going on with people in the Trackless Parts unless there's a reason to or until they confront us. People have autonomy; they can live 'as of themselves,' as we say, as long as they stay within parameters. Of course, those who think they are running things don't stay within those parameters, and when they hurt others, which they invariably do, they're brought into some sort of order or they go to their home in hell." He looked up as a tall, slender woman in a sky-blue uniform appeared at the door. She tapped on the doorjamb and came into the office.

"Layla, come in; glad you're here." Jerry got up and moved a straight-backed, padded chair to one side of the desk. "Percy, Frank, this is our field agent for the Trackless Parts," he said. "She can probably give us more information about what's happening. Layla, can I get you coffee, juice, water?"

"Water, thanks." The woman smiled at Jerry as she sat down.

Frank heard a muffled sound beside him and looked over to see Percy staring past him, mouth open, eyes round. Percy abruptly closed his mouth, swallowed, opened it again. No sound emerged.

"What?" Frank whispered under the cover of Jerry getting a glass from the counter and pitcher of ice water from a corner refrigerator.

"Look at her," Percy said at last, his voice barely audible.

Frank looked. The dark-haired woman was smashing, no

doubt about it, but there were lots of beautiful women on campus. Frank couldn't see what had put his friend in this state of advanced catatonia.

Layla took the water glass from Jerry and turned to face the two men in the leather chairs. She saw Percy's dazed stare and her eyes widened, her pleasant expression turned to puzzlement, and then to something that Frank thought might be alarm. But as she lowered her gaze Frank realized the look in her eyes was not one of alarm, but a flash of glowing acknowledgment.

Jerry had gone back to his seat behind the desk and was watching the two with smiling interest. "So what do you have to give us?" he said to Layla.

Layla cleared her throat. "I talked to Hannah about this earlier." She darted a glance at Percy who, aside from an occasional involuntary twitch of his large hands, had not moved since his first abortive start. She cleared her throat again. "Hannah was worried about Birgit leaving the campus. Apparently Birgit thinks Dan needs her help."

"Don't know why it is that everyone seems intent on saving that young man's delicate hide," Jerry grumbled.

"Of course, since Janet went with her Hannah's not overly concerned," Layla continued. "Hannah says Janet knows more about this world than most arrivals, and she also says Kate is nothing if not level-headed, so—"

"Kate's in the Trackless Parts?" Frank said, frowning.

"Along with Janet and the little clergyman who came to give Birgit the message."

"What's with him?" Jerry asked her. "Is he one of Zaroth's crew?"

"He's hopelessly enthralled with the friend he knew on earth," she replied, "and so far he has continued to make excuses for what he's seen here. Whether he'll be able to see clearly enough to resist Zaroth's influence, we don't know."

Jerry rose, took his coffee mug to the little sink beneath the shelves, and rinsed it. "Now that you're here, Layla, these two don't need me. There are a couple of things that I should see to, so if you people don't mind I'll leave you to finish this by yourselves."

The three stood. Even Percy managed to hoist himself from the depths of the blue leather chair. "We don't need to use your office," Layla said to Jerry. "We can have our meeting elsewhere."

"Good idea," Jerry looked from her to Percy, not bothering to hide the glint in his eye. "Why don't you use the garden courtyard for your conference?"

Layla was tall, but she had to tilt her head upward to thank Percy as he held the office door for her. When they reached the empty courtyard Percy pulled out a wrought-iron chair for the field agent and, still not saying a word, took the seat beside her.

"Look, you two go ahead and start," Frank said, "and I'll see if I can rustle up some iced tea or something." It sounded incredibly lame to his ears, but the two at the table simply nodded absently.

At the door leading from the courtyard Frank stopped and looked back to see Percy reach out and take both of Layla's hands in his. She hesitated for a moment, then said something that seemed to release Percy from his trance. He leaned his head close to hers and whispered to her, and on receiving her reply threw back his head and laughed. It was a joyously raucous bellow. Only then did he release her hands, but Layla quickly grasped one of his, reclaiming it and lacing her fingers with his.

Frank let the glass door close behind him. So this was how it worked. At least for the two out there, who since that first extraordinary moment of meeting seemed to be attuned to each other's every thought. Was it possible that he'd be given what they had? Frank's felt a constriction in his chest. *Maybe.*

He walked over to the mahogany counter that stretched the length of the lounge and ordered three iced teas, wondering just how long he could he make his errand last.

22

Kate could make out very little in the gloom of the cellar room. At least, she thought it must be a cellar. It had taken a long time to get here. She'd followed the uniformed guard into whose charge the thin woman had given her, stumbling down narrow, slanting hallways that seemed to lead to the bowels of the building. The stone walls of the room emitted a dank, musty odor, and the stone bench on which she now sat felt as though it had spent time in a freezer. The only light in the room came from a small, square, wire mesh opening set high in a door that led to a central, high-ceilinged room.

"What has he done to you? What are you doing here? Is this some sort of prison?" Kate stared at the young man slumped beside her, who sat head down, hands clasping the curved edge of the stone bench.

"He says I can leave if I want," Dan mumbled, "but if I do he can't be responsible for what might happen."

"Dan, look at me," Kate commanded. "What are you afraid might happen? Who are you afraid of?"

"There's a guy who's looking for me. He, he came here just before I did."

"Why is he looking for you?"

Dan shivered. He crossed his arms about his chest and rocked back and forth, as though trying to warm himself. "It's the guy who thinks I'm responsible for him being here." He looked over at her. "But it wasn't my fault. When I saw the cop car roll up, all I could think about was getting away. What could I have done, anyway? He'd probably have bought it anyhow."

"And you think this Zaroth person can protect you?"

"He says he can. He's a pretty powerful dude."

Kate put a hand on his arm. "Can you think of someone else who could help you, someone who is truly powerful?"

"Maybe not someone, but something." Dan felt the back pocket of his jeans. "Damn. Not long ago all I wanted was to get rid of that little pistol, but now I'd give a lot to have it back." He slumped again. "But I don't know how much it could do against these people. When I had that first interview with Zaroth," he stopped and swallowed. "The guy made my flesh crawl."

"I'm not surprised," Kate murmured.

"But now, I don't know. He doesn't seem so bad. He didn't actually do anything or even threaten me. And he did promise me I'd be safe here," Dan paused. "If I stay until he finds a better place for me to hide." Dan gave Kate a sideways glance and lapsed into his own thoughts, oblivious to her presence. *How much does Zaroth know? How did he hear Tiny is looking for me, anyway? It's the uncertainty about everything here that's so hard to take.*

"Dan! Dan, snap out of it!" Kate's sharp command jerked him to the present.

"Sorry."

"I asked whether anyone here has treated you badly," she said.

"No. Well, at least not at first." Dan studied his fingernails. "It was when I said something about going back to the Academy, that I was put down here, that Zaroth . . ." he paused.

"What?" Kate prodded.

"He showed me some kind of documentary." Dan shuddered at the memory of the grainy pictures taken by what seemed to be a handheld camera. They were pictures of a person doing horrible things to someone, but the quality was so bad he couldn't make out exactly what was being done. The screams had made bile rise in his throat.

"That's it? He showed you a movie?"

Dan flashed her a look of dislike. "Easy for you to make fun. It, it was awful."

"Oh Dan, I'm sorry; I wasn't making fun of you."

Dan brushed this aside. "He didn't say why he showed it, just hinted about what might happen if I didn't take advantage of what he called his 'generous offer to be part of the organization.'" His voice grew shrill. "I, I don't even know what's real and what's not anymore—what I've maybe just dreamed. They've left me alone so much—for days—with nothing to do but look through that little mesh opening at the rituals they do every night. At least I think it's at night. It's hard to tell, it's so dark down here."

Kate sat up straight. "Rituals? What rituals? And why do they want you to be part of their organization?"

"Who knows? Why would anyone want me? Why am I some sort of prize all of a sudden?" Dan's lower lip thrust out. "Ever since I woke up in this world no one has given a damn about me, not really. Except Birgit."

Kate's jaw tightened. She took a breath and let it out. "Birgit is upstairs," she said slowly. "She heard you wanted her so she came here to see you."

Dan's eyes widened. "She came into the Trackless Parts? She shouldn't have done that." *Do I really want Birgit here? In a place like this? Yeah. I do. I need all the help I can get. She'll be all right; that naïve innocence of hers will protect her.*

"Oh, I doubt that." Zaroth responded to this thought as he uncoiled himself from the doorpost and sauntered to the stone bench to stand before them, hands on his slim hips. "At the moment your friend seems, shall we say, in need of a bit of help herself." His eyes on Dan, his voice became whip harsh. "Apparently you don't remember how to act when I address you?"

Dan scrambled to his feet and in a vague simulation of standing at attention. He attempted to square his shoulders.

"Ah, better. Not good, but better."

Kate stood too, outrage crowding her mind, her fuzzy thoughts attempting to push past and be spoken. But before she opened her mouth, she realized with astonishment that, like her nephew, she was standing at attention. She consciously lowered her shoulders, and assuming a casual stance, slowed her quick breaths. "Just who the hell do you think you are?" Icicles dripped from the words.

"Your host, dear lady, your most accommodating host, remember?" Zaroth bowed. His gaze slid down her tall figure. "Frumel, take the lady to her room; she will wish to freshen up for the banquet," he said. As the burly guard moved from behind him to place a hand on Kate's arm, Zaroth continued, "You'll forgive me if I don't escort you upstairs, my dear, but I have some important matters to attend to."

Kate knocked away Frumel's hand. "I have no intention of attending any banquet. And I'm staying right here."

"No, dear lady, you are not." Zaroth's smile exposed sharp, gleaming teeth. "Don't worry about Dan. I think I can assure you that your nephew will join us later this evening. Now I suggest you go." The last word was encased in steel. He nodded to Frumel, who again seized Kate's arm. She tried to twist away, but this time the guard tightened his grip.

"Come, come, Frumel. I'm sure the lady will accompany you without your resorting to force," Zaroth said, his tones dulcet.

Kate shot Zaroth a look of loathing, but she let the guard lead her, stiff and grim faced, from the room.

Zaroth clasped his hands behind his back and rocked on the balls of his feet. "I'm going to give you another chance to join us, my young friend. I really don't know why you're making such a thing about throwing in your lot with us. You were with us whilst you were on earth, you know. Oh, don't look so shocked, my boy, you weren't aware of it of course, but we were certainly aware of you, saw you in our midst, as it were. Matter of fact, you were with us a good deal of the time toward the end."

"No," Dan moaned.

"Oh yes. That's why I was so interested when I heard you'd arrived; it's one of the reasons I suggested you come visit us." Zaroth stretched his mouth into a smile. "Now I know you've watched the exercises, games really, that we have down here each evening. I came to invite you to participate in this evening's workout. We're planning to meet with the ladies afterwards for the festivities; if you perform well you may join us. I think I can arrange it so that your friend Birgit will be your, ah, partner."

Dan looked at the greenish glow that seemed to emanate from Zaroth's scales, at the curiously hopeful expression in his yellow eyes. "I, I don't think I'm up for much exercise right now," he said.

"Pity. Ah well, I'll leave you then." Zaroth half turned away and then stopped to regard Dan. "I'm sure you're tired of being here by yourself; probably you could do with some company. I shall ask the sergeant to bring in the new man."

Dan flinched at Zaroth's tone. "Who? Who are you putting in with me?"

Zaroth tapped his high forehead. "Let's see. I think you know him. His name is Tiny. Yes, I'm almost sure it is."

"No! No, please," Dan said, his voice strangled. "Look, I'll go with you. I'll do these games, if that's what you want."

"Oh, not what I want. Not at all. Make sure it's what you want. Can't have people saying there's any coercion here, can we?"

Dan's shoulders slumped. He hung his head. "Okay," he mumbled.

"Pardon?" Zaroth cocked an earslit toward Dan. "I can't hear you."

"Okay," Dan said. "Okay, I want to go with you."

"What is it, Birgit? Talk to me." Janet knelt by the silent girl.

But Birgit continued to sit on the edge of the narrow bed, knees tight together, hands clasped in her lap, her eyes fixed on a spot halfway up the dingy, pale-green wall. She did not appear to hear Janet's question, and seemed unaware of the rabbit that crouched, quivering, on the bare floorboards at her feet.

"Birgit, you can't just sit there and wait for the water to rise," Janet said, impatience clipping her words. "You've got to do something." She waited a moment, then reached out to brush a tendril of dark hair from Birgit's face and said more gently, "I guess you have done something, haven't you? Reverted to the silent Birgit who tended her roses." She jerked upright at a sharp rap at the door. "Who's there?"

"Your hostess," came Pegeen's dulcet tones.

Janet made no move to go to the door. "Thanks Pegeen, but we don't need anything. We're fine." She gave an involuntary gasp as Pegeen appeared inside the room, standing with her hand resting negligently on the knob of the closed door.

"This is my place; you can't keep me out," Pegeen said. She looked at Birgit, sitting like a carved statue staring into space. "Shouldn't our little horticulturist be lying down?"

"She won't." Janet looked at Birgit, her face troubled. "I tried to get her to rest, but she just sits there stiff as a board."

"Well, let's hope she unbends," Pegeen said crisply. "Zaroth wants you both to join us for the banquet." Her voice lowered. "And let me give you a word of advice; if you know what's good for you, you will do exactly as Zaroth wishes."

"Where's Kate?" Janet said, her voice sharp.

"Oh, don't worry about Miss Kate; she'll be at the banquet too."

Janet looked at Birgit, who gave no indication she was aware of the conversation. "Well, you can count me out. You can tell your friend Zaroth that it doesn't look like Birgit is going anywhere, and I'm not about to leave her alone."

Pegeen's lips parted in what could have been a smile. "Why all the concern for your gardening friend? Isn't this buddy arrangement a bit sudden? From what I heard on your precious campus, you were definitely in the running to win the 'Miss Uncongeniality' award. Of course, maybe that's the attraction—your mute little friend is probably the only one you can get to listen to your pronouncements about all the clever things you learned on earth. Things you learned as a fourth-grade teacher, no doubt."

Janet flushed but said nothing.

Pegeen fluffed her mane of platinum-white hair and shrugged. "Whatever. I came to let you know you're expected downstairs and give you adequate time to freshen up. I'd suggest you and the little gardener here pull yourselves together and grace us with your company." Pegeen gave a tiny grimace. "Zaroth's not the only one who doesn't like to be kept waiting."

Janet's jaw tightened. "I can't believe I felt sorry for you when we first met," she said. "I guess I sort of admired your honesty about wanting to be beautiful, about getting a kick out of wowing people who wouldn't have given you a second glance during your life on earth. But now I realize that honest or not, that's the whole you—there isn't anything else. You don't have the slightest interest in anyone but Pegeen."

For a moment Janet thought she actually saw sparks shoot from Pegeen's eyes. The woman's long fingers contracted and she tensed, poised as though to attack. Janet took a step back and raised her hands to defend herself, but before Pegeen could strike there was another knock on the door.

"Who is it?" Pegeen snarled.

"Cadmium here," came the high-pitched voice.

Pegeen strode to the door and flung it open. "I hope you're going to tell me Zaroth sent you and you're not just wandering about poking your nose where you're not wanted," she said.

"I, I thought I'd look in on the ladies," Cadmium said, wiping his forehead with a large, not-too-clean handkerchief. "Thought I'd offer whatever aid might be needed, ah, that is, if any is needed."

Pegeen gave a snort of disgust and grasped the rotund clergyman's arm, pulling him into the room. "Come in then, don't just stand there," she said. "I've had enough of these two anyway." She marched to stand before the silent Birgit a moment, then gave an angry snort and swirled her long silk robe about her. "See if you can talk some sense into them; we expect you to have them downstairs by dinnertime." And with this she swished from the room.

Cadmium's hesitant smile had already faded. His face ashen, he darted to the bed and knelt beside it, taking Birgit's unresisting hand in his pudgy one. "What's the matter with her?" he asked Janet. "What has put her in such a state?"

Janet simply crossed her arms and regarded him levelly, and though Cadmium continued, his voice was defensive. "I admit the incident with the guard was unsettling, but Zaroth explained why it happened and he promised me there won't be any more of that sort of thing. Perhaps you can assure her—"

"I can't believe you're making excuses for that, that man," Janet interrupted him. She brushed her face with an impatient hand. "I can't understand what you see in him."

"You find Zaroth objectionable?" Cadmium said, astonished.

"Frankly, I do. There's definitely something odd about your friend. When I looked at him downstairs, he seemed almost," Janet hesitated, "almost reptilian."

"Oh, surely not." Cadmium got to his feet. "You must be mistaken—a trick of the light perhaps. The rooms here aren't terribly well lit, I must admit. But reptilian? My dear, he was considered one of the handsomest men in seminary. But that's neither here nor there. Perhaps if I tell you about him, explain what kind of man he is—"

"Please do," Janet said dryly.

Cadmium brightened, oblivious to Janet's sarcasm. "I'll try, but it's hard to do justice to a man like John—ah, Zaroth. You see, he's incredible, protean, if I may say so. It's not his brilliant mind that astounds one, though of course his intellect is incredible, and it isn't just that his sermons made Christianity come alive to thousands, sermons which, by the way, he gave without referring to notes, often quoting whole chapters from the Bible with no apparent effort. He was, and I'm sure continues to be, a genuine force for good. I can tell you John made a real difference during his lifetime. You must have heard of the Third World Food Program? He was responsible for starting that, though of course now it's called the Emerging Nations Food Program. Despite the fact that everyone said the donated food would end up in government warehouses he went ahead with it—meeting with world leaders, tirelessly traveling the globe. He kept at it until the program was a resounding success." Cadmium folded his hands and made a steeple of his fingers, looking at Janet from beneath wispy eyebrows. "And you know the Brandencrag Hospice for Children? That came about entirely through his efforts. You just couldn't stop John when he decided to do something. He went right to the top, to the movers and shakers, and made them listen. But what I liked best about him was that he didn't just hobnob with important people, he was aware of the little folk too. He always asked the help about their families, made them feel he really cared.

"When he was taken from us at such an early age, at the height of his career, I tell you the world mourned." Cadmium shook his head sadly.

Janet looked unconvinced. "If he's the one I'm thinking of, I remember hearing about him when I was young, but from what I've seen here—"

Whatever she'd seen remained unsaid, cut off by a small, despairing cry that seemed to bounce off the pale-green walls. Janet turned to see Birgit bent over, staring at the floor, her hands at her throat. "What is it?" Janet said.

Birgit looked up, her eyes brimming with tears. "Shoma," she whispered.

It was a moment before Janet realized that Shoma was no longer sitting beside Birgit's feet. Janet squatted to peer under the bed and then rose to look about the small room. The large brown rabbit was nowhere to be seen.

Frank held onto the side of the rear seat as Layla took the jeep around a corner on two wheels. "We're trying out for the Indy 500?" he yelled over the engine.

Layla flashed him a glinting smile and turned back to the road, but Percy, sitting in the seat beside her, shot Frank a reproachful look. "She knows what she's doing," he said.

Frank leaned forward and tapped him on the shoulder. "Just because you've found your heart's desire doesn't mean we all have to end up in a heap on the roadside."

Percy took a half-hearted swing at Frank, but the wide grin that had not left his face since first meeting the field agent remained intact. "Five will get you ten, Layla gets us there in one piece."

"Where's 'there'? No, no, you tell me," Frank said hastily as Percy turned to Layla. "Let her concentrate on driving."

Percy gave him another look, but said, "She thinks we should reconnoiter before we show up at Zaroth's headquarters, maybe talk to a few of the residents. Seems there's been more changes in the city recently than just Elida B. leaving. Something big is about to happen, and the more we find out the better."

Frank nodded. "Has she heard anything about Kate and the others?"

"They were escorted to the main municipal building Zaroth's using as his headquarters," Layla called over her shoulder. "But since they went to the Trackless Parts of their own accord we can't interfere."

Frank swore quietly.

"Say what?" Layla turned in her seat.

"Sorry," said Frank. He looked at Percy in appeal as the jeep hit a pothole and all three bounced into the air.

"I think you're scaring my friend, honey." Percy smiled at Layla. "Humor him?"

Layla gave Percy a lingering look and put a hand on his knee, causing the jeep to veer dangerously close to a roadside drainage pit. "Oops," she said. With an apologetic glance at Frank, she gripped the wheel with both hands and leaned forward to concentrate on the road. Frank let out the breath he'd been holding.

The first citizen they asked refused to acknowledge any unrest in the city or having heard of political maneuverings, but the second, a woman at the edge of a crowd in front of a pawnshop, was more forthcoming. She turned away from the people watching a surly clown juggle five dented tin cans, and said, "Oh yes, there's plenty of goings on these days. You won't catch me taking sides, but there's those who thought it was high time for a change even before she left."

"You mean Elida B. Mitchell?" Layla said politely.

The woman sniffed. "Never did cotton to her, her with her

fancy ways, thinkin' she was so much better than the rest of us. Now this Pegeen person has some of the people atwitter, but I wasn't all that impressed. Seems to me it's only a matter of time before that handsome bugger takes over."

"Zaroth."

"Shush." The woman put a finger aside her nose. "Doesn't do to talk too much about these things. But stay around and watch; you'll see." She turned back to the clown, who had finished his act. He held out a tattered hat to the crowd, but after desultory applause his audience melted away.

"Come on, put the hat away, Claude," the woman said to the clown, "these buggers never give nothing anyway."

"Is he part of a circus?" Frank asked her. "I mean, you don't often see clowns performing solo in front of a pawnshop."

The woman eyed him scornfully. "Now why would there be a circus here? Circuses are for kids and I don't see any children about, do you? Matter of fact I haven't seen a kid since I can't remember when. But then it wouldn't make much difference if there was a circus, would it, seeing as Claude here isn't allowed around 'em. "

Frank didn't ask if it was circuses or children Claude wasn't allowed around. He figured he knew.

The woman went forward to help the clown pack up his tin cans, and Layla signaled Frank and Percy to follow her. The field agent led them to a crowded alleyway lined with stalls selling all manner of paraphernalia. "This is a good place to hear what's going down," she said. "Let's scatter."

Percy looked at the dented kitchen appliances, scuffed plastic dishes, broken lamps and tarnished picture frames that filled the stalls. "People buy this stuff?"

"No one buys anything. It's all junk and people don't want to spend their money anyway. I know this section well and it's mostly populated by . . ." Layla hesitated, her eyes shadowed, "by people who loved money more than anything when they lived in the world. I mean really loved it. They just gather here to browse and gossip."

She was right. In the time it took Frank to saunter from one end of the alley to the other he heard plenty of haggling, a good many derisive comments about and offended defense of the merchandise offered, but saw no one open a wallet or purse. He did, however, hear more than he'd expected about what was going on.

"Bloody palace coup, it is. Better be careful which party you side with. Wouldn't do to be caught backing the wrong one."

"I hear Zaroth is holed up in the municipal building and isn't letting anyone in except his followers."

"His followers? His gang, you mean. First thing he did when Elida B. left was get the whole brigade of guards to report to him."

"Hasn't gone in for rough stuff though, not that I've seen. And the man's smart, has all those intellectuals eating out of his hand."

It was near the end of the street that Frank heard something that, though he gave no outward sign, made his stomach contract.

"Did you hear about the three Academy people he has with him at the center? I hear he has plans for 'em."

"Like what?"

"Dunno, but I wouldn't like to be in their shoes. Saw 'em with my own eyes this morning when the guard brought 'em in. There was a girl in one of those Eastern getups, and two other women and a man. I'm not sure if the man was from the Academy. Had a clerical collar on, but you can't tell anything by those. Anyway, the younger girl was mighty scared; looked like she was about to pass out."

Frank craned his neck to search the crowd and, seeing Percy, shouldered his way to him. "I heard someone talking about the women," he said. "Doesn't sound as though they went to Zaroth willingly. A guard brought them."

Layla had come up behind them. "That's interesting," she said.

"Why don't we just go and get them out?" Frank asked her.

Layla shook her head. "We can't. Not unless they ask. Help can be given only when a person asks for it. There's real evil in this place, but until the women realize that they have no power of their own against that evil they will be helpless against it. Resistance will be useless."

"Can we at least let them know we're here if they need us?" Frank asked.

"We don't decide when to help them," Layla reminded him gently. "It's up to them."

Frank lifted his hands. "Then what do we do?"

Percy had been regarding him, a quizzical look on his face. "Patience, bro," he said. "Remember that little session you had with me a while ago in that coffee shop?" He looked at Layla. "I had to learn things don't necessarily get done when we want them to."

Layla looked from one to the other, but didn't comment. "Just what do you know about these women?" she asked.

Percy waited for Frank to speak and when he didn't, said, "Kate is a friend of Frank's and the aunt of Dan, the boy Zaroth persuaded to come here, and Birgit is a good friend of Dan's. And Janet, who knows them both, originally offered to come along because she didn't want Birgit going into the Trackless Parts alone."

"Wise woman," was all Layla said.

They headed back toward where they'd parked the jeep and Frank fell into step with Percy.

"You think we're going to have trouble getting them out?" he said, his voice low.

"Worried about Kate?" Percy asked.

Frank looked at him in surprise. "I'm worried about them all," he said shortly. Then he put a hand on his friend's shoulder. "You don't need to worry, Perce. I meant what I said before. I am totally and absolutely over that. But I *am* worried, about Kate and about Janet and about that lovely, frightened, incredibly stubborn girl."

"I wouldn't," said Percy. "Worry, that is. We do our job, stand in reserve and follow Layla. You'll see, things will be fine."

Frank didn't look convinced, but he nodded and Percy lengthened his stride to catch up with Layla.

"Look, you don't have to go if you don't want to," Janet said. She adjusted the mirror on the high dresser and ran a comb through her hair. "I'm going to this banquet, if only to find out what's happened to Kate. If we're lucky, she's seen Dan and persuaded him to go back to the Academy with us."

Birgit did not look up. She had not wept for her lost rabbit. Since that first agonized wail, she'd sat quietly, her hands folded, frowning in concentration.

Janet picked up a lipstick and liner. It was mildly annoying that Birgit was unwilling or unable to share the thoughts that held her like a marble statue. After all, she, Janet, had accompanied the girl only because Birgit had so plainly wanted her help. The clock beside the bed chimed a tinny tune. *Six o'clock. Okay.* Peter Cadmium had pleaded that they come downstairs by six o'clock. Better get going, with or without Birgit.

"Are you sure you'll be all right?" Janet said, watching the silent girl.

"I will go with you." Birgit rose, the silk of her sari falling to her feet in graceful folds. The tears in the fabric Janet had noticed earlier were no longer visible. Or had they disappeared?

"Sure you want to?" she asked the girl.

"I want to," Birgit said quietly. She looked at Janet. "It was wrong of me to think I could help Dan. I know that now."

How could it be wrong? Janet waited for more.

"Gregory told me my stubbornness helped me during the bad times. It did. It helped me stay alive. He said I don't need it now, but it is still there, I think. It is what made me want to help Dan all by myself."

"It's not wrong to want God to use you to help him," Janet observed.

"No, it is not," Birgit agreed, "but I was mostly thinking of how I could help him by myself. I will go to this banquet and see what God wants me to do."

Janet's eyes widened. "And how will you know that?"

"I don't know."

It might be an unsatisfactory answer, but Janet knew it was all she would get. She smoothed on an extra dash of lipstick and followed Birgit down the winding stone staircase.

23

At Birgit and Janet's entrance the twenty or more diners lining the hall's long table fell silent. The table was covered with sparkling white linen; the places, set with silver and crystal, glinted in the light of tapers that jutted from walls papered with flocked velvet. Zaroth sat at the head of the table, Pegeen on his right. One of the few not to look up when they entered, Zaroth now raised his head and smiled benevolently as the women were ushered to their seats. Janet took the seat she was shown next to Cadmium, who was on Pegeen's right, and looked across to where Birgit was seated next to—Janet stared at the shaggy-haired young man hunched in the chair next to Brigit's. Yes, it was Dan!

"Impressive, isn't it?" Zaroth said. "I'm quite pleased with our renovations, though of course there's much more to be done." His smile broadened as he saw another woman being ushered into the great hall. "Ah, Dr. Douglas joins us. Bring her here." He watched, amused as, much to Pegeen's obvious displeasure, a stone-faced Kate was escorted to take her place in the chair at his left. "How very pleasant it is to have you all here." He turned to Birgit. "I understand your rabbit is missing. How distressing! I hope I need not say that we have been doing our utmost to find your pet." He took a long draft from his goblet, a gold tankard rather than the crystal that sat at the others' places. "But let's not discuss sad happenings. We are delighted we could persuade you ladies to join us. And of course we are happy that our friend Dan has graced us with his presence."

Dan slouched lower in his chair. He did not look up. He had not, Janet realized, looked at them when they'd entered, had not looked at Birgit when she'd been seated next to him. *Is he drugged?* Janet moved aside slightly to let a servant put a heavy tureen in the middle of the table.

"Yes, yes," Zaroth rubbed his hands together and reached for the ladle. "Let us begin."

Cadmium coughed. "Ah, John, that is, Zaroth," he began. The little man's high-pitched voice had a quaver in it, but he plowed on. "I'm sure you want—I mean, I know you would not wish to begin this wonderful feast without, ah . . ." he held his hands up, palms together, and looked an appeal at his friend.

For a moment Zaroth's eyeslits narrowed, but then he said jovially, "Of course, of course. We cannot begin our festivities without, um, a proper prayer."

"Zaroth always asked the most marvelous blessings before meals," Cadmium told the assembled diners. "They were so appropriate, so full of Biblical allusion, so meaningful. He could always come up with a verse that would capture the occasion's spirit. Quite remarkable, really."

"Yes, well. Let us bow our heads," Zaroth began.

Though there were those at the table who looked at each other in surprise, all bowed their heads. Except Janet. Though she dipped her head a fraction, she did not take her eyes from Zaroth's face and therefore saw an interesting amalgam of emotions cross his scaly visage. Zaroth closed his eyes, lifted his chin, and confidently opened his mouth. Nothing, however, emerged. As the silence grew, one or two at the table began to fidget. Zaroth's mouth snapped shut. He opened his eyes and looked into space, startled. He cautiously opened his mouth again. And quickly closed it. A general rustle of uneasiness rippled among the diners. A few raised their heads, darting glances at the head of the table. The silence grew thick, impenetrable.

"Well, well," Zaroth said at last, "my fabled memory seems to have deserted me." He chuckled. "If I were a gracious host I would ask my friend Cadmium to take up the duty, but as you all know, I don't enjoy giving up my prerogatives—" there was a nervous titter at this "—so I suggest we bypass the formalities and serve ourselves what I can promise will be a delicious meal. Do help yourselves from one of the serving dishes before you." He scooped a large ladleful from the embossed silver tureen and, with a smile at Pegeen, dished a portion onto her plate. "You especially will enjoy this, my sweet."

Pegeen's previous annoyance had changed to a glinting smile. "Thank you," she purred, "but don't you think you should serve our little guest?" She gestured to Birgit.

"Of course." Zaroth dipped the ladle again and deposited a large serving of meat and vegetables swimming in rich brown gravy on Birgit's plate. "Do try some, my dear."

Birgit gave him a long, considering look and turned to the boy next to her and said quietly, "You wanted me to come. I am here."

Dan raised his head enough to slide a darting glance at Birgit. He nodded.

"Are you glad I came?" she asked him.

He nodded again.

Birgit leaned forward, frowning at a dark stain at the corner of his mouth. "What is that on your chin?"

Dan wiped his face with his napkin, glanced at the linen, and quickly stuffed it out of sight.

Birgit looked at him, her eyes solemn, knowing. She pushed back her chair and stood, looking first at Janet, then Kate. "I don't know if we will be able to leave," she said, "but I think we should try." She held out her hand to Dan. "Will you come with us?"

"Enough!" The word cut the air. Zaroth's yellow eyes shot venom at Birgit. "You will stop this ridiculous nattering. You will sit down. *Now!*"

Birgit held his gaze and remained standing. "I know what you've done."

Zaroth's greenish scales paled. "You know nothing."

"I do. I know that lady," she pointed to Pegeen, "took my Shoma. I do not know how she did it, but she did."

"Nonsense." Pegeen exchanged looks with Zaroth. "What reason could I possibly have to take your rabbit?" Her laugh seemed to catch in her throat.

"I do not know what happened then," Birgit said as though Pegeen had not spoken, "but the spot I saw on my friend Dan's face—I think it is blood, dried blood." She turned to Zaroth. "And I am sure I know what you believe is in this stew you gave me. When you served me and asked me to eat, I felt evil flowing from you like the waste from privies."

Zaroth didn't seem to take offense. "Now, now. I don't know what your overactive imagination may have conjured up, but the truth is far less horrific. My men regularly take part in various exercises—keeps them in shape. It was just a game, a childish one really, rather like a version of fox and hounds. Very like it, actually. Your friend Dan got right into the spirit of things; he did astonishingly well for a beginner. Caught the prize, in fact."

Dan put his fist to his mouth. "I didn't know it was Shoma," he cried to Birgit. "I thought it was just some stupid game, something to show I was tough enough to be one of them."

"Do you want to be one of them?" she asked.

"No, of course not." But he would not meet her eyes.

"Then come with us," she said gently.

He spread his hands, palms up. "You don't understand. I can't go with you. They wouldn't take me back."

"They? Do not worry about asking anyone at the Academy. I have learned some things since I set out to come here and help you. I can tell you there is only one you should ask to take you back."

But Dan stubbornly shook his head. Then the words burst from him in a torrent. "I'm so sorry about your rabbit, Birgit, but, but aside from that, well, when I was doing the, the exercise with the other men instead of just watching, it felt sort of . . . comfortable. For the first time since I've been here, I felt I was with people who wanted me to be with them."

Kate had risen to her feet. Now she came around the table and grasped Dan's shoulder. "Listen to Birgit," she said. She leaned close, willing Dan to look at her. "Whatever you may have felt a while ago, you don't really want to be with these people. Remember the pictures you told me about?" Her voice became low, urgent. "You don't have to stay. You can't."

For a moment it seemed as though he would lift his head and meet her eyes, but then his head sank still lower. "I, I don't want to leave. Not yet," he mumbled.

"We must go." Birgit said quietly. She looked at Janet, who'd been fixed in her chair, staring at them all.

"Stop those women." Zaroth whipped the command at the two guards stationed in the doorway. "Don't let them leave the room."

The men advanced toward the table, but before they could reach it the sound of pounding at the Municipal Building's great wooden door filled the hall.

Zaroth rose to his feet. "Secure the door," he snarled to the guards, who immediately scuttled out to the hallway. "Yes, yes, you too," he said as several of his men half rose in their seats. "And you," he pointed a talon at Birgit, "You will not move—not a step."

Birgit appeared not to have heard him. She looked at Dan, her face awash with pity, her eyes bright with tears. "I'm so very, very sorry," she said. She adjusted her shimmering sari about her and nodded to Janet and Kate.

Kate, still clasping Dan's shoulder, hesitated, but Janet rose and numbly walked to the hall's entrance. After a long moment Kate joined Birgit and walked the length of the table. Despite Zaroth's order, the diners had subsided into their seats and now sat watching uneasily. As the two women joined Janet at the entrance to the dining hall, Kate glanced back at Cadmium, who'd sat stunned ever since Zaroth's abortive attempt at prayer.

"Reverend Cadmium," she called out to him. "Please— come with us."

The little man blinked and looked at Zaroth.

The creature at the head of the table fixed him with a questioning gaze. "What about it, old friend?" Zaroth said gently. "Do you, my most ardent supporter, intend to desert me too?"

For a moment it seemed as though Cadmium would rise, but then he sank back in his chair, a shaking hand to his eyes. "I, I don't know," he stumbled. "I can't believe you intend to harm—"

"Harm the ladies? The furthest thing from my mind," Zaroth said. "It's true I raised my voice, but it was simply because I want them to enjoy our hospitality. I will not stop them, but I'm hurt," his eyeslits drooped shut, "hurt, I tell you, that they wish to disregard my poor attempts at welcome."

"Come," Birgit whispered, taking Kate's hand.

The pounding had stopped. The guards who stood before the great bronze door fingering the weapons at their waist hesitated, but then stood aside as the women approached.

"Is it safe out there?" Janet asked.

Birgit shrugged. "I don't know. Help me with the door."

Together the three women lifted the heavy handle and pushed the door open to a pelting rain that smacked at them, snatching their breath and momentarily blinding them. The muttering rumble of an angry crowd came at them in pulsing waves, punctuated by individual shouts.

"About time they let us in!" snarled a ragged man at the front. "Come on, let's see what they're planning in there!"

"Look, it's the women the guard brought in this morning," cried a scarred man with close-cropped hair. "Make them tell us what's going on."

"Stand aside!" At the bellowed order the crowd separated, and like two moving boulders dividing a stream, Percy and Frank made their way up the steep steps. Making a protective barricade with their arms, the men escorted the women through the driving rain to the lamp-lit street at the rear of the crowd. Frank firmly deposited Janet and Birgit in the rear seat of a jeep that sat at the curb, motor running. Kate clambered into the front seat beside the woman at the wheel and Percy came after, perching beside her on the seat, half his large frame hanging precariously out the opening where there should have been a door.

"I'm Layla, the field agent," the sodden woman said as Frank leaped on the rear fender and gripped the jeep's roll bar. "And I say we get out of here."

No one spoke as they roared through empty streets and left the village behind. The rain had stopped. A watery moon shone down on the desert ahead, making black shapes of the boulders and leafless shrubs that littered the landscape.

When they reached the end of the narrow road that rose from the plain and began the broad, pitted stretch that led to the Academy, Layla stopped the jeep. She shook her head, causing a cascade of shining droplets to fly about. "Frank," she said, "if we three can fit up front, you can squeeze in the back. You'd better, or you're going to be rolling down the road on your can."

"True." Frank put a careful leg inside. The women moved as far as they could to one side of the seat as Frank brought his other leg in the jeep. "Not going to work," he grunted and, scooping Janet from the seat, pulled her onto his lap.

"Now wait a minute," she protested.

"Layla's right," he said firmly. "I don't feel like falling and landing on my ass." He turned to Birgit. "Glad you decided to vacate the premises," he said to her. "We were waiting for you; Layla told us you'd be able to get everyone out who wanted to come."

"I know," Birgit said quietly. "I prayed when I sat in that room they gave us. And as I prayed something came to me. I realized that no one in that place had the power to hurt me. Suddenly I knew they have no power at all."

Janet stared at her. "You knew? And you just sat there and let Zaroth serve you—serve you . . ." she stopped.

"The man they called Zaroth thought it was Shoma, but it wasn't. Many of the things in that place are only . . ." Birgit hesitated, searching for a word.

"Appearances?" Layla supplied.

"Yes. Things that seem to be so, but are not."

"What things were appearances?" Janet asked. She held herself very still, trying with limited success to ignore her embarrassment at the unusual position in which she found herself.

"All sorts of things," said Birgit. "Like the banquet hall. I know others saw fine dishes and silver there; I saw a poorly made trestle covered with a stained cloth. I saw chipped plates and misshapen spoons and forks."

"Oh," Janet said in a small voice.

"Don't feel bad," Frank whispered in her ear. "I have a feeling she's an angel. We're not."

"I think you got that right," said Layla, smiling at Frank.

"Let's get you folks back to the Academy. Though my guess is that for our friend it will be just a stop to say goodbye. Right Birgit?" she said, looking in the rearview mirror.

Birgit smiled shyly and nodded.

Layla gunned the motor. The jeep shot off, squealing as it took the next corner.

24

Frank took a seat at the rear of the sanctuary. The medium-sized room was alight with sunshine that poured through the clear glass side windows. Soft lavender and crimson rays from the windows above the chancel filled the inner sanctuary and painted its creamy white carpet with vibrant, jewel-bright colors. Frank settled back to enjoy the mingled voices of the choir. He couldn't quite understand the words, but he knew the choir sang of joy and praise. During the hush that followed one of the songs an usher came to Frank's row and beckoned to him.

"Me?" Frank gestured, disconcerted.

The usher smiled and nodded, and Frank obediently followed him to the curving front row where the usher showed him to an empty seat next to—*well, how about this*—next to Janet. Frank sat. "Have any idea what we're supposed to do?" he asked her.

"We don't do much at a betrothal," she whispered. "We're here to witness the consent and pray for their happiness and have a party afterwards. There'll be more for us to do at the wedding."

Frank was about to ask about the wedding, but at that moment Percy and Layla and a robed priest entered the chancel from an inner door.

Percy, immaculate in a white suit that perfectly fitted his massive body, held Layla's hand tightly as they took their place before the priest at the center of the chancel. Layla's periwinkle-blue chiffon dress fluttered against Percy's white trousers as she inched closer to him. Frank saw her look at Percy and smile, saw Percy's shining brown face echo her smile, and saw that whatever nervousness Layla may have felt had vanished.

The priest held out an open book to them. "Percy, Layla," he said, "I stand before you to hear, receive, confirm, and consecrate your consent." The brief ceremony had begun.

"Thank you." Janet took an hors d'oeuvre from the plate held out by one of the many children helping pass trays of food. "It was lovely, wasn't it?" she said to Frank. "I'd read about betrothals here, of course, but this was, I don't know, even more moving than I expected."

Frank nodded. "Despite its simplicity." He paused. "Or maybe because of it." He considered her. "You're feeling better?"

She reddened. "I'm fine. Why wouldn't I be?"

"Beats me. You skedaddled out of that jeep so fast I thought you were looking for the nearest infirmary."

"You're kidding, right?"

"Yes," he said solemnly.

"Okay, you two," Percy called out. He stopped mid-dance step and, still holding Layla's hand, came over to Janet and Frank. "Any reason Layla and I have to search all over for you? I thought guests usually make it a point to come congratulate the ones the party's being given for."

Janet kissed Layla. "It was lovely; I can't wait for the wedding."

Percy looked over their heads at Frank and raised an eyebrow.

Frank shook Percy's hand. "Stuff it, friend," he murmured.

"Mm-hm," was all Percy managed before Frank stifled him with a bear hug.

"Can anyone join this love fest?" Jerry said as he held out a hand to Percy. "Congratulations, Percy, Layla. And I understand the congrats aren't only for this occasion, but the new assignment, Percy. This morning I found out I'm not losing a field agent; I'm gaining a team."

Percy beamed.

"Hey, that's great," Frank said. He pumped Percy's hand again.

Jerry turned to Janet. "And this is the brave lady who volunteered to accompany Birgit to the Trackless Parts?"

"Brave? I don't think so." Janet ducked her head.

"Well that's the report I got from Percy and Layla," Jerry said. "You two go along and enjoy your party," he said to the betrothed couple. "I want to talk to these two about that little escapade."

The three watched Layla and Percy move onto the dance floor, their steps flowing to the music. "Always good to see two people find each other," Jerry murmured.

"You want to ask us about what happened? I thought you'd be the one to know," said Frank.

"I do. What I meant was, I know you're interested in what occurred after you left Zaroth's town. I can fill you in if you'd like." He saw that he had their attention. "Yes, there was a whole lot going on after you took off. A minor earthquake, you could say."

Janet's gaze sharpened. "Literally?"

He nodded. "Not everyone in the city, but a large portion found themselves quite literally tumbling toward the home they've chosen."

"Dan?" Frank asked quietly.

"Dan escaped the major cataclysm, but he didn't head back

to the Academy. He's still in the Trackless Parts, but not for long, I'm afraid."

They digested this. "Did Zaroth and Pegeen . . . are they gone?" said Janet.

Jerry shook his head. "Zaroth is. When Pegeen was last seen she was gathering as many of the former acolytes of Elida B. Mitchell as she could and trying to form a society of her own."

Janet's lips quirked in a half smile, but then she said slowly, "There's something I don't understand about Pegeen. Why was she allowed to come to the Academy in the first place? She practically never went to classes; matter of fact, from what I saw, she didn't do much of anything except cause trouble with those ridiculous ideas of hers."

"Pegeen had a real use to perform here. The opinions she presented allowed what was inside some of the students to surface."

Janet cocked her head. "Say what?"

"If, despite living an orderly, conventional life on earth, they inwardly agreed with her, they couldn't help but have their acceptance of those ideas come out in the open. If, on the other hand, her listeners didn't agree with her wacky ideas, they sloughed them off—no harm done. We just stepped in and suggested she change venues when her 'conversations' got out of hand and she started disparaging marriage." Jerry's easy smile sobered. "Zaroth's insidious mixture of good and evil was a different matter. He could have caused a lot of trouble at the Academy if he'd been allowed to stay."

"Zaroth certainly didn't have much time as head honcho of his little realm before it and he toppled," Frank observed.

"He did not go alone, however," Jerry said cryptically.

"You don't mean Mr. Cadmium is with him?" Janet asked, distressed.

Jerry gave a brief shake of his head. "You remember Zaroth's secretary?"

"The woman who served us tea?"

"She's finally got what she wanted." Jerry answered Janet's raised eyebrow and unasked question. "Her boss. She has him to herself—at least for the moment. Imagine Zaroth's surprise."

Janet giggled. She couldn't help it. The picture of the stick-thin woman and Zaroth was just too ludicrous. Then she sobered. "But Mr. Cadmium, did he get away? He seemed so interested in coming to the Academy."

Jerry's face was grave. "It appears he hasn't been able to shake off Zaroth's influence. He's still looking for the friend he called John. I pray he doesn't find him." And with that, Jerry took a small plate of fruit from a little girl's proffered tray. "Thank you, my dear," he said to the child. He popped a grape in his mouth and returned to Frank and Janet. "There was another reason I wanted to corner you," he said. "Come around and see me tomorrow morning, Frank. I think we may have something for you." He nodded to them both and headed across the dance floor.

"Sounds like you're going to be asked to join Jerry's group," Janet said. "Congratulations! That's wonderful."

Frank wondered if she realized how wistful she sounded. "There's nothing I'd like better," he said. "If it happens. How about you? What would you like to do if you had your druthers?"

She thought. "Something I'm really passionate about, I guess," she said at last. "But what that would be, I don't know. I taught because it was the easiest thing to do. Got my degree and a fourth-grade class the same year; never did anything else." She stopped, aware of the discontent in her voice. "There I go, whining again," she said with a short laugh. "You'd think on a lovely day like this, I could manage an occasional positive thought."

"You know kid, sometimes I think you're too tough on yourself." Frank took her plate from her and put it on the nearest table. "Let's go for a walk in the garden, shall we?"

Kid? But Janet followed him out to the garden beside the sanctuary and then on up the hill. "It's strange not to see Birgit here," she said as they passed the rose garden. "I can't understand how she could forgive Dan for what he did—or thought he'd done."

"I guess that's one reason she's already found her home and we haven't," Frank said. "Well, here we are." They had reached the latticed trellises at the top of the hill and Frank gestured to one of the benches that looked out over the countryside and sat down.

Janet stood scowling at him, her hands on her hips. "Did you have to choose this place? You couldn't manage somewhere else?"

"What's wrong?" he said. Then he regarded her with the hint of a smile. "Oh, this is where we—" He did not finish, but he didn't get up, either. "Come on," he patted the bench beside him. "Sit down. If only to prove to yourself that you're a different person than the wailing woman I first met."

Janet remained standing. "I can't believe you could be so insensitive."

"Cops are often accused of being insensitive," he said mildly.

"Now you're trying to make a joke of it. I'm serious." She tapped her foot on the flagstone in exasperation. Frank looked at the tapping shoe. Janet, following his gaze, immediately stilled her foot, an unwilling grin tugging at the corner of her mouth. "I don't know why it is that I act like a complete idiot when I'm around you. Either I dissolve into tears or I say something stupid. You, you're absolutely maddening, you know."

"I know."

She sat down beside him. "Absolutely maddening."

"Do you think you could do something about that?" Frank gave her a sideways glance. "I mean, could you work on my more maddening qualities and maybe help me improve whatever redeeming qualities I might have?"

"I may just haul off and smack you."

"Oh, don't do that." He caught her hands. "Why don't you kiss me instead?"

For a moment Janet sat, incapable of speech. She wondered whether the heart-stopping rush of joy she felt was reflected in the light she saw in Frank's eyes. She laughed aloud. "Yes," she said, "I think I will." And she did.

Kate stood at the edge of the floor watching the dancers. She felt a catch in her chest at the thought of Dan out in the Trackless Parts. The catch became a sharp jab of pain as she remembered his lowered head, the way he turned from Birgit, from all that could have been. *No, don't dwell on it. Dan will be as content in the life he has chosen as he will let himself be.* This was a day to celebrate, a joyous occasion. She'd concentrate on how pleasant it was to be here sharing Percy and Layla's happiness.

She'd seen Frank and Janet leave. Unless she was mistaken, something good was happening there too. *Thank you for letting me see it.* Hannah and Gregory gave her a smile as they whirled past. *Please, Lord God, give me what they have.* When would she be able to laugh and talk with Howard like the couples spinning past? When would she and Howard be able to hold each other? Kate suppressed a tiny ache of longing. *Be happy. Be happy for the happiness of others if you can't have your own.*

It happened so quickly that at first Kate wasn't aware that she was no longer in the reception room. Then she realized she was in a garden. No, it was more of a meadow than a garden, daisies and wild indigo and rose mallow sprinkled among the grasses in haphazard clusters. The colors were not the jewel-bright tones of the Academy gardens, but subtle, pastel shades whose hues varied even as Kate looked at them. And the music that wafted on the freshened breeze was not dance music, but gentle notes that could have come from wind chimes.

She was alone.

Kate closed her eyes and raised her face to the warmth of the sun. *Why am I here? What am I to do?*

She gave an involuntary yelp as something wet and cold brushed her hand. "Buster!" Kate gave a shaky laugh and scratched the dog's big head. "What are you doing here, fella? Keeping me company?"

Buster thumped his tail and leaned against her knee. His head went up and he sniffed the flower-scented air, staring intently into the distance. Kate followed his gaze but could see nothing. Buster barked. "What is it, boy?" Kate asked, her voice sharp.

Then she saw them. At the far end of the meadow two shining figures led a halting man across the flowered field, holding him by the elbows and forearms.

"Howard!" Kate gasped. She was too far away to see the man's face, but she knew it was Howard. She ran through the knee-high grasses toward them, Buster bounding beside her. "Howard," she called out. As she came closer the shining figures vanished, leaving Howard to sway, his arms outspread in an attempt to keep his balance. Kate lunged to catch him before he fell. "Howard!" It was a half-sob.

Howard struggled from Kate's clasp and regained his feet. He stared at Kate uncertainly. Then the clear, sharp gaze she remembered replaced the confusion clouding his eyes. "Kate?" he said. "My Kate?"

"Yes, my darling. It's your Kate."

He took a stumbling step and stopped. "Kate," he said. "I'm walking!"

"I know." She held out her arms. "I know."

"You're," his eyes widened, "you're beautiful."

She held him then, and kissed his lips, his cheeks, his withered neck. "You are too—to me," she whispered.

Howard returned her embrace, awkwardly at first, but then his arms closed about Kate with unaccustomed strength. "Kate, Kate." They kissed and kissed again.

Howard raised his head and looked at her in wonder. "The pain," he said. "It's gone."

Kate leaned against him, feeling the sharp bones of his shoulder. She traced the hollow of his thin chest. "Just you wait, my darling, just you wait," she murmured. "You ain't seen nothing yet."

ACKNOWLEDGEMENTS

Once again I want to acknowledge my debt to the eighteenth-century theologian, sage, and scholar Emanuel Swedenborg. This novel might well have been called *The Sojourners,* for Swedenborg tells us that in the Bible the term "sojourner" means one who receives instruction. Like the characters in this novel, I too have been a sojourner, and in writing it I have borrowed freely from Swedenborg, especially the vivid descriptions of the spiritual world found in his book *Heaven and Hell* and other of his theological works, such as *Marriage Love* and *Secrets of Heaven.* For this and much more, I am deeply indebted to him.

QUESTIONS FOR DISCUSSION

1. The Academy in this novel is depicted as a place between heaven and hell where students—newly arrived from Earth—learn spiritual truths. In the two previous books in this series, *The Arrivals* and *The Wanderers*, new arrivals were left to explore the world of the spirits with no formal instruction or explanations. Which of these two modes would appeal more to you? Which seems more logical?

2. In the beginning of the book, Dan ends his own life, only to awaken and find that he can't get rid of the gun that he used. It's only once he starts to talk about the reasons for his action that it vanishes. What do you think the gun represents? Its disappearance? How do you interpret the fact that Dan later wishes he had the gun back?

3. Kate is drawn to Dan as soon as he arrives in the afterlife, despite her own status as a newcomer. Do you agree with the way she handled her nephew? What would you have done in the same situation?

4. Horribly abused in life, Birgit brings her fear and mistrust of others with her in death. How do the angels and new arrivals around her try to draw her out of her shell? Who eventually succeeds? How does Birgit change as the story progresses, and what do you think those changes signify?

5. Pegeen's views on sex and relationships reflect a view held by many in today's society that marriage is not necessary for

a romantic relationship to succeed. Do you agree that such views are harmful?

6. Over the course of the story, Frank struggles with his attraction to Kate, whose husband is still alive. Frank's feelings are depicted as an evil of which he must purge himself in order to be accepted into heaven. Yet Janet's husband, Richard, met another woman after his death, married her, and the two moved on to heaven long before Janet arrived in the world of spirits. Compare these two sets of relationships. Do you believe Frank and Richard should be judged differently? Why or why not?

7. As she progresses spiritually, Birgit visits a community in heaven. Did the community match your expectations of what heaven would be like? Why or why not? What kind of heaven would you like to live in?

8. The people and places in hell are depicted in this story as not being what they seem. Zaroth, for example, looks handsome to his followers, but reptilian to the heaven-bound spirits; the place in which he lives looks like a large city to some visitors, but like a collection of huts to angels. What do these illusions suggest about the nature of hell?

9. Peter Cadmium reveals that Zaroth in life was a minister who helped many people—but was far from moral in his private life. Do you think Zaroth ever truly had a chance to go to heaven? In this story, what is the difference between the heaven-bound spirits and the hell-bound ones?

10. At the end of the book, Dan is lost in the Trackless Parts, and seems to be bound for hell. Do you think this is fair? Why or why not?